Grand, Gloomy, and Peculiar:
Stephen Bishop at Mammoth Cave

Books by Roger W. Brucker

*The Caves Beyond*
By Joe Lawrence, Jr. and Roger W. Brucker

*The Longest Cave*
By Roger W. Brucker and Richard A. Watson

*Trapped! The Story of Floyd Collins*
By Robert K. Murray and Roger W. Brucker

*Beyond Mammoth Cave:*
*A Tale of Obsession in the World's*
*Longest Cave*
By James D. Borden and Roger W. Brucker

# Grand, Gloomy, and Peculiar: Stephen Bishop at Mammoth Cave

## A Historical Novel

## By Roger W. Brucker

CAVE BOOKS
Dayton, Ohio

Published by CAVE BOOKS
4700 Amberwood Drive
Dayton, Ohio 45424
www.cavebooks.com

CAVE BOOKS is the publications affiliate of the Cave Research Foundation.

Publisher: Roger McClure
Editors: Richard A. Watson, Hilary Lambert
Layout: Paul Steward
Cover Painting: Bonnie Curnock
Cover Graphic Design: Gary Berdeaux

The original Map of Mammoth Cave by Stephen Bishop, published in *Rambles in the Mammoth Cave*, by Alexander Bullitt, 1844 was 11.3" x 16.8". A second edition with corrections was published later and was 13.5" x 20".

Library of Congress Cataloging-in-Publication Data

Brucker, Roger W.
  Grand, gloomy, and peculiar : Stephen Bishop at Mammoth Cave : a historical novel / by Roger W. Brucker.
      p. cm.
  ISBN 978-0-939748-71-6 (pbk. : alk. paper)
  ISBN 978-0-939748-72-3 (hbk. : alk. paper)
1.  Bishop, Stephen, 1821?-1857--Fiction. 2.  Tour guides (Persons)--Fiction. 3.  Mammoth Cave (Ky.)--Fiction.  I. Title.

PS3602.R8327G73 2009
813'.6--dc22

                                                      2009021769

To Lynn Weller Brucker

## Author's Note

Caves are fragile. Their features may be thousands or millions of years old. Cave animals are rare. They live precarious lives on the knife edge of ecological balance. During the period covered by this novel, explorers and visitors disturbed cave animals and wrote their names on walls. Today cave features and cave life can be destroyed through ignorance by visitors who do not understand the fragility of underground relationships. Irresponsible people have removed stalactites or crystals that will never grow again. They have killed bats by entering habitats at a time when food supplies were low. They have defaced cave walls with graffiti. Caves are unique places for adventure and discovery, but before you enter a cave, I urge you first to learn about safe caving. Please contact the National Speleological Society, www.caves.org. They will guide you to a safe and fulfilling adventure in caving.

*After Stephen crossed the Bottomless Pit, we discovered all that part of the cave [passages] now known beyond that point . . . as Stephen was wont to say, they were 'grand, gloomy, and peculiar.'*

—Franklin Gorin, Stephen's owner, quoted in William Stump Forwood, *An Historical and Descriptive Narrative of the Mammoth Cave of Kentucky, 1870.* The word "peculiar" at that time had the connotation of unpredictable or surprising.

Engraving of Stephen Bishop by N. Dmitrieff published in *Scribner's Monthly Magazine*, October, 1880, 23 years after Stephen's death.

Mammoth Cave, Kentucky
December 1, 1878

Mr. James Ross Mellon
President, City Deposit Bank
Pittsburgh, Pennsylvania
Dear Mr. Mellon:

When you visited Mammoth Cave last month you wanted to know more about Stephen Bishop, my late husband. You promised that if I would tell you his story you would furnish a suitable headstone for Stephen's unmarked grave.

I did write the account of my life with Stephen two years after his death. Stephen is the father of my late son, Thomas Bishop. The story was for our son and his children so they would know what kind of man Stephen was. When Thomas died without children during the war years, I plunged into despair. My heart cracked with sorrow and I thought I would never show this story to a living soul.

Your kind offer has moved me to send you my story. More than anything I want Stephen's life to be ~~rembor~~ remembered for what he did, not how he was treated. He often described the cave as "Grand, gloomy, and peculiar." In my heart he was the first guide and explorer of Mammoth Cave. Thank you.

Your servant,
Charlotte Bishop

# Chapter 1

## 1859, Mammoth Cave, Kentucky

I am Charlotte Bishop. That has been my name since 1843. Before that, I was Charlotte Brown. I was a runner from the time I was a little girl on Red Rose Hall plantation near Columbus in Mississippi. Slaves like us didn't get to run much because it made us look like we were trying to escape. But nobody worried about me escaping. Another thing, black people learned not to run or anything else that made them look like they had too little to do.

Addie Wells brought me up as her own child, which I was not. My mother was sold when I was three or four, so I don't remember her. I had an older brother Jim, who was sold at the same time. Addie said mama gave me to her so I would have a better life than where my mama and Jim were going. Addie taught me many things, like how to count my fingers and toes. Things like how many? How far? How big? How much? I always liked numbers. She taught me to ask questions.

Addie encouraged me to run fast. Although I was small, I had the long legs for it. I liked to feel the wind in my face and I loved to explore the woods to see the shapes and shadows shift. Addie told me that men and boys want one thing from a Negro girl, and if I could outrun them, I would not have to let them have their way if I didn't want to.

Early on I didn't know what she was talking about, but when I was eight or nine, I was cornered by old Asa Woodworth at a patting one dark night. He clapped in rhythm with the others around the fire, but he kept slapping me on the leg, higher and higher. He said I was pretty and he had something to give me. I didn't like the way he kept touching me, so I said to him, "Tell you what. If you can catch me, you can do what you want."

I didn't wait for his answer, but took off running back through the paths in the woods. He took after me. I was afraid I had guessed wrong about his speed. I imagined his fat old belly and smelly hands all over me, and I ran faster. I could dodge pretty good, and I had often run through the same pines, so I knew where the stumps were. I headed that way. I jumped some of the stumps and ran around others. He yelled for me to stop, and a lot of other angry words.

I heard a thud behind me, then no more running. I circled back softly to see if I could see him. He was lying on the ground near a stump. I think he hit his head on a rock or a stump. My heart pounded. I sweated a gourd full, but stayed quiet to see if he would move or get up.

He didn't. They buried him the next day, and said he had tripped up trying to lay out. Or maybe run away. I said nothing.

When I was fourteen, Red Rose Hall fell on hard times. There was an estate sale and the slaves were to be sold. Some of the people I loved best had been sold off before that sad time. I hoped I could stay with Addie and Tom Wells, but I knew that would depend on luck more than anything. Half the time sold-off slaves got a better deal, half the time worse, but getting sold was no way to freedom.

A few slave owners from down the road came to look us over and we lined up. Mostly they wanted one or another of us, but the estate wanted to sell the whole lot of us. Two slave dealers showed up, one from Jackson and one from Nashville. The one from Nashville went down the line looking close at each of us. He didn't spend much time looking at the field hands, including me. But he did fix me with a gaze that was like he was sizing up a hanging ham. After we spent a long time standing in the sun, overseer sent us back to work. We wondered which of us would be going. We found out that evening. Overseer said to pack our belongings to set out for Nashville the next morning. The dealer bought the lot of us for one price.

Eight of us climbed into a wagon at first light. We had our clothes in bundles and there wasn't much room. Overseer waved goodbye and behind him the son of our old master and his wife wept as the horses picked up the slack and started us off to Nashville. Addie thought they were sorry to see us go, but I think they were sad because the plantation was about broke.

The wagon journey was bad. Four long days. We'd get a bit of cornbread and salt pork late in the afternoon. About dark we would be turned out in a fenced barnyard to pee and sleep. The driver chained the men together. At cock's crow the driver ordered us back into the wagon. When the sun was high he might stop at a water pump once or twice.

We crossed the Tombigbee River on a small ferry and got onto the Natchez Trace. In Nashville we pulled up to a holding pen at a slave market. There I met an old crippled woman who had been there four days, had stood in eight sales, and got one bid of $30.

Next day at the sale I fetched $210 on the bid of a

man named Bell. He was Robert Bell, dressed in a white linen shirt, brown boots, with an elegant brown hat. His face was red. Not quite as red as Tennessee dirt, but redder than pink. He bought two of the men for $385 and $395, but he didn't buy Addie and Tom Wells. They sold as a pair to someone else for $970. My heart cracked and I choked back tears as they were led away. I will never forget their parting look as the closest thing to a mama and papa I ever knew left for good. I do not know how anyone can rip love in two like that. I was alone and scared. Even now I cry inside when I think of the last time I saw them.

Robert Bell told the three of us that he picked us because he liked our looks and heard a good report from the driver, passed on from the overseer. He ran a tavern up in Kentucky on the stage coach road between Nashville and Louisville. We'd be his kitchen, inn, and farm help, and he hoped we'd all get along. "I own you, and you will obey me and do an honest good job."

Later, Bell's wagon came to Three Forks, Kentucky, five days north of Nashville. I met Stephen Bishop for the first time in Bell's Tavern, which brings me to why I am telling this story.

Many years have gone by since Stephen came to the tavern with his owner, Franklin Gorin, from Glasgow, Kentucky. This is how I came to notice Stephen before he became famous or married me. I am sure others will tell about the famous Stephen Bishop, explorer guide at Mammoth Cave. I'll tell about that, too, but I will tell the truth about how Stephen was the most curious man on earth. He could turn bad times into good times. He was the bravest man I ever knew, I'd say fearless. He could get along easily with anyone, and that included the ornery and hateful ones. He could tell stories to charm anyone. He wasn't what I call handsome. He had nappy black hair that was bushy and medium long. His skin was the golden color of molasses in the sunshine. He stood a head taller than me, and while I have long legs, the rest of me is short. Stephen would give you a smile in a flash and listen to you with his eyes. He taught me to read and write.

I wanted our son, Thomas Bishop, and his sons and daughters to know the truth of his father and their grandfather. Stephen was a slave but he wanted to be free more than anything. When he became free, Stephen stayed a slave to the cave. He provided for us. He was affectionate, passionate, a loving man and husband and father in every way. I think, though, that his passion for that old cave was as strong as his passion in bed. Most of all, he listened to me, he understood me like nobody else, and he cared about me and Thomas more than himself.

To tell the truth, I am telling Stephen's story now because I am coughing. Stephen was coughing like I am now. He took sick and got weaker and weaker. Then he died. I must tell his story now or never.

I always wanted to be free. Free to save Addie and my real mama. Free from Asa. Free from being sold and free from Mr. Bell and Dr. Croghan. I am free now, except from the ache in my heart for want of Stephen.

# Chapter 2

## 1836, Bell's Tavern, Kentucky

The truth was Robert Bell didn't exactly buy me. He rented me from John Bogsdon of Nashville, for $70 per year. I learned later it was against the law for owners to bring new slaves to Kentucky, but we could be rented out. I never laid eyes on Bogsdon. I believe this was a way to get around the law. Would my ownership pass to Bell when $210 was paid?

Robert Bell's tavern was a collection of farm buildings beside the trail to Louisville. Our wagon pulled into the place late in the afternoon. There were two buildings, one brick and the other log, about twenty feet square on the first floor, separated from each other by a porch about ten feet wide and around both buildings. Rocking chairs on the porch were empty when we arrived. There was a second floor. It covered both buildings and bridged over the first floor middle porch. A stairway led from the middle porch to the second floor.

Our wagon turned in and we passed a hitching rail where three horses stood switching flies off their backs. Behind the inn I saw a kitchen building. Smoke rolled out of its tall chimney. We stopped in front of the stable. Mr. Bell told the two men to wait by the stable. He showed me to a slave cabin, second from the end of the line of four near the stable. "This is your bed in the corner. You stay with Mildred, the cook. Put your things in here and follow me to the kitchen." My new home had a smooth dirt floor, like Addie Wells's cabin in Mississippi. Mildred's bed was in the other corner with a white quilt over it. I dropped my bundle on the straw mattress, and followed Mr. Bell to the kitchen.

Mildred was a big-boned jet-black woman who moved around as chief cook of the whole place. "Got me some help, Mr. Bell? About time. George, he do the best he can, but he is old and slow." She shot me a glance, then nodded toward George, a white man with gray hair and most of his left ear missing. George just looked into the fire in the hearth.

Mr. Bell spoke: "This is Charlotte Brown. Charlotte, Mildred." I flashed my eyes down, then looked Mildred in the eye. She looked me up, down, and sideways holding a wooden spoon like a club.

"How old? You run good?" She jabbed the spoon toward me.

"Fourteen. Yes." I waited for her next questions.

"You good in the kitchen? Can you stir up corn pone for tonight?"

I took the spoon from her. "I can learn, yes." I picked up the bowl of corn meal, pinched salt from the cellar, and dipped out water from a bucket. When I was little, Addie taught me how to make corn pone better than most, and how with bacon drip and a little sorghum mixed in it would taste better than regular old corn bread. Mildred turned away to attend roasting meat. Where was the bacon fat and sorghum? I asked George. He handed me a fat pot from the back of the hearth and a sorghum bucket from the shelf. I added the two to the corn meal mixture, beat up the batter and ran it into a pan. I placed the pan over the hearth coals.

Mildred ordered me and George around getting the evening meal ready for the tavern. I was tired to the bone from the long wagon ride and kitchen chores on top of that. Mildred seemed not to notice. After we cleaned up from the meal, Mr. Bell came back to the kitchen from the inn.

"More corn pone," he ordered.

"Kitchen's closed!" Mildred announced. "Fire's down. You got three paying guests and your family. We put out enough corn pone for ten or twelve."

"They ate it all up and want thirds." Bell was agitated now. "They say it's the best corn pone they ever ate. I agree."

"Too late. You want to give everybody thirds on twenty-five cents a day? You want midnight corn pone? Take that long to get the fire up." Mildred knew how to get to Mr. Bell, through his pocketbook.

George added, "How about for breakfast then? Mildred's right."

"When I need your advice I'll ask for it, old man." Bell turned out the door to leave. "Just make sure it's the *good* corn pone!"

Mildred planted her fists on her ample hips and said to me, "What did you put in that corn pone? Do you know something I don't?"

"Bacon fat. Sorghum. Made good corn pone in Mississippi, too. If you got some onions or peppers I can make better yet."

If Mildred resented me stepping up, she didn't show it. She said we'd get up at first light tomorrow, lay a fire, and make breakfast. After that she and George would show me around. Bell's Tavern had a steady trade of travelers on the stagecoach from Galt House in Louisville on Monday, Wednesday, and Friday. Travelers could continue on to Nashville the next day. Bell's Tavern was about halfway between the big cities. On Tuesday, Thursday, and Saturday the stage from Nashville arrived. Lone riders and small groups in ox carts or wagons arrived any time of the night or day, but not so much after dark. Bell charged twenty-five cents a night for supper, bed, and breakfast. Noon dinner was fifteen-cents.

As I lay on the straw in Mildred's cabin, my head swarmed with everything new. How come George's ear was missing? Did a bear bite him? Would Mildred teach me to cook? I only knew a few things Addie taught me, and I didn't like to cook that much. Mr. Bell said he wanted me to do a good job. If true, he could pay me ten-cents a week, or better yet, set me free. I would certainly respect him for that!

Next morning after breakfast George took me out to the pantry where they stored the corn meal, wheat flour, hams, yams and potatoes. Two slaves who tended garden and worked at the farm also unloaded food from Mr. Bell's wagons to keep bins and shelves full. He took me across the lane to another building made of logs. It looked more like the small privy out back than anything. We opened the door and George lighted a lantern. We went down a set of steps into a cold room underground. The walls were wet stone and I heard water gurgling. I never saw anything like it before.

"This here is our storage cave. We keep the milk, cream, and butter in here." George held the lantern high, but the shadows made it hard to see much. "Over here is where we get our water, out of this cold stream. It runs year around like this. In fall, when it gets cold, we move apples, some of the cabbages, and other vegetables down here." I shivered some because it was cold in that storeroom. Got goose bumps.

George enjoyed showing me what was where. I

warmed to him right away. I asked,"Did you get in a fight with a bear?" Then I thought I might have ruffled his feathers some by speaking direct.

"No, my ear was bit off in a fight with Rufe Skaggs over by the Forks of the Nolin River. He bought a mule off of me. Paid two-dollars. Said he'd pay the rest in a month. Six months later I went to his place. Put a halter on the mule to take it home. Rufe came out mad as hell, yelling for me to git off his place. He claimed it was his mule, paid in full, and I had cheated him. When I grabbed hold of the rope Rufe came at me with a hoe handle. He slammed it down like to break my head open, but I ducked over."

George trimmed the lantern, and went on, "He laid that hoe right across the mule's back. The mule snorted, and turned and kicked Rufe hard in the leg. Rufe grabbed hold of me howling in pain and rage. He hugged me tight and bit my ear hard. He jerked back like a dog shaking a rat. About the third pull he ripped my ear clean off. I come near to passing out from the pain. It was like getting hit with a hot poker and a bucket of blood all at once. I took off running and didn't stop for a mile. Rufe hollered after me if I came back, he'd kill the mule and stuff it inside me. I still believe he would."

I asked George how long it took for his head to scar over where his ear used to be.

"Long time. Got so sore and sick I couldn't move much. Hot fever and a pounding head. Scabs came and went, but the most hurtful part is when anybody looks at me. They see a loser in a fight. I feel like a nigger."

He stopped. His eyes glistened with tears welling out. I felt pity for the man. It would be terrible to find out all of a sudden you were treated like a nigger, rather than get used to it in a hundred ways as you grew up.

"Looks like you found friends here." I tried to cheer up the old man. "It could be worse."

"Worse? I buried my two babies and my wife. I couldn't work my place, even the garden. Then my neighbor came by with a court paper saying he owned my land because I never got around to getting a patent on it." Plainly, I had not succeeded with cheer. I tried to switch the subject, but he went on. "I hired on with Mr. Bell for seventy-cents a week, but he's behind on that."

"Mildred will miss us," I cut in. "We'd better get back." We climbed the stairs out of the cave, George carrying a bucket of water. He blew out the lamp and set it on the shelf. When we opened the door we were nearly blinded by bright sunshine.

Around noon I heard horses pull in. A young Negro drove a buggy with two white men in it. They climbed down and the driver tied the horses. The slave looked sixteen or seventeen, was medium tall and lean, likely of face. He had nappy hair on the long side. That was the first time I saw Stephen Bishop. One white man was taller, maybe forty (you can't tell how old white people are). He wore a striped frock coat, loose white shirt and brown trousers. I sidled around to the desk with my broom to hear who they were. The second man was young, about nineteen and with white hair.

"Hello, Frank," said Robert Bell. "You here to meet someone? I'll have your boy get your horses some water." Bell told the slave to take the horses around back for a drink. I swept the last of the dust out the door, and went back into the kitchen with the broom. Only I kept walking right out the back door to see if that young slave needed anything.

He removed the horses' harness at the trough. "How far did you come?" I asked.

"Glasgow. Ten miles south." He started to wipe the sweat off their flanks. "Name's Stephen."

"Stephen, if I can get you anything, let me know." I turned and hung the broom on a peg on the wall.

"Haven't seen you before." Stephen brushed the mane of one horse.

"Mr. Bell bought me in Nashville, me and two men. I come from Mississippi. How about you?"

"I was born in Glasgow seventeen years ago. Mr. Franklin Gorin, the lawyer, owns me. We came over to meet a cave man, Hyman Gratz. He owns Mammoth Cave. Charles Harvey, Jr. is with us. Got anything to eat around here?"

"I'll see Mildred." I stepped into the kitchen and asked Mildred about feeding the horses and slaves. She poked her spoon toward the stable in back, "Have the boy take the horses back there. A stable hand will put out some feed. Dinner's not ready, so get that boy an apple to tide him over. It's in the barrel."

When Stephen returned, I took him with me to the storage cave. I had not seen apples there, but maybe there were some. In the glow of the lantern we looked around and into some of the barrels. Stephen fished one out of the apple barrel. He wanted to know about the cave, so I showed him the running stream of water, the wet walls and ceiling. There were crickets on the ceiling. They looked like the brown crickets in the privy, but they were a lighter color. I saw a brown mouse hanging on the ceiling. Stephen said it was a bat.

Did I know where the water went, he asked. I told him no, but it set me to wondering, too. "Water has to go someplace," he said, "else we'd be underwater right now."

"Why?" I asked.

"If the water couldn't get out, it would fill up to the top, like a horse trough with a roof on it." Stephen was a good explainer. "And we'd be soaked to the skin, and then some."

"You're so smart about things, where does the water come from?" I think I stumped him. His little laugh turned serious. He looked upstream, shielding his eyes from the lantern light. He finally said he didn't know, but we could go see. Since I had to work in the kitchen, I said not now, and we climbed the stairs to the outside.

I asked George about the bat. He said bats won't hurt people. They live under the roofs of buildings and in caves. They fly out at night but come back.

"Is that the honest truth?" I didn't believe him.

"Yes, I always tell the truth." George looked hurt.

Later I told Mildred about what George had said. She said, "When a man brags about how honest he is, I start to count the spoons."

# Chapter 3

## Mammoth Cave is Sold

Mildred scolded me for staying away so long, and kept me hopping through dinner. I brought platters of pork chops to the big table where Mr. Gorin, Mr. Abner Harvey, Mr. Gorin's partner, and the cave-owning man, Mr. Gratz, ate dinner. Charles, Jr. just listened. I got the broom down and swept the floor some so I could hear what they were saying. Gratz said he wanted to sell Mammoth Cave. He was getting old, sixty, and wanted to do something else besides own a cave for visitors to see. He'd sell it to the right party for $5,000. Gratz said Franklin Gorin seemed like the kind of go-getter that would put Mammoth Cave on the map. Mr. Gorin looked interested, but said he could not pay for it all at once. Mr. Gratz said he could take several years to pay it off, and he could easily make enough to pay it off from the tourist trade.

Mr. Gratz ordered brandy, so I stopped sweeping and nodded and went to the kitchen. Mildred put four glasses and a bottle of brandy on a tray, and I carried it to the gentlemen. When I set it down in front of them,

Gratz took Gorin and Harvey by the hands and began to pump them. "It's settled then. I'll have a deed drawn. You're the new owners of Mammoth Cave. You won't regret it, and it will be a damn sight more fun than law-yering!" Mr. Gorin, Mr. Gratz, and Mr. Harvey talked about some things I missed, until I heard Stephen's name. Then I moved closer to the table to hear better.

"Your boy, Stephen, is a likely fellow. He'll make a good guide in no time. I'll have some of the help teach him the cave," said Mr. Gratz. Mr. Gorin was putting away his papers and Mr. Gratz drained his glass. I cleared the dishes.

Outside the door I saw Stephen looking over some mules in the pen. I picked up a pot of table scraps and went out to feed the chickens, near Stephen. "Looks like you are going to be a cave man yourself. You know about Mammoth Cave?" I watched Stephen's eyebrows squint.

"What? What are you talking about? Did you hear something?"

"Just that your owner is buying Mammoth Cave and you'll learn to be a guide there. Mr. Gorin, Mr. Harvey, and Mr. Gratz drank to it and shook on it." I thought Stephen would bust with curiosity, but I waited patiently.

"You should be ashamed listening in on somebody else's business," Stephen scolded. "They really shook on it? You aren't making this up to rile me, are you?"

I told him I thought he should know. At least, I'd want to know. Just then Mr. Gorin called Stephen to bring the buggy around front, and Stephen did. Mildred sidled up beside me and said without looking at me, "You overheard what went on in there. Keep it to your-self, or there'll be trouble."

She told me she'd be keeping an eye on me, and she smiled and waved as Mr. Gratz rode off on his horse. Stephen, Mr. Gorin, Mr. Harvey, and Charles Harvey,

STEPHEN BISHOP AT MAMMOTH CAVE

Jr. headed their buggy down the road toward Glasgow.

Later I asked Mildred what she knew about Stephen. She said he is a fine boy, and that she slips him a piece of fried chicken when he drops by. I asked her where Mammoth Cave was. She said to ask George. She was too busy.

George said that Mammoth Cave was about seven miles northwest of Three Forks. He'd heard it was a big saltpetre cave. Back in the war with the British, a saltpetre mining company moved in with about seventy owned and rented slaves. They set up a big manufactory at Mammoth Cave, and made saltpetre for gunpowder for the army. After the United States fought the 1812 war with the British, they quit making saltpetre there, and the cave was pretty much just a big hole in the ground. George said he had never been there, but expected to go see it one day. Mr. Bell said he did not intend to see Mammoth Cave, "I'll spend my time underground when I die."

Most days were interesting but some were dull in the months that passed. Guests came and went, and I got along with everyone, including Mrs. Bell. But things began to change after the fire.

I was peeling potatoes in the kitchen when I heard George yell, "Fire!" I ran out the door and saw flames and smoke at one corner of the smokehouse where the hams were hung. George was waving his arms and making a rumpus. I thought about the horse trough and ran over there. It was nearly empty, so I dipped up the last of the water in a bucket and ran to the fire. The water hardly did anything to put out the fire.

I thought about the cave, so I ran over and bounced down the stairs two at a time. Couldn't see nothing, but I could hear the water running. I felt the stream on my feet so I scooped up a bucket of water and ran up the stairs. The fire was bigger now. I ran over and tried to aim the water more carefully this time. It drenched the base of the flames so smoke rolled over me. I beat it back to the cave, down the steps, scooped more water from the stream, and ran up the steps. It took six or seven trips, but I put the fire out. Good thing. I was all sweaty and stumbling. One of the other slaves took the bucket and made several trips to the cave stream for more water.

Robert Bell was all over the place looking at the damage. He asked George what had happened. George said he was smoking some new hams when the fire spread. He tried to stomp it, but the flames were too hot. So he called for help. That's where I came in. Mr. Bell thanked me for running for water and saving the meat. I felt happy the fire was out but happier still that Mr. Bell didn't punish old George. I have seen slaves whipped for less than that back at Red Rose Hall.

George said afterward that Mr. Bell kept watching me when I wasn't looking. When I did look up and catch him, he would say something like, "Thank you for running fast," or "You saved a month's worth of meat and I appreciate it." It made me feel good to hear it from Mr. Bell, but there was something about his eyes and voice that told me I'd best watch out.

In the next few weeks I learned to clean and make up the rooms. This was on top of helping in the kitchen and serving food when trade picked up. When a guest left the tavern, I'd empty the chamber pot and slop water. I would strip the bed to air out the feather quilt. If the sheets were too wrinkled or muddy, I put them in the wash basket and put on clean sheets. Sometimes drunk men slept with their boots on, and the mud and dirt stuck to the sheets. I would plump up the pillows, and sweep the floor out into the hall. The last thing was to take the pitcher to the cave to fill it with fresh water.

One morning I was tending a room where a man and his wife stayed until the stage came. Robert Bell walked in the open door of the room I was cleaning. He closed the door behind him. "Looks like those two tussled around some." He was pointing at the rumpled bed where the sheets were twisted and the comforter was on the floor. I allowed it was more mess than usual. "You know, I'm indebted to you for how you jumped up and put out that fire."

Mr. Bell circled around the bed to where I was loading the crumpled sheets into the wash basket. He said in a soft voice, "Now, if you continue to be nice to me like that, I think we can talk about manumitting you some day." The thought of freedom shocked me, but at the same time I was getting scared of him closing in on me. He reached for my hand.

"Oh Lordy, Lordy!" I shouted, and pulled away from him. I jumped up on the bed. "You'd let me go free? Oh, thank you Mr. Bell. Thank you!" I raised my voice a notch or two so I could be heard through the open window. "You are too good, Mr. Bell. Saving the meat from the fire was nothing at all." I spread the curtains at the window and half leaned out, shaking a feather pillow. "I is so happy you is pleased! I is grateful." William Bell, the master's young son, looked up from the yard below. I shouted to him, "Mr. Bell so kind, he just thank me again for putting out the fire. He be a wonderful man!"

"Shhhh, be quiet. Get back in here." Mr. Bell was pulling my hand. I pulled the pillow in and swung around, cuffing him alongside of the head with it.

"Oh, I so sorry, Mr. Bell, I didn't mean to hit you like that. But I got work to do." I fished under the bed for the chamber pot, pulled it out and whipped off the lid. "Whooee. Sure do stink!" I held out the china pot in both hands for him to behold the mess inside. He made a grab for me, but I whirled around fast and near emptied that pot on Mr. Bell. "Lordy, Lordy," I yelled, "I sure have made a mess. You stay right there. I'll get help and clean you up. I'll get Mrs. Bell." I threw open the door and ran out.

"No, stop. Come back. No need for help. Come back!" But I was almost down the stairs running at top speed with that chamber pot, yelling for help as loud as I could. I may have stopped Mr. Bell from what he had in mind, but I decided right then I would not stay at Bell's Tavern, promise of freedom or not.

Mr. Bell kept his distance for a time. When he got too close, I'd talk louder and praise him to anyone who might be listening.

George said, "Mr. Bell still has his eye on you. Don't get alone with him. Unless you got another pot of shit ready."

Mildred said Mr. Bell was unhappy with his wife, Maria. If he got the right chance to grab a pretty slave girl like me, he would. That's the first time anyone said I was pretty. I was fairly small, but solid, and like I say, long-legged. I looked younger than my fourteen years, didn't have big breasts, but I was a full woman for a year or so then. And I knew how to run.

"There's three kinds of people in this world," Mildred said while we fixed the noon dinner one day. "There's a few people that give and are kind. There's a lot of people who give and take. Be nice to them and they be nice to you. Then there's a lot of folks that just take. George is one of the givers. Maybe Stephen is, too. Mr. Bell is one of the takers. Reckon the rest of us is in between."

Mildred reminded me of Addie. Addie used to say things like that back in Mississippi. I was too busy then to understand, but now I could see it better. My heart cracked a little, wishing Addie could hold me.

# Chapter 4

## Stephen Saves a Friend's Life

Maria Bell was about sixteen or seventeen, too young to be married to an old man like Robert Bell. But they did have a small boy, William. Mrs. Bell kept to herself mostly, and she hardly said anything when her husband was around.

Days grew shorter as the year wore on. I made it a point of telling Mrs. Bell how wonderful her husband was, and how I appreciated his kindness. I was cleaning a room when Mrs. Bell walked in. "You are so lucky to have such an attentive and loving husband," I said to her. "He just can't seem to thank me enough. He makes me feel like a $20 gold piece!"

She wrinkled up her nose and pointed at the candlestick, "Make sure you save those candle ends. We render them into new candles, and you're throwing them out. Money doesn't grow on trees. If Mr. Bell has failed to tell you that, he should have."

I aimed to tell her just enough to make her suspicious and watchful. And the talk about the gold piece was sure to get noticed because Mr. Bell is one of the tightest men around when it comes to spending money. She did seem to keep more careful track of him after that.

One day Stephen pulled in to the tavern with a wagon. He had bulging sacks of corn in the bed. Beside him was Cato, a slave who also belonged to Franklin Gorin. Cato was older and bigger than Stephen. "I need to fill my water jug," said Stephen to Mildred, who poked her head out of the kitchen door.

"I'll fetch it," I said, and grabbed his jug from his hand. I ran toward the cave.

"Wait," said Stephen, "there's another jug. I'll fill it, too." Stephen was beside me now. I opened the door to the cave and lit the lantern, and we went down the steps and over to the babbling stream.

"Got to wrench it out first." I filled the jug and poured it out. Then I filled it again. "Are you going to Mammoth Cave?"

"In a couple of months. Mr. Gorin is closing his law practice and land sales office in Glasgow. We're starting to pack because the deed is all signed. Right now I'm taking a load of corn over to the floating mill at Goose Spring Farm to grind it into cornmeal. I brought Cato along to do the heavy lifting." Stephen emptied and filled his jug, then hoisted it up and drank deeply. He topped off his jug with more water.

"Wait," I said. "Come back this way when you get the cornmeal. You're going to need more water."

Stephen looked at me curiously. "More water? Yes, I guess I will. And it's on the way home." We went back to his wagon and he told the team, "Giddiap." The sun shone through the golden leaves and outlined Stephen's wagon. It made me wish I could go along.

All day I could see in my mind Stephen dribbling water down his chin and chest when he took that drink of water in the cave. It made me laugh to think about what a mess he made.

Later that afternoon Stephen and Cato drove their wagon back into the yard. I noticed that Cato had blood running down his back from a wound that he tried to hide by turning one way and another. Mr. Bell greeted them and asked what they wanted. Water, they said, and delivered Mr. Gorin's greetings to Mr. Bell. Mr. Bell lightened up some, and pointed the way to the cave. Both Cato and Stephen toted their jugs after letting the horses drink from the trough. I told Mildred I would bring back a pail of milk and followed them into the cave.

"What's a floating mill?" I asked.

"It's a set of millstones on a flatboat." Stephen explained every detail. "The flatboat is tied fast to trees along the bank of a swift stream, and there's a paddle wheel on one side of the boat. Water rushes by and turns the wheel. The wheel turns a shaft that rotates the top millstone. You pour the corn in a hopper and it falls down a hole in the middle between the millstones. Ground up cornmeal comes out at the edge and falls into a trough. You shovel it into sacks and load it back on the wagon, and the miller collects a tenth of the cornmeal for his price."

"So you went to the river? The Green River?" George had told me you had to cross the Green River to get to the Forks of the Nolin River, where he used to live.

"No, this is a different river. It's at Goose Spring Farm, about three miles from here. Farmers from all around bring their corn to be ground into cornmeal. You go west and south on the turnpike, then turn north and up the hill where there's a lane that leads to Goose Spring Farm and mill. This little valley is a deep hole in the ground. A river maybe thirty feet wide comes out of a spring at one end, flows along the bottom for a little piece, then sinks in a pool. The floating mill is tethered along that stream. You drive the wagon down a steep road and unload the corn into the mill and load the cornmeal back into the wagon after it's ground by the millstones."

It struck me odd that a wide, swift river could be so short and be down in a hole in the ground. "Where does the water go? And where does it come from?" I wanted to know.

Cato answered angrily, "Nobody knows and nobody cares. It's a mystery. Just like that damn miller. I'd like to kill him!" Cato's eyes flashed hot fire beneath his narrowed brow. Their water jugs spilled over the top now.

"Where?" I asked again. Stephen answered.

"Like Cato said, we don't know, but I'd like to know. We might have found out, but Cato got uppity with the miller and almost got himself killed." Stephen said the miller ordered Cato to shovel somebody else's wagon load of corn into the mill when it arrived after they did. Cato pretended he didn't hear, but looked evil at the man. The miller uncoiled a leather bullwhip and cracked Cato a bleeding cut on his shoulder. Cato was ready to strike the miller with his shovel. "But I stepped between them."

Cato interrupted, "What the hell did you say to the miller? You took him off a little way and whispered to him. He kept looking over your shoulder at me. Stephen, what did you say to him, that he let us go?"

Stephen said, "No need to go into that. It's late and we need to be on the road."

I said, "Tell us what you told the miller, please?"

Stephen said, "Well, I told him that we both belonged to Franklin Gorin, the lawyer over at Glasgow. He asked if he was the one whose father killed a bear on his farm the day he was born, firstborn in Glasgow. I said yes, that's him."

"That's it? He let us go after that?" Cato was more agitated now.

"That's not all of it. I told the miller you were Frank Gorin's son, and if Cato got a beating or ended up dead, Mr. Gorin would bring the sheriff and the regulator patrols, and have him thrown in jail, forfeit the mill, and get 100 lashes. So it's best to let bygones be bygones." Stephen was grinning now. "The miller decided he better not punish somebody else's property!"

Stephen and Cato were fixing to drive their wagon back to Glasgow when Mr. Bell said, "It's twelve miles to Glasgow. If you leave now you won't get home until daybreak. You can stay in the slave quarters if you want. I'll ask Mildred to get you something to eat. Get a fresh start in the morning. I'll charge you twenty cents, or a peck of cornmeal."

Stephen and Cato agreed. While they put the team up for the night, I got two plates of salt pork, beans, corn pone, and greens ready.

It was after dark when I finished cleaning up the kitchen and went to my cabin. Stephen was sitting in front of one of the slave cabins when I went by. "You're not going to tell me where the water came from and went to?" I said to him. "Not sure I can sleep, wondering about that."

"It's peculiar, and here's why. Every little trickle of water after a rain runs into a little crick and that crick runs to a bigger crick. Then it joins a stream and then a river. Know what I mean?"

"Yes, back on the plantation we had the crick. It flowed to a bigger river then to the Mississippi River. When that old river slid past New Orleans it went into the sea, where ships could sail all over the world."

"How do you know that?" Stephen asked if I had seen the river.

"No, I heard about it." Tom Wells told me. I always wanted to see it for myself. So did Tom.

Stephen and I talked about mysterious things like

disappearing water, what it was like being a child, about memories of being young, about sneaking off and exploring. He told me he liked to hide from his mama, and his favorite hiding hole was inside an old brick oven where his mother never thought to look. Then one day she started to build a fire in the oven, and Stephen had to cry out. She was surprised and scolded him and switched him good. "My baby brother, Schuyler, will probably vex her, too."

Stephen said his mother was part Creek Indian. I asked what that meant. He said his mother was yellow, a light-complexioned Negro. As a small boy his friends teased him about how his mother looked, until one day he told them she was part Indian. That caused their eyes to roll in wonder. It shut them up pretty good, especially when Stephen told them he would cast an old Indian spell on them if they told anyone this secret.

Nosey folks were forever curious about who your parents were, whether they were white or black or mulatto. I began to turn over in my mind the notion that my great grandmother was an African princess who was kidnapped by slavers. When she came missing, her mother and father, the king and queen, were grieving so hard they wept and cried. Their tears flowed along the ground and became a mighty river—the Charlotte River—and that's why my mama named me Charlotte.

I told Stephen about how I loved to run, and about the time I took off running and old Asa Woodworth chased me, hit a stump, and died. I never heard anyone like Stephen before. His stories made me laugh and some of them made me feel bad. When I couldn't keep my eyes open anymore I said goodnight and hoped he would come by again.

At first light of morning Stephen and Cato didn't wait for the cock to crow. They had left with the whipoorwills.

One guest at Bell's Tavern was a preacher from Oberlin up in Ohio, who was heading to Nashville. He seemed kinder than most of the guests. He asked if I was born in Kentucky. I said No. He asked was I a slave or free woman of color. I told him I was a slave. He asked how that could be, since Kentuckians could not bring in slaves to the state after 1833. The Kentucky legislature had made it illegal to do so. I told him John Bogsdon in Nashville, who I never laid eyes on, bought me and rented me to Robert Bell.

That preacher said this is how slave owners in Kentucky get around the law, by claiming not to own their slaves, but to rent them from owners in states where slavery is the law. He went on to say God hated slavery. Well, so did I. But if I could be rented out to one man, couldn't I be rented out to another if I didn't work out? The idea stuck in my mind.

Maybe I was too valuable to Robert Bell. Many slaves worked as little as possible. They'd lay out from time to time, returning just before their master got upset at their absence. Some slaves ran away. We talked about those we knew who ran, but most of those were caught and returned. Some slaves ran off to find their parents or their children. I had thought about running off to find Addie Wells, but had no idea where she might be. Now and then runaways would appear at the kitchen door or slave quarters just after dark. It was dangerous to give them food or help them, but Mildred sometimes just happened to leave some food out, or delayed until dark taking table scraps to the chickens.

If you were careful, it wasn't a problem, because everyone knew that slaves had a five-finger wage that was not money. Since masters took money earned by the sweat of their slaves, it was only right and wise for the slaves to help themselves to the master's bounty, which they helped earn. It wasn't thieving. It was just changing one form of property to another form of owned property. Mr. Bell sometimes complained that Mildred was using too much food. She told him he was a stingy manager rather than a storekeeper who knew his stock. She delivered him ten dollars of value for every dollar he spent on food.

If I hoped to get out of Bell's Tavern, I'd have to find a money way of doing it.

Anything else was too risky.

# Chapter 5

# Running to Mammoth Cave

The following spring we had a couple of passengers stop off at Bell's Tavern from the Louisville stage. Mrs. Cooper looked eight or nine months pregnant, sort of pale and frail, but stuffed. Mr. Cooper asked Mr. Bell about staying over a few days, due to his wife being weary from traveling. During his stopover he wanted to see Mammoth Cave, so Mr. Bell arranged for a wagon to take him there for two days.

About mid-afternoon of the first day Mrs. Cooper became ill. She threw up her dinner even though she had not eaten much. Mr. Bell grew concerned about Mrs. Cooper, and Mildred told him she might deliver the child any minute. They talked about sending one of the slaves to bring Mr. Cooper back from Mammoth Cave. I said I would run to Mammoth Cave and tell Mr. Cooper to come back at once.

"I appreciate your offer, Charlotte, but it's seven miles through the woods to Mammoth Cave," Mr. Bell said. "You would get tired, or worse, a bear might catch you and eat you." I told Mr. Bell I could run to

Mammoth Cave in an hour. I told him George said the last bear was seen over thirty years ago. If he would write me a pass I would be on my way. He scribbled with his quill pen on a piece of paper and sealed it in an envelope." Here, show this if you need to, and get back as soon as you can."

George said the way to Mammoth Cave was to follow the road from Three Forks north. Mildred gave me a piece of corn pone wrapped in a cloth. I tucked the pass down the front of my calico frock and drew up my belt to hold it in. I ran off like a scared fox.

This was my first time away from Bell's Tavern since I first came, and it felt wonderful to be running free. My bare feet flew along the dusty road. I skipped over the ruts left from the last rain. The road led over little hilly rollers between little dips that looked more like slop basins than valleys. I thought I would find a stream to get a drink, but there wasn't any. Two dogs that were lazing on the porches of cabins got up and barked at me. It was hot, but running fast made a wind in my face and cooled me some.

The road started up a steep hill and led sideways up the steepest part of the slope, until it broke over the crest of the hill. From the top I looked back south and could see the bottomland with knobs rising out of it in the distance. Ahead the road stretched along the top of the ridge among tall trees and after a couple of miles the road forked. One way lay straight ahead, the other had a sign I could not read. I figured that must be the way to go. I followed that road down a steep hill to a valley bottom. Immediately the heat of the day became cooler as I ran under the big trees. Once or twice I felt a cool breeze, sort of like I was sinking into water, and I was partly in it and partly out.

Where was that breeze coming from? I had felt cool air like that in our cave back at the tavern, but out here in the woods there were only holes at the edge of the road. One strong blow of cold air made me stop and approach the hole. Air rushing out of a hole in the ground fluttered the leaves on nearby trees and felt refreshing. I stopped and let the cool air wash over me until I shivered a little, and then I went on.

The road was climbing uphill now and I reached the top of the ridge where I ran along under big trees. I ran past several cabins, but followed the biggest ruts. When I crested a little rise I could see a large log cabin nestled among the trees. Several horses were tied to the hitching rail switching flies off. Smoke rose from the chimney of the kitchen house off to the side of the main cabin. I ran to the porch and asked a lady for Mr. Gorin. She said she was his wife, Louisa, and she would get him.

"Mammoth Cave around here?" I said.

Franklin Gorin had stepped out of the building and nodded Yes to my question. He asked, "Why are you running?"

I told him that Mr. Cooper's wife was feeling poorly and that Mildred thought her baby might come anytime. Mr. Bell told me to fetch Mr. Cooper and ask him to return at once to Bell's Tavern.

Mr. Gorin fished out a pocket watch from his frock coat and opened it. "Mr. Cooper is in the cave with Stephen. They won't be out for a couple of hours. By then it will be getting dark."

I had thought Mr. Gorin might loan Mr. Cooper a horse for the quickest return trip. "Guess I could spare this mare," he said indicating a bay tied to the rail. "Go around to the kitchen and get something to eat. You ran all the way here from Bell's place?" I nodded.

He followed me around to the kitchen. "How long did it take you to run here?" I told him it took about an hour. He shook his head, but it was no big thing to me. At the kitchen door a slave handed me a large plate of fried chicken, some biscuits with honey on them, and beans.

As the sun sank, through the long shadows I saw four men walking slowly up a path from down the hill. The man in front carried a basket and a lantern. Two of the others carried lanterns. Closer up I saw Stephen was in the lead with Mr. Cooper just behind him. Mr. Gorin met them on the path and spoke to Mr. Cooper in low tones, pointing toward the bay mare.

"Can I leave now?" Cooper said.

Stephen said, "If you wait for the full moon to be out, you will be able to see just fine. "Gives you enough time to clean up and eat supper. Rest a little before you set out."

Cooper told Gorin, "That cave trip was the most wonderful thing I have ever done in my life. Stephen, here, knew the answers to all my questions. He showed us wonders nobody else has ever seen!"

Franklin Gorin and Stephen exchanged a flash of a smile as Cooper went on: "We came to a giant chamber where there were saltpetre dirt vats made of split logs. It looked as if the slaves had left yesterday. Stephen produced for our inspection some actual digging tools, several shovels, a hoe, and a pickaxe. We went on ten miles into the cave."

"More or less," Stephen said.

"I'm sure it was ten miles, to where we had the most delightful picnic by lantern light sitting on the rocks. It was the most delicious fried chicken, biscuits, raisins, nuts, and a draft of exquisite wine. A most delicious luncheon indeed! And Stephen, my how he can tell stories. Tell them the one about the ghost that lives in the spring."

Stephen said, "I believe they have heard it." Gorin rolled his eyes up into the trees. "You'd better get ready to eat," Stephen warned, "it's a long ride ahead of you."

Cooper pressed a coin into Stephen's hand, then went into the log inn with Mr. Gorin.

Stephen turned to me and asked, "So you ran all the way over here from Bell's? Weren't you scared?"

I rested against the doorway and said, "Yes, I ran, I like to run, it gives me time to think about things. After a while part of me is running along and part of me is thinking and flying over the ground. And, no, I wasn't scared."

The lantern grazed Stephen's light brown face and his eyes sparkled as he smiled. He seemed softer than when I first met him. To tell the truth, he seemed a little uppity when I showed him the cave at Bell's Tavern. Now he was more at ease.

I continued, "Can you answer me a question? When I was running down into a valley between Bell's and here, I ran into a pool of cold air, sort of a breeze. I stopped to find out where it came from. It flowed out of a hole in the ground. What is that?"

"Same kind of cave that you showed me at Bell's that day. Caves are cool, so when they breathe out, you can feel the air rush, like standing in a high wind in winter. Sometimes you can see the cold air, like when you go past sinkholes in the ground early in the morning and the air makes steam. It's like fog, and it can shake the leaves."

I believe Stephen could explain why the sky is blue and trees are green, and why some people are kind and some are mean.

"Want to see Mammoth Cave?" Stephen blurted it out.

"Sure do. But I have to get back. Mr. Bell said come back as soon as I can." Stephen pointed out it would be dangerous to run back at night, even in a full moon. Between the ruts and roots, I'd trip up for sure. I asked was he worried that I'd run into wild animals or ghosts.

"Ha! You? You are too small to eat, and probably you could outrun any ghost."

There was that sly smile again. I wanted to see Mammoth Cave with Stephen, and he convinced me I could set off at first light and get back in time to help in the kitchen.

"You got anything warm beside that dress?"

"No, that's it, but I go into Bell's cave a couple of times a day with just this on. I'll be all right."

Stephen said he would get some food, oil for the lamps, and a warm coat for me to wear. I watched him go into the slave quarters, come out, talk to a couple of other slaves, head for the kitchen, and come out with a small basket. Slung over his shoulder was a small metal can that sloshed. "Lamp oil," he said. He slipped a worn coat over my shoulder and we set off down the path.

# Chapter 6

# A Grand Cave

Stephen pulled out a match and struck it on a rock. "Don't breathe the smoke, it'll kill you," Stephen said. He held it to the wicks of both lamps. We stood in the middle of a pool of yellow light. I put my finger through the wire loop on top of the heat shield, lifted it, and we set off. Our footsteps crunched along the trail that led down the steep hill. The only other noise was crickets singing. A perfume of honeysuckle drifted by. At the road edge the path ended and we crossed the ruts, then back onto the path again. We stopped at the top of a big hole in the ground. I heard the sound of falling water at the far end.

We climbed down some rough stone steps, to the right of the splashing water, and into a blast of cold air. "I'm glad you found me this coat." I turned up the collar.

Our lamp flames fluttered and danced. At the bottom of the steps a flat path went down a short dip and up into the cave. Along the right side of the rock-lined path were two pipelines made of hollowed-out logs. Stephen said it was part of the saltpetre manufactory, and that they used one pipeline to carry water into the cave and the other to carry the niter-liquor out.

We came to a large round room, bigger than the biggest room at Red Rose Hall, which I had seen once. Our lights dimly reached the walls and ceiling of the room. Our bodies formed giant shadows on the wall. I set my lamp down on the floor behind a rock and made a wolf head shadow on the wall with my hands, like Tom Wells showed me when I was a little girl. When I opened my little fingers to make the wolf's mouth go, I heard a piercing wolf cry. "Oooooowwwoooo. Woop, woop, woop, oooouuuuwww!" It startled me, but I knew right away it was Stephen and he laughed when I looked surprised.

"The Rotunda was discovered by a hunter, who chased a bear into this hole. He held his long rifle in one hand and a torch in the other. If he had met the bear head-on and eye-to-eye, how could he shoot the gun and hold the torch up at the same time?" Stephen waited for my answer. "Well?"

I picked up my lamp and moved it up against the wall where my wolf shadow had been. "The hunter didn't need a gun. He put his torch over near the wall like this, and the bear disappeared."

Stephen laughed again, "You should be a guide."

In the floor I could see the rim of a log wall like a corncrib, but square and larger, and there was another next to it. A couple of long hollow pipeline logs lay nearby. It looked like piles of earth heaped up and covering the floor of the cave. "Slaves dug cave dirt and hauled it to these vats. They dumped it in and ran water over it. Muddy water trickled down through the dirt and came out the bottom of the vat as niter-liquor that was pumped up to the top of a tower by slaves, where it ran out a set of wooden pipes to the entrance. That's where they boiled the niter-liquor in iron kettles to make salt-petre crystals. Saltpetre crystals, charcoal, and sulphur mixed together make gunpowder." Stephen pointed out the drain lines, pieces of the collapsed pump tower, and its pipeline back toward the cave entrance. There were passages leading left and right.

We walked deeper into the cave, to the left through a passage bigger than a church. He showed me stone cubbyholes in the wall, like letter holes in a desk. There were remains of another pipeline, mountains of rocks, dried shit from oxen and people, and a dripping spring of water in a little hole in the wall. We came to another room with passages up and onward. "How do you know where to go? Will you get us lost?" I asked.

"No, I'll show you. Did you bring anything to draw on, like paper?" I fished Robert Bell's slave pass from my dress. He spread the envelope on a rock, took a pencil, and drew a wiggly line. "We came in here to the Rotunda, see?" He drew a circle. "Then we went left like this, and we're right here." His second line ended in a little circle. "Back at the Rotunda we could have gone to the right," he said pointing ahead. We'd come to a mountain of rocks, and a little passage leading onward, and it ended, too. The lines were cave passages, and I could see he knew just how it all fitted together.

"I'll keep this map," Stephen said.

"No you won't," I said. "That's my pass if I get stopped on the way back home." Stephen turned the envelope over and studied the words Bell had written in ink.

"Do you know what it says?" Stephen asked.

I took it back from him. "How could I know? Mr. Bell just told me it's a pass and if anyone stops me, I am to show them this. Then they'll know that I belong to Mr. Bell and I travel on his business. Didn't you and Cato have passes when you traveled on the road?"

"No, we didn't need a pass where we went." Stephen moved ahead down the passage.

We passed more cave earth vats and more halls off in different directions. We came to a big rock, bigger than a stagecoach. Stephen said we'd stop for a bite to eat. He pulled out two apples and gave me one. It wasn't the best, a little mushy, one of last year's apples. He had brought one drumstick and a part of a chicken breast, which he handed me. "This is from a one-sided chicken — it was in a fight," he said.

"How come you didn't bring me the winner?" He fell over on the floor. I thought I'd pee laughing at Stephen who rolled on the ground flapping his arms like chicken wings and clucking like an old hen.

Stephen told me the cave passages were like a river bed. They split where a side stream came in. Once in a while the passage would divide around an island of stone, and then the passages would come back together. I could picture water in a crick flowing along slow on a sunny day, and boiling along after a hard rain. I yawned, gentled by Stephen's voice. We must have been in the cave a couple of hours. I wasn't tired until now, but that run was making me sleepy.

I felt Stephen's hand on mine, and he said, "You look tired so we'll go back." He helped me to my feet. "Race you back," he yelled as he ran off.

I jumped after him and ran fast, scared that he'd leave me behind. He crested one hill, leaving me with my feeble light. I lunged ahead, picking up speed and raced ahead of him at the bottom of the hill. I was wide awake now. There seemed to be only one path ahead, and my feet on the rocks on the floor made them clunk and clank as they shifted. Stephen was behind me but I lengthened the distance between us, pounding on toward the entrance. I had a brief picture in my mind of the trees flying by that night in Mississippi with Asa in hot pursuit. Now I was alone, skimming over the trail in a big cave instead of a forest. Stephen's footfalls faded behind me and I was running alone and free through the glorious Mammoth Cave. The cave widened to where I could not see the walls. I stopped and the lamp flame picked up again. I walked from one wall to another. Nothing looked familiar; I had never been here before! Now I felt real fear in my stomach. I listened, but there was no sound behind me. Had I taken a wrong turn? But I hadn't turned at all.

I turned and trotted back the way I had come. Around the corner was the vast round room, the Rotunda, and in the bottom of a square vat Stephen's lamp cast a patch of light on the ceiling high above me. I stopped at the edge and looked down at Stephen stretched out on his back on the floor of the vat, like a field hand at rest.

"You're fast. You wore me out." Stephen's eyes sparkled and he grinned up at me. "You like to run?"

"Sometimes, when nobody is chasing me." He asked who would chase me, not counting Stephen, the guide. I told him more about Asa Woodworth, and how scared I was, and how I ran for my life that night he died. I thought Stephen would make a joke about what he would do if he caught me. Instead, Stephen got up and hit his clothes with his hands as dust rose in a cloud.

"Well, I've been scared, too. This cave has some scary places in it. And some of the visitors have made me fearful. Cato said something the other day that scared me. He said he was planning to escape to freedom. He was angry, being a slave and all. I was afraid he'd be overheard, and get both of us in trouble. I told him in a loud way that we have it better off than most slaves. Of course, that made him madder, mostly at me." Stephen quietly told me of other times in the cave when he had felt frightened.

He climbed up beside me and brushed my hand.

"Out we go. Nothing to fear on your first trip to Mammoth Cave. Maybe next time." We walked to the entrance steps and climbed up to a dark blue sky with a full moon touching everything with cool light.

Stephen showed me to an unoccupied cabin and said goodnight. As I lay back on the straw mattress I heard in my mind Stephen's laugh, his musical voice, and his wonderful stories. I could be a friend with Stephen, who gave me so much to remember that night.

A rooster woke me. I sprang up and went to Franklin Gorin's cabin. I asked if Stephen was about, so I could give back the coat and thank him for the cave trip. Mr. Gorin said Stephen was planting corn in a bottom field down by the river today, but he would give the coat back. I asked about Mr. Cooper. He had ridden off last night when the moon rose high enough to see by. Gorin wondered if I needed a bite to eat for my trip back to Bell's. I made him some corn pone, the way I do, and he gave me a piece to eat.

"Are you the cook at Bell's yet?" he asked. "This is the best corn pone I ever ate. We need a cook here some days when we have more visitors than we can handle."

I told him Mildred was the cook, but I was getting my hand in now and then. He said, "Charlotte, can you read? A cook needs to be able to read and write a list."

I suppose my face revealed fear. If I told him yes, there would be trouble. Slaves who tried to learn to read could be punished continually. Also, if I told him yes, it would be a lie. If I told him no, would it rule out leaving Bell's to come to Mammoth Cave? Mildred could not read or write. It certainly did not prevent her from cooking. She memorized the supplies list, and I had taught her to cook several dishes I had learned in Mississippi. Carefully I said, "Would it help me to become a cook here if I learned to read?"

Gorin thought before he spoke. "Somebody smart might get by even if she couldn't read. I know slaves aren't supposed to read. But a smart slave who can read is more useful than one who can't."

I thanked him for the food. I told him I'd like to work at Mammoth Cave. I said goodbye and ran through the forest like a swift wild turkey. The morning sun slanted through the trees making islands of light on the forest floor. I pretended the light spots were rocks in the cave and I was bounding from one to another. I felt free to avoid the shadows and thankful to be alive and running fast.

Near the bottom of the long hill leading to the rolling land a man stepped out from the trees and looked at me approaching. I recognized Cato and stopped.

"Can you keep quiet about seeing me?" Cato moved back a little into a tree shadow.

"Why?"

"Because I'm laying out."

"They'll miss you and come looking for you." I told him it was a bad idea, and he could expect less food or the lash when he was caught. He should go back.

"I'm running, heading north. I have nothing to lose. If I make it to the Ohio River, I think I can get to Canada."

That was Cato's plan? Even I knew it wouldn't work. Any Negro traveling north could expect questions. Slave catchers had a strong network of informers, slave owners, government officials, drovers, and teamsters. A black face without a pass would get you twenty miles and a set of leg irons.

"Listen, go south instead of north."

"South? That isn't the way."

I cut Cato off short. "No Negro heading south will be questioned. Why would he be? And do you have a pass?"

"No, I don't have a pass." He looked down at his feet. I took out my own pass, the one on which Stephen had drawn the cave map. I worked my fingernail under the flap of the envelope and drew out the folded paper. "You keep this, and head south. If anybody stops you, say you are on an errand to Nashville for your master in Louisville. Don't show the pass unless you must." I stuck the envelope shut and put it down my dress. "Good luck."

Cato waved as I ran off. I had a bad feeling I would never see him again.

I ran to the back door of Bell's Tavern in time to clean up the breakfast leavings and dishes. The guests were sad because Mrs. Cooper's baby had died of a fever shortly after it was born, and before Mr. Cooper had arrived. Mrs. Cooper wept and Mr. Cooper did his best to comfort her.

Their baby boy was buried in Bell's graveyard, and it was about a week before the Mrs. was strong enough to travel.

I learned that Cato was caught in Elizabethtown, about thirty miles north of us. He came to the back door of a stagecoach inn there and asked for food. The proprietor gave him a big plate of food, slipped out and knocked on the door of a slave catcher guest. The slave catcher asked if Cato had a pass. Cato produced it. The slave catcher unfolded the pass and read it, then he laughed out loud.

"Is your name Charlotte?"

"No sir. It's Cato, sir."

"Well this pass says I can take you back down the road thirty miles and collect ten dollars. Then you, me, and Mr. Estes here will be square. Is that all right with you?"

"Yes sir."

Getting away wasn't an easy or sure thing.

After word came that Cato was caught running, Robert Bell asked if I had his pass. I was scared because that was the pass I had given Cato. "Mr. Bell, I have the envelope. I will get it for you." When I handed the envelope to him my heart was pounding. He looked at the front of the envelope, then turned it over. He was looking at Stephen's map.

"What's this?" he sounded mean.

"Writing, sir."

"Whose writing?" he demanded.

"Stephen's. Stephen Bishop at Mammoth Cave." That should take Bell onto a new trail.

"Do you know what this says?" He handed the envelope back. I looked at the lines and turned the envelope around a few times studying it.

"No, I can't read it."

"Neither can I. If Stephen told you that was writing, he lied to you." Fury shone in his eyes. "Charlotte, where's the pass I wrote out for you?"

"I gave it to Cato. He had never seen a pass before. He wanted to see it." I thought the truth was as good as a lie, because Bell would not believe anything I told him now that Cato's name was out in the open as a runaway.

"That's what Cato told his owner, Franklin Gorin. He said he took it from you when you were running back here. Why didn't you tell me that?"

"I was afraid you would be angry if I came back without it." I began to cry. Mr. Bell was more distracted by that than he was when I brought up Stephen's writing. He moved toward me and slipped his arm around my shoulders.

"Now, now, Charlotte. Don't cry. I'm sorry I frightened you, it's all right. I am sure you didn't mean to help Cato run away." His comforting touch was becoming uncomfortable for me, so I began to sob and wail so loudly that he let me go.

It might not be easy to get away from Bell's Tavern, but I did not intend to stay one day longer than necessary.

# Chapter 7

## Brandied Peaches and
## a Slave for Rent

Robert Bell owned many slaves besides Mildred and me and the men who Bell brought north with me from Nashville. The other slaves lived on the Bell farm about a mile away. They mostly tended the fields and livestock. Pigs and chickens were plentiful, but we had beef cattle and some milk cows. Every third day one or another slave would bring a wagonload of food from the farm to the tavern. In the summer there was fruit. In winter we got our potatoes, yams, carrots, and onions refilled as needed. In late summer and fall we dried beans and put up some of the fruit and pickles in crocks to tide us through the winter. My favorite time was when the peaches ripened. For a couple of weeks we stored peaches in crocks of sugar water and moved them down into the cave. I sneaked a peach now and then.

Visitors at the tavern liked to end a meal with a peach or cornbread with honey or sorghum. One day I served a gentleman from Baltimore a peach at the end of his dinner. He asked for sorghum without cornbread, so I brought him the pitcher. He had been drinking brandy before and during his meal. It surprised me when he dumped his glass of brandy and a dollop of sorghum on top of that peach. People eat strange things sometimes, like eggs on top of pancakes and sorghum or molasses, but I never saw anybody mess with a peach. "Is that good to eat?" I wanted to know. Sorghum tasted sharp with a little bite, not as mild as honey.

The gentleman dabbed his mouth with his sleeve. "If anyone offers you a last meal before hanging you, ask for a brandied peach. Can't do any better than that. I learned that from a harness maker in Atlanta." He cut the peach into small pieces and swirled each one over and over before he ate it. I could not imagine how that would taste.

My curiosity got too much of me the next day, so I sneaked a peach, sorghum, and a little brandy. Well, you had to get used to that! It tasted like a peach sure enough, but the sorghum gave it an extra kick. Honey was better. The brandy cleared out your nose and its fumes carried that sweet peach flavor all through my head. I wondered what a little thick cream would do to it, so I added a couple of spoonfuls. That mixture with honey instead of sorghum made about the best taste I ever enjoyed, and the cream hid the brown color.

That evening when Mr. Bell and his family had nearly finished eating, I brought him a dish of my new peach mixture. He took a little taste, like it might be poison, and then a great grin broke out on his red face. "What is this? I see the peach and the cream. But what did you put in this?" When I told him the guest from Baltimore had ordered it and I had improved it some by adding cream, he told me to bring some for his family. Mrs. Bell said it was the tastiest sweet ever and that Mr. Bell should serve it to guests.

From then on, brandied peaches became the dish of the tavern. Folks coming through on their return trip asked for a brandied peach first thing. Soon guests came for the first time asking for the brandied peach they had heard about. After a little while he just left out the cream. Later he was serving mostly brandy and just a little peach. Peach brandy, as he called it, didn't appeal to me, but he would pour some for every arriving guest.

Robert Bell came after me again, saying how much he appreciated me telling him about brandied peaches. I made a loud fuss over his praise and escaped to the kitchen or dining room a few times. If I didn't figure out some way to get him to stop, or to get away, he would get me off in a corner alone. He may have been old, fat, red, and ugly, but he was stronger than me and he owned me.

It was a cold day in November when Mr. Bell came down the steps in the storage cave while I was collecting potatoes, milk, and turnips for Mildred. "Charlotte, I am fit to be tied because I want to get to know you better. Every time I come near, you howl and carry on. I get the feeling you don't like me. I do want to be your friend, and I'd like you to be friendly back." He put his arm around my waist. I could smell whiskey on his breath. Nobody could hear me if I yelled and he would not be stopped.

"Tell you what, Mr. Bell. I believe you do like me. I believe I could make you like me even better than you do now." His eyes widened. I had his attention pretty good. "And I could treat you real fine, if only —"

"If only what?"

"If only it wasn't that time of the month. See, I just started to bleed. And when I bleeds I use up maybe a dozen corn husks. It stink pretty bad, but I am ready now if you want me. Or we could wait a few days when I could clean up and be all fresh for you."

He was backing off with a worried look and his eyes shifted to make sure he would not fall over something.

"You would wait? Wait for me?" His eyes glassed over.

"It will be hard to wait, but it will be better in a few days." I gave him all the hope I could. He turned and went up the steps out of the cave.

The next day Bell's Tavern burned to the ground.

I don't know exactly how it burned because I wasn't there.

Before first light of that morning I asked Mildred to give me the list of food and supplies she needed from the farm. She said there wasn't any list. She remembered what was needed and recited the list to one of the stable slaves who would run out to the farm. I asked her to send me instead. She said no. She needed me.

I couldn't think of any other excuse to get away, so I told Mildred about Mr. Bell's intentions. It was embarrassing, but told her about using my monthly time as a reason to make him leave me alone.

She seemed to think that was amusing at first, but then her eyebrows narrowed and she sounded more serious. "You remember this list." She rattled off about fifteen things she needed from the farm, and told me to ask for Noah when I got there.

I put on an old sweater and a cap, because the weather had turned colder. My breath steamed like a horse after winter running. Noah opened the door of the overseer's cabin when the dog barked at my coming. He nodded after each item Mildred wanted. Then he slowly repeated each item out loud. "I have to get back," I said after warming myself at the fire. He handed me a wool cloth to wrap around my face to keep the cold off, but I didn't need extra because running keeps me warm. I set off in a different direction.

The trail to Mammoth Cave was hard and frozen. Ice sparkled from some of the ruts. Bare tree limbs jutted into a gray sky. It felt wonderful to be running again. I slipped off two times a week to run, but it had been three days since my last run. I wasn't cold in the least, it was like floating, so I took off the sweater and tied it around me.

My feet picked the right spots without thinking about it. My mind was racing too, not knowing exactly what to do. I must get word to Stephen about the fix I was in. He might not be able to do anything, but he would have some ideas. I never met anyone who knew more about people than Stephen, and I needed good advice. I rehearsed my story: *Stephen, can you help me? Mr. Bell means to take me by force. I have about used up the excuses. What can I do?*

Stephen had to be at the Mammoth Cave Hotel or Franklin Gorin's house, or in the cave. I would come to Mr. Gorin's house first. He seemed decent when I talked to him before. I knocked. Mr. Gorin opened the door. I didn't see Stephen anywhere, and I was afraid I had made a terrible mistake, but Mr. Gorin stood aside to let me in, and asked, "What brings you out on a winter day? Come in and warm yourself at the fire." He took a seat and beckoned me to sit in a chair opposite him.

I was flustered some, but I allowed, "I need to find Stephen Bishop right away and ask him something important. You know where I can find him?"

"What do you want to ask him?" He waited a long time for my answer.

"I was sent—Let me start again." The room was turning around and I felt like a simple-minded girl. "I want to ask Stephen what to do about Mr. Bell." I began to weep and I could not stop. Mr. Gorin handed me a kerchief and I dabbed my eyes with it. Then I decided to tell the truth why I had come.

"Mr. Bell, who owns me, is trying to take me and use me. He is married and I don't want to be used by him. I am afraid for my life. Stephen, he is the smartest man I know. He can tell me what to do, what to say. See, I lose no matter what I do. Mr. Bell can whip me or sell me. Even kill me if I don't let him take me. I do not want to run away. Runaways get caught. Please, can I talk to Stephen?"

Now my fix was out in the open. Mr. Gorin could either help me or return me to Bell.

"Are you sure Robert Bell owns you? Legally owns you?" Mr. Gorin was standing up now and pacing back and forth in front of the hearth.

"Guess so. He bought me at the slave auction in Nashville. Then I found that somebody I never met in Nashville owns me. His name is Bogsdon, but I was rented to Mr. Bell, who claims he owns me. Makes no difference, does it?"

"It might. Since 1833 it has been against the law in the Commonwealth to import slaves into Kentucky." I had forgotten about Mr. Gorin's lawyer schooling. Where was he going with this?

"But Stephen is your slave. Is that against the law?" Maybe I spoke too quick.

"Yes. Stephen is my slave, and so was his mother. Both were born in Kentucky, so the law does not apply." Mr. Gorin spun around and fixed me with his blue eyes. "Tell me, Charlotte, are you interested in Stephen? What's your attraction to him?"

I began to tear up again. "He treated me right and he is smart. He stays out of trouble better than most. I trust him. That's all."

"Stephen is a good judge of character. He tells me you are a hard worker and that you know how to help cook, wait table, and make up the rooms. He said you are smart, even if you can't read." Gorin began to pace again. "And brave when you put out that fire. We may be able to use you here, at Mammoth Cave, if we can figure out a way to get you here without stealing you."

Mr. Gorin's face clouded over. "And another thing, Maria Bell is my daughter. We don't get along well since I was unhappy about her marrying Robert Bell. On the other hand, I want the best for her," said Mr. Gorin. "Perhaps there is a way to reduce the temptation."

There was a knock at the door. Mr. Gorin opened it and Stephen was there. "Come in. We were just talking about you." Stephen's eyes rolled as if to say, *What is this about?* Gorin said, "Charlotte is in a bit of trouble. Mr. Bell is trying to get romantic with her. She wants to know from you what to do about that. She believes you are clever and can be trusted to tell her what to do."

Stephen looked back and forth between Gorin and me. He said to me, "Has he threatened to hurt you? Does his wife know what he intends?"

I relaxed a little and sat back in the chair and said, "No, he hasn't. He just tries to corner me when nobody is near. And I don't know for sure, but I think his wife doesn't know. Mistress Maria would be angry if she knew. She would probably think it was my idea, or order that I be sent to the farm or sold." Robert Bell was the ideal tavern keeper and inn host. He tried to be jolly with everyone, and maybe he could talk his way out of anything. I just didn't know. I felt like crying, but this wasn't the place. I hadn't guessed that Maria Bell was Mr. Gorin's daughter, so I was in trouble over my head.

Stephen turned to Franklin Gorin. "Sounds like ownership is one question. Mistress Maria's jealousy is another question. Maybe Charlotte can be rented out until this quiets down?"

Mr. Gorin pointed his finger at me, "Charlotte, your problem is your own to work out with Mr. Bell. We will think about it for a couple of days and get word to you.

Stay out of Bell's way. Tell him you have the fever, or ague. But go back at once."

I ran back toward Bell's Tavern, afraid I had failed. The farther I ran the more worried I got. I was one of many slaves. Mr. Bell wasn't soft-hearted. Of the things he cared about, I think money was on top. Second came talking and being liked by guests. As I came over the last rise of land beyond the last sinkhole I saw a column of smoke in the sky and a heap of embers where the tavern was. People were carrying furniture to some of the other buildings.

Plainly something terrible had happened while I was gone. There had been fires every couple of years, but now the tavern was burned clear to the ground. What had happened? How did it start? Was anybody hurt or killed? Would Mr. Bell think I had burned the place? I decided to circle around the back, keeping out of sight. I ran up behind Mildred's cabin and climbed in the window. Nobody there. I walked out the door and over to where Mildred was directing some of the stable hands on where to put things.

I asked her what had happened. She said that George had demanded his wages from Mr. Bell early in the morning. The two got in a loud row. She heard Bell say he would rot in hell before he paid any money to George because George ate too much and didn't work hard enough. George got in a rage. He poured out a can of lamp oil on the floor and torched it off with a fire-brand from the hearth. George ran away toward Smith's Grove yelling, "Damn you Bell! Burn in hell! Damn you Bell! Burn in hell!" My name had not been mentioned and nobody missed me in the confusion.

Robert Bell stood giving orders to three slaves on horses down by the path to Nashville. He sent them off at a fast gallop, then turned and walked toward Mildred and me. "Old man won't get far. He didn't know a good life when he had one. If I get him back I will bite off his other ear." Bell stared in the direction of the departed riders.

"We are ruined," said Maria Bell.

But her husband said, still looking, "Actually, it is not as bad as it seems. I wanted to build me a new all brick tavern soon. I just have to get started now instead of later." He went on to say that he wanted the new inn to be all brick so it couldn't be burnt. And it would make Bell's Tavern look more elegant, "More like the Galt House in Louisville," he said.

We worked hard to turn part of the stables into a rough sort of tavern. We moved our beds out of Mildred's cabin and put some kitchen things in it. The make-do stable was shabby, and would not accommodate many travelers, but at least Bell wasn't out of business. Mildred and I settled our beds in a corner of the hayloft.

Almost a week went by before Stephen pulled a wagon into the few remaining buildings of Bell's Tavern. He said he had a letter from Franklin Gorin to deliver to Mr. Bell, and was on his way to the Goose Spring kiln to fetch a load of bricks to take back to Mammoth Cave. Then Stephen walked over to me.

I smiled and asked, "Anything for me?" I hoped Stephen would have an encouraging word.

"No, I am hard pressed to get over to Goose Spring and back before sundown. I'll be back late today if the bricks are ready." Stephen's tone was far away, all business. He pulled the team onto the path to Nashville and I felt my hope fading.

Tell the truth, there wasn't much to do all day. We had only two guests. Originally there were three, but the one who arrived on his own horse took one look at the smoldering ashes and the stinky stable inn. He left in disgust. Mr. Bell scurried around poking in the still-warm ashes of the inn, fishing out a bit of metal here and a bit of china there. I pitied him some, but not too much. I kept out of reach.

Around sundown Stephen arrived with a wagon-load of red bricks nested in straw and hay. He asked to see Robert Bell.

I was cutting potatoes in the kitchen so I moved closer to the doorway when I heard Stephen call out, "Mr. Bell, I have a letter for you from my master."

# Chapter 8

# Farewell to Bell's Tavern

I looked out the doorway of Mildred's cabin to see Stephen walking to Mr. Bell with a letter. I reached for the broom and started to sweep the front steps so I could hear what they said.

Robert Bell slit open the envelope and got out the paper. He read it, forming words silently with his lips. He said, "Franklin Gorin wants to rent Charlotte for six months. Did you know that?"

Stephen said, "No sir," then he added, "We are short of help, I know that much."

Bell studied the letter some more, folded it, and tapped it on his hand. "I'll think about it."

I saw Mrs. Bell coming, so I rounded the corner where I could hear but not be seen. She said, "Robert, we need that money. The sooner Charlotte is out of here and we have her money, the better." There was a little silence, then she said, "The sooner the better." I think Mrs. Bell knew her husband wanted me.

A couple of days later Mr. Bell came to me and said,

"Mr. Gorin is short-handed at Mammoth Cave. I believe in helping a friend, so I'm sending you over there to work for a while. It is just to tide him over."

I knew there had to be money in it for Bell, but I also knew there wasn't much to do around the tavern until the new one was built. And with the place in ruins, there weren't rooms to corner me in. I tied my clothes in a bundle and set off for Mammoth Cave the next day, carrying a sealed envelope to hand to Mr. Gorin when I got there.

My bundle slowed me down some. It took two hours to walk to Mammoth Cave. Cato hailed me as I came up to Mr. Gorin's house.

"Running away for sure, are you?" He was jollier than the last time I saw him. "We can use some more help around here. *I* can use some more help from you." I felt for the envelope, making sure Cato didn't see it. I did not need another run-away attempt by Cato, and I didn't want to get stuck to him like I almost was.

Mr. Gorin said I'd have to work hard, because the cave business wasn't really good. I'd have to earn my keep. Stephen showed me to the slave cabin I had stayed in that one night, and then took me around to the back door of the kitchen at the Mammoth Cave Hotel. The fragrant smell of baking bread and vanilla filled the air. Sally Lively was the head cook. Archibald Miller and Joseph Shackelford were kitchen help and waiters when they were not off guiding tourists through the cave. They were white and came with the cave when Mr. Gorin bought it. Mr. Miller was Mr. Gratz's former manager of the cave. I got on fine with the kitchen slaves. They all pitched in when visitors arrived, but between times our work slacked off. Our produce mostly came from the big garden on the place, but they told me it was nowhere near as big as Robert Bell's farm.

Stephen came for meals most days, but he guided

more cave tours than Archie and Joe. From what guests said, Stephen was the guide most folks wanted. I said to Stephen, "When are you going to show me the rest of Mammoth Cave?"

"Haven't you seen enough of it? If you have seen one cave, you've seen them all. Isn't that right?" He waited for my answer.

"No, I've not seen enough of it. I want to see what's down some of those dark halls and passages. Have you been down all of them?"

"Every time I go off the regular route I find some new place. Some of the visitors pay me to show them some new and unexplored passages. Do you want to see a big pit I discovered?" Stephen's eyes were alive and glittering. "We can go after tonight's meal is put up."

After we washed the dishes and fetched the eggs for tomorrow's breakfast, Archibald and Joseph left the kitchen. I put a couple of biscuits in a cloth and tied the ends. Since it was cold in the cave, I brought a shawl to keep warm. Stephen stood by the door with two lanterns. I followed him through the trees and down the hill to the steps at the entrance.

"You aren't scared, are you?" Stephen had a big grin and was up to some merriment.

"Nawsuh, I is got dis here fire on mah finger, an' a likely nigger to protect me." He laughed when I held up the lantern. "Besides, any bear would rather eat you than me."

We went to the bottom of the steps and past the waterfall. In the Rotunda room we went to the right in a passage that was bigger than any I saw on the last trip. We moved over piles of dirt on the floor and I could see the ruts made by the ox carts hauling cave dirt to and from the saltpetre vats. There was a low black hole on the left wall.

I asked Stephen where that went. "Want to see? We

can go that way," he said. When we got closer I saw the hole was a passage we could walk in. It just looked small from out in the big passage. We picked our way over the rocks and walked into a round passage a little bigger than a smokehouse. I could see more of the walls and ceiling because they were closer to our lights and there were turns you could not see around.

In one place our voices made an echo. Stephen sang a little of "A King Came Riding," but it sounded ordinary instead of wonderful when we rounded the next bend. There was a crack leading to the left and I felt air blowing out of it. Stephen said it got too tight, but I wanted to try it. I squeezed in, holding the lantern ahead of me. If I could climb up off the floor and turn sideways, maybe I could push on. Stephen said, "What did you find?"

"Nothing except the sound of water. It sounds like a waterfall."

"Like the one at the entrance?"

"Yes, maybe louder, but far away." Stephen told me to come back, which I did, but my clothes bunched up when I backed up. He had heard the water before, but to me it was like I had found it because I had to push around some small corners to get to a listening place. I called back, "Is it a waterfall? I think I could push farther. There's a wind in here. Is that like the wind that comes out of the ground hole?"

Stephen said I asked a lot of questions he couldn't answer. Maybe I'd have to find out for myself.

A little farther on we stopped where the floor sloped up to the ceiling. Some black rocks stuck out of the mud and the floor was wetter here than back in the passage. I asked Stephen how come the passage stopped like that, and he said the roof just fell in. Maybe that roof leaks, what with the mud and the waterfall back in that crack. "Are we under the hotel?" Maybe the cistern sprang a leak. Or maybe the privy. Stephen didn't know. But my mind raced ahead, "You drew a map for me on my pass the last time. Can you draw one now to show where we are?"

Stephen said, "Hold out your hand." I swapped lantern hands and held out my right hand. Stephen moved to my side and took my hand in his two hands. His hands were warm and felt good in the chilly air. I could feel the warmth rise up my arm and into my body, a kind of shiver I never felt before.

"See those lines?" He tapped the palm of my hand. His mouth was next to my ear and I bent my head sideways so his lips brushed my ear. He pointed, "See that line? That's the way we came from the Rotunda. And see this branch coming down from that line? This is where we turned off into Big Bat Avenue. We are down here where the line ends in Little Bat Avenue." I stared at his pointing finger, not wanting him to let go with his other hand, or do anything else except hold onto me. How could I keep him here with him so warm?

I asked, "But these other lines, what about them? Where do they go?"

His warm breath and close voice continued. "We'll go back and continue in the main cave. At the next branch is another blocked passage, and the other way gets smaller and finally ends like this one. The floor comes up to the ceiling." To keep him there I turned my head and brushed him on the ear with my lips. He slid to the side a little and I kissed him on his cheek.

Stephen turned and planted his lips on mine for a count of twelve or thirteen. I began to tingle all over as he slipped his arm around my waist and pulled me to him. His body was like a warm tree, solid and welcome. I put my arms around him and hugged him tight. Nobody will ever know how powerful and attractive Stephen Bishop was to me at that moment, and from then on. We kissed for quite a spell, then kissed some more. I felt limp as a kerchief and didn't want him to stop holding me.

"Charlotte, you are the first doer I have seen."

"Stephen, I hope you'll take me in the cave again." I've never kissed anyone like that, never wanted to. We kissed again, and then he led me back to the main cave where we turned to the left. Sure enough, we came to a place where a high pile of rocks as big as valises and travel trunks sealed off the passage, another roof cave-in but without the mud. We followed the one remaining branch which got lower and finally pinched to a close. I grabbed Stephen's hand and we kissed again. Oh, he was sweet. We held hands to the steps out of the cave. I knew that night that I wanted to be with Stephen and believed he wanted to be with me. I watched how he moved, and talked, and made things clear.

I had never felt attracted to anyone before this. Back at Red Rose Hall I remember Addie and Tom Wells would cling together and make soft pleasure noises in the night. I hoped I could find someone to be with like that. Asa Woodworth and Robert Bell wanted to grab me. The things I felt for them were fear and anger. But Stephen made me feel different altogether, like I mattered. Wherever he goes in the cave or on the ground above, I wanted to be with him more than anything. My heart beat faster. To tell the truth, it still does as I write this.

During the next few weeks, business picked up at the cave. I asked Stephen if we could go in the cave some more. He said he was guiding four or five tours a day, and most nights. We had the same problem in the dining room and kitchen. We served two and sometimes three settings, and Sally and I would not finish until late at night. Occasionally I could hand Stephen the lunch basket full of fried chicken, biscuits, corn pone, apples, and a bottle of wine. When I passed off the basket his hand would light on mine and we'd linger a little, feeling each other's warm touch and not wanting to pull apart. Sometimes Mr. Gorin would come by just as Stephen came to the kitchen door. He would give Stephen orders to take good care of a special tour, and maybe take a small jug of brandy in addition to the cider. Once he told Stephen the guest drank like a riverman and to make sure he didn't run out of brandy. Other times Stephen told me about some of the questions visitors asked, "How many miles of cave yet to be explored?" and "Is the cave air good to breathe?" Sometimes they'd ask, "Was your mammy or your daddy white, since you are so yeller?"

Stephen thought most of these questions were stupid, but he always gave a pleasant answer, and visitors returning from tours he led said he was a "proper gentleman" and unusually agreeable and bright for a Negro. To the first question, he used to say he didn't know how many miles had not been explored. He then started to use Joe Shackelford's answer, "There's one hundred and fifty miles of cave altogether, but only about fifty miles that's been looked at." To the second question about the goodness of cave air, he said, "The cave air is wonderful healthy, so healthy that during the war with the British, the saltpetre miners would stay underground for months at a time and never be sick a day."

He used to answer the third question as honestly as he could, but it never satisfied. Most of the time his answer led to other questions as to why would his white daddy wanted to breed his black mammy, and other ugly questions. Stephen fixed a hateful man on one trip. When he asked about Stephen's parents, Stephen put his hand up like to pretend to guard his answer and said in a loud voice for all to hear, "My mother was a Negro and my daddy was a full-blooded Indian." This raised a

chorus of ohs and ahs. Sometimes the questioner wanted to know what tribe, and Stephen said his mother was
sworn to secrecy on the subject, an Indian oath.

I didn't get any closer alone with Stephen for weeks.
Mostly a slave's time belongs to his master. Sunday was
a day off for most of the field hands, like Cato, but the
rest of us worked from dawn to way after dark taking
care of the visitors. Stephen found me one Sunday afternoon between dinner and evening meal preparations.

"I need your advice," he said. We were out behind
the hotel a piece, so I heard him out. "I have to work
every Sunday. Seth Charles and Aiken Lively get off on
Sundays and they are black."

"Yes, but they are freedmen, you know that."

"I do know that. Let me finish," he said. "We have to
lead twice as many tours when they are gone. They have
'privileges' slaves don't have. Then there are the white
guides, John Wigglesworth and Casey Dunn. They only
work Friday, Saturday, and Sunday, and get off Monday and three more days. I am angry about the way Mr.
Gorin is running things. I have to work twice as hard for
no money. Seth and Aiken get one dollar for six days
work, or twenty-five dollars a month. Wigglesworth
and Dunn get one dollar for three days, which is twelve
dollars a month. It isn't fair."

We walked back to the hotel and I said, "Stephen,
your figures for Seth and Aiken should be twenty-four
dollars, but you missed the food and lodging that Mr.
Gorin provides you for free. Then there's that little
money some visitors slip you when you do a good job
guiding. You are a better guide than the others, and old
Archibald is getting lame." I was going to show him that
everyone was in about the same pickle when it came to
money: Always too much work and not enough money
no matter what.

But Stephen was getting hot and said, "I don't

understand why a freedman should earn less than a white man when they are both about as good."

"From one slave to another, what don't you understand about that? God put white folks on top of black folks, and that's all there is to it."

"Woman, you don't understand! I want time off. The time to explore the cave, time to take you into the cave, time to talk to you, time to be with you. Your body and soul and work belong to Mr. Gorin, but him owning all my time and all your time makes me want to run away."

If anyone had heard Stephen complain, he would be punished, maybe whipped. So I interrupted, "If you run away you can't explore the cave. Stephen, it's your cave. Everything you find in there is yours. Not Mr. Gorin's, not anybody's. When I heard that waterfall back in that crack in Little Bat Avenue, you said you heard it before. Well, that's not true. The water I heard was *my* water — different from *your* water. Different water every day." I felt desperate to get his mind off running away and on the cave exploring, which he loved.

"You're right, I hate to say it," Stephen confessed. "Cato said running was a bad idea. It got him stuck in the hot fields all day. And Cato said having two days off isn't all fine when Charlotte works on Saturday and Sunday, too."

Was Stephen talking to Cato about me? I knew Cato had his eye on me, but he was like Mr. Bell, up to no good. I had my eye on Stephen, and only Stephen.

Stephen saw Mr. Gorin coming up the path so he turned away, saying to me, "Cato has got time for you, Charlotte, so maybe you would be better off with somebody who has more time off than I do."

He left me vexed and wanting to run after him. What happened? Had I scared Stephen away by giving him a kiss? Had Cato told lies about me?

After the last dish was put away and Sally had gone to bed, I left the kitchen and walked into the cool night. I headed for a stand of chestnut trees down the road. I picked up speed and started to run through the low grass between the big trunks. Chestnut burrs would hurt, so I kept a sharp eye out. Moonlight patches flashed at me through the high branches. Faster and faster. Some twigs hurt my feet but I didn't care, I was free and fast. I could outrun Cato, and Stephen, and Mr. Gorin, and anyone. That wind licked my face and whispered, "Run, Charlotte, run. If you can't have what you want, you can run." Nobody was awake when I got back to my cabin a long time later.

# Chapter 9

## Big Discoveries

Stephen took me on a cave trip several weeks later. The stream of visitors had turned to a trickle. We all worked hard to make sure they ate good and stayed over several days to go on more cave tours. Archie Miller and Joe Shackelford had made two ladders out of cedar poles. Stephen wanted a "mule" to carry in one of the ladders, and I guess I was it. My warm feelings for Stephen had died down some, but only because we were all tired from each day's hard work.

I asked Stephen where we were headed as we moved down the hill and into the entrance. The oil lanterns hanging on our fingers made spooky shadows on the ceiling. He said, "We're going beyond the Rotunda, past the saltpetre works to the Coffin." I asked if it was a real coffin. He said it was a large, coffin-shaped rock with flat sides. We carried that ladder through the Main Cave and stopped to rest at the Coffin. It looked like a coffin made for a giant. "There's another level beneath this passage. It is not so big, and it has not been explored much. I found a pit, but I can't see into it. This ladder will let us see it."

We continued until we came to a smaller passage to the left. We crawled over rocks, heaving the ladder. At a drop-off, Stephen climbed down and set the ladder and told me to climb down. "I need somebody to test the ladder. To see if it is safe." I threw a small rock at Stephen.

We crawled over more rocks. Black soot rubbed off on our clothes. Stephen said the soot came from Indian torches. I asked why Archie and Joe didn't carry the ladder into these tight passages. Stephen said they took the first ladder in, but it was too much work for white folks. We came to a place where the floor dropped into a big hole. We left the ladder and Stephen led me through a passage to the right that came to a deep hole. It was so deep that the rock he threw over the edge took three seconds to smack on the bottom far away. We could not see the bottom when we leaned over with our lanterns.

Back at the ladder, Stephen said, "We will use the ladder to climb down into the canyon in the floor." I asked *him* to test it this time, and he laughed. "Where does the cave go straight ahead?" I asked.

"It runs into a big pit, so wide we can't cross it or climb to the bottom." He said we could go the other way carrying the ladder. We came to a balcony overlooking a big pit and peered down. Stephen said, "I believe this is the same pit we threw the rock into a few minutes ago."

We must have spent an hour climbing down and up into passages that ran into the same pit. Each opening into the pit gave a view of how vast and black that pit was, but our lanterns were too dim to see the whole thing. We had figured out how different passages on different levels led to the dome, and discovering connections brought us closer together. I had an idea of how to see more of the pit. It was time to leave the cave, but not before I kissed Stephen and he kissed me back.

A couple of days later we went back to the big pit with its many windows. This time I brought my sack of candle stubs I had been saving at the hotel. At each window we set a candle and lighted it, then crawled or climbed to the next window. We placed seven or eight candles at different levels opening onto the pit. From the bottom the pit glowed and looked so large I believe the Mammoth Cave Hotel would fit inside it. It was the finest, most wonderful thing I had ever seen in my life.

Stephen told Master Gorin about the new dome and offered to take him there. Gorin was excited. I was lucky to have some more candles for Stephen to take. That night when Gorin and Stephen returned to the hotel, Gorin gathered all the guests together to tell them all about "Gorin's Dome." He said it was finer and more spectacular than anything else in Mammoth Cave, 150 feet high and 80 feet wide. People would cross the ocean to see it. Gorin wrote letters to newspapers far and wide, and even to London. Gorin said that Stephen had discovered the dome and praised Stephen as the best cave explorer in the world. I asked Stephen if he really was the first to find that pit. He said no, but until the candles lit it up and you could see it as a glowing dome from below, it might as well be "our discovery." I asked him if he meant Stephen and Charlotte's discovery. He just smiled and winked.

It took months of labor to move rocks and clear trails so visitors could see Gorin's Dome without crawling on their hands and knees. The guides dug a shortcut from behind the Coffin to the Wooden Bowl Room, and from there down through the Snake Hole and its broken rocks. Archie, Joe, and Stephen worked from early morning to late at night to improve the trail. Scattered through the tight passages they found burned pieces of river cane, used by Indians to make torches to light their way. On one of these trips Stephen crawled into a passage to the left of the ladder. This low and sooty crawlway led over and past some deep covered pits, and finally to a ledge overlooking the pit they could not cross. Stephen said he might be able to climb up with one of the ladders.

His chance to try the high unexplored passage across the deep pit came in October, 1838. Gorin introduced Hiram Stevenson to Stephen and told him Mr. Stevenson had come all the way from Georgetown to see "all of Mammoth Cave and more." Stevenson told Stephen that he had heard about Gorin's Dome and wanted to discover something grander than that. I handed Stephen the basket of victuals for the two of them each day for three days, but I went to bed every night before the explorers returned to the hotel.

On the fourth day they came out of the cave just before supper. "We made a big discovery!" yelled Stevenson. He swept up hotel guests and visitors. They burst into the dining room. "Come hear what we found!" Mr. Stevenson carried on about how they crossed the Bottomless Pit on the ladder we had carried in. He waved his arms and showed how he had lunged to safety just in time, with Stephen following close behind.

In the kitchen I asked Stephen what had happened as he ate a cold fried chicken leg. "We came to where we left the ladder, leading down to the bottom of the floor canyon. Then we went the other direction to the deep pit. I was starting to smoke Hiram Stevenson's initials on the wall, when he said, 'Let's go across.' That man was an exploring fool, but I am not.

"So I picked up the ladder and said, 'Follow me.'" Stephen bit off another piece of chicken and went on, "We ducked into the small crawlway to the left. I dragged the ladder and Stevenson carried the back end. We crossed one covered pit and then turned to the right to cross another pit using the ladder for a handrail. That pit was only eight feet deep. We climbed onto a ledge where one side dropped about a hundred feet.

"This was the high passage I saw when you and I were there. With the ladder, we could climb up to the high cave. I climbed the ladder and Mr. Stevenson followed. We were on a rocky shelf perched on the other side of the Bottomless Pit. Ahead of us lay a passage with no footprints in it. Stevenson asked why there were no prints." Stephen broke off a piece of corn pone and told how Stevenson and he were now walking in unexplored cave where there weren't any footprints.

Stevenson was wild to see what was around the next corner and the corner after that. They scrambled down a slope and came to a nice passageway, not as big as Main Cave. Several passages joined and the ceiling went up out of sight, and they found beautiful crystals, formations, and curved walls. They counted off 600 paces before they came to a very low crawlway. Here they found a few burned torch fragments on the floor. Later they called this Pensacola Avenue.

Stephen and his visitor retreated to the head of the oval passage and turned into a passage that wound its way downward, still without footprints. Stephen was relieved to find bigger passage again. Deeper yet into the cave they began to smell mud and water, and they felt colder as a breeze sprang up. Stephen pushed Stevenson into the lead so he could be the first to press his footprints in the sand floor, and they walked a long way.

They came to a high room with a drop off. They stood on a cliff in a thirty-foot-wide room that looked to be forty feet from the bottom up to the ceiling. Moving down to the left a long distance there was a patch of black they thought was a hole in the floor, but a rock tossed into it splashed. They had found a river, the first in Mammoth Cave. Stephen kicked steps into the slippery mud bank and approached the water. The river passage led into the gloom and out of sight. It was time to go. Stevenson agreed they had better return, so they retraced their steps.

Back at the hotel Hiram Stevenson raved about their discovery. He told and retold about using the ladder to straddle the "deep pit" that really was only eight feet deep, and to climb up to the far side to the big pit that he forgot was more than a hundred feet deep. He described every rock in the long passage, every slippery step down to the river.

Stevenson insisted that Gorin build a bridge to cross Bottomless Pit directly. Actually, Stephen had suggested a bridge when he saw they were on the far side of the big pit. Now Stevenson became the chief champion of bridge building.

I scolded Stephen for putting the visitor up to insist on a bridge. Mr. Gorin would not venture such an expense if Stephen himself had suggested it.

Hiram Stevenson's enthusiasm for the wonders on the far side of Bottomless Pit caused Gorin to make plans for building a wooden bridge in the cave. Archibald Miller and Joseph Shackelford didn't want to build a bridge because they would have to carry in lumber. "There's too damn much cave already. We don't need any more miles," said Archie.

Stephen's spirits picked up in the days after his big discoveries. When he came by the kitchen one morning, I said I would like to go with him. He seemed more interested in the next cave trip than in me. That hurt after how tender I felt when he had kissed me last. But his eyes sparkled and his voice grew lively as he went on and on about the discoveries awaiting his next visit. I wondered if he knew how much I wanted to be with him. I would go anywhere with him. He was living for that cave and to know its secrets. I wished he felt that way about me.

We made one trip together that winter. He told me to roll up another dress in a bundle and keep it dry as we'd likely get wet. He wanted to explore Lake Lethe and the River Styx—the new name for the new river. A visitor who said he was a preacher and a college teacher had told Stephen about Greek mythology, Charon and all. Charon was the ferryman on the boat that crossed the River Styx, carrying the properly buried dead to the underworld. Lethe was the river of forgetfulness. Stephen committed the preacher's story to heart and could repeat it word for word.

After a long walk past familiar cave places, we came to a drop-off to water far below and a narrow ledge up to the left. We scooted along the scary ledge carrying the ladder, and then used it to climb down. At the lake's edge Stephen rolled up his trousers and removed his shoes. I hitched up my skirt. I was afraid the lake bottom would be muddy. The cold water shocked me. I waded in deeper and the water climbed higher on me, wetting my dress to my knees, then to my waist.

We waded to the far bank, then up and through a sand floor passage to the river. The river bottom was sand, packed firm, and not muddy. We waded around a corner and the river became deeper. Down below, my body was warming up as it grew used to the water, but my breasts tingled as cold water rose over them and then up my neck. "Keep close to the wall and walk on your toes," Stephen said, his voice echoing. I followed him around several more turns. It was scary and hateful at first, but better and more comfortable the farther I went. I wondered where the river would go, and felt my curiosity rising. I could see why Stephen was on fire to know more and more about the cave. We rested against the wall, up to our chests in the water, Stephen said, "We need a boat to paddle on this river." He knew how far into the cave we were. Carrying a boat this far would be too much work for anyone. "With a boat we could look at all the river."

Down in the clear water I saw a white cave fish as long as my finger. It swam away slow.

Stephen said we had done enough for one day, that we should change clothes and leave. Back on the shore Stephen stripped off his wet trousers revealing his muscular, glistening legs. His chest was handsome. I began to shiver and climbed out of my wet dress. Stephen looked at me, but I didn't care. My teeth chattered. I slipped on my dry dress and felt warmer immediately. Stephen helped me up the steep bank. At the top I threw my arms around him. He hugged me to him. "Keep me warm," I said.

"Maybe if you keep caving, I'll just keep you," Stephen said. "I can't get Archie or Joe to get in the water to see where the river goes. And I sure wouldn't hug them none, no matter how cold they get."

We left the cave weary and climbed the steep steps into the land of winter stars.

I didn't get much sleep that night. I was tired, but too excited by our adventure. On my way to the kitchen a few hours later Cato asked where I had gone and what we had done. I told him Stephen took me to the Styx River and we went to Echo River fishing for white cave fish.

Cato spit and snarled, "You'd better stay out of that damn cave if you know what's good for you. Stephen will have his way with you and then throw you down one of those deep pits. Bright girl like you should stick with me. I have got what you need. And it ain't some haunted cave." Cato grabbed at my hand but I spun around fast and danced away into the kitchen. He meant me no good, just as Asa and Robert Bell did. I had tried to be nice to Cato and help him, but now I intended to avoid that man who thought he could scare me.

One day Charles Harvey and his son, Charles Harvey, Jr., rode in on white horses. The father had long white hair to match. I recognized the younger man. He was with Franklin Gorin and Stephen at Bell's Tavern when Mr. Gratz sold Mammoth Cave, and was Franklin Gorin's nephew. Today he had accepted his uncle's invitation to his father and him to go on a cave trip.

They asked for Stephen as a guide, but Mr. Gorin gave them Archibald Miller instead because Stephen had left with a tour three hours before that. Archie Miller seemed peeved, but he handed each of the Harveys a lantern. They went to the cave.

In a couple of hours Archie returned without the younger Charles Harvey. Archie explained, "Junior left his hat at the spring in the cave. We were at the Giant's Coffin. I sent the son-of-a-bitch back to get his hat and said we'd wait for him. He never came back, so his father and I left the cave. The boy wasn't at the spring, so we headed out of the cave. Has he showed up yet?"

He must have tried to find his own way back to the entrance, we decided, since we had not seen the young man. Old man Harvey tossed down several glasses of whisky and ate a slab of ham.

Franklin Gorin came by and when he heard the boy was missing, he sent for the guides, Stephen, Joe, Archie, Seth, and Aiken. "Boys, we got a missing visitor. Been gone three hours. No telling where he is. We'd better go look for him." Mr. Gorin added in a low voice to the guides, "We can't afford to lose relatives or paying visitors."

Stephen told Mr. Gorin it would be wise to send the

five guides into the cave at once to hunt for Harvey. Gorin agreed and sent them. He said that one of the slaves
should be sent in a couple of hours later with a basket of
food, to wait at the Giant's Coffin. Since I had been there
with Stephen, I was to take food right after the evening
meal was over.

That basket was heavy. I switched hands with the
lantern and basket all the way to Giant's Coffin. I hoped
I would hear the guides calling for Charles Harvey, but
all was silent. While I waited, I imagined that Stephen
crept up behind me and wrapped his arms around me.
We'd kiss and hold each other. Then we'd go down a
side passage and find Harvey sitting in the dark with
his lantern oil gone. The lost man would be frightened,
cold, and glad to see us.

I dozed off and woke up later to see my lantern was
low and about out. I set off walking to the entrance, hop-
ing I would make it before the flame snuffed out. The
rock walls glided by me just as the trunks of the chestnut trees did when I ran through the woods. I felt free,
but not scared. At the bottom of the steps to the outside,
my light quit. The stars in the sky at the top of the stairs
lighted my way.

Mr. Gorin was waiting in the hotel near where old
Mr. Harvey slept with his head on a table. None of the
guides had returned. Everybody else had turned in.

Sunday came and went with no sign of Charles Harvey or the five guides. Around midnight I was sent into
the cave with another basket of food. I had left the first
basket at Giant's Coffin and it was empty, so I knew
Stephen and the others were still searching. They must
have come together to eat, then spread out to continue
the search. Around seven o'clock Monday morning the
five guides and Harvey walked into the dining room.
Junior looked a fright with red eyes and wild hair. Sally
Lively set food before young Mr. Harvey. I spooned out

plates of food for the guides, who ate outside the back door. They all ate like they were starved.

Stephen said they found Charles Harvey many hours down one of dozens of side passages, hunkered behind a large rock. After he found his hat at the spring he tried to return to the others but went down a wrong passage. He didn't recognize anything, but he had not paid attention on the way in. When he felt he was lost he did what men do, he panicked. His light grew dim. He thought a small crawlway might be a shortcut back to the Main Cave, but his lantern died. He yelled for help, then wrapped his coat around him in the dark and waited and waited. Young Harvey slept now and then but lost track of time until Joseph Shackelford found him.

Stephen gave me a sly smile. "His hair was white when we found him—that's how scared he was." I pinched Stephen. Young Harvey's hair was white when he went *into* the cave with his white-haired father. Stephen would tell that story many times over. I knew that for certain.

The guides learned that it paid to warn visitors about the dangers of getting lost. They told about Charles Harvey, adding little details about how he went insane in the cave. They made up a story about a woman who wandered off from a tour and never was found. The guides felt such stories enhanced their reputations and resulted in larger contributions from those "lucky enough to get back alive."

Only a few visitors came those late winter and early spring days. We kept busy in the kitchen putting up potatoes, turnips, and dried apples. When we butchered we hung the hams in the smokehouse and made sausage. I ran in new directions through the piles of dead leaves, but my favorite run was still out and through the chestnut trees. There was a little spring out there where

I could drink from a pool. I told Stephen about it and he asked me to show it to him. So I did one Sunday. Stephen couldn't run as fast as I could, but he could keep going a long time.

We both drank deep at the spring and wiped the sweat from our faces. I asked Stephen if he had ever thought about taking a wife. (I knew someone who loved him.) He said once in a while, but things were unsettled. His life was not his own, since he belonged to Master Gorin. Kissing me was what he would like to do more, but with me going back to Robert Bell any day now, we might not see each other again.

What did he mean I would go back to Bell? My eyes teared up. Did Stephen know something I didn't?

"Dear Charlotte, Gorin just rented you, he didn't buy you. You have to go back to Bell's Tavern in a few days. So I won't see you." Stephen had tears in his eyes. "I pleaded with Gorin to rent you for a year, but master has about run out of money. He can't keep you. Likely he can't keep the cave either. Maybe he will have to sell me, too." Stephen's tears turned into rivers down his cheeks. We reached for each other and cried. My heart felt pain like it did when I saw Addie and Tom Wells led away forever back in the Nashville slave market.

Stephen said he wanted to be with me forever, to take me into Mammoth Cave and find wonderful discoveries. He said he wanted to explore me and live with me and love me. We held each other that warming afternoon and loved each other on the sunlit grass near the spring. We would figure out something to break the shackles that kept us apart and owned by others.

Maybe the anger we felt on that sunny Sunday was like Cato's fury at being a slave. Cato's passion to run away didn't seem so stupid after all. Could Stephen and I run? Escape from slavery? All the runaways I heard of were caught, whipped, and sometimes chained. Well, the pain outside could hardly be more than the pain inside.

We walked back toward the hotel hand in hand. At the edge of the chestnut stand he gave me a little nudge and took off running. I caught him easily and stayed beside him. I swore then I would never leave Stephen, but I did in the next few minutes when he puffed to a stop. I ran off easily around the bend and into the hotel.

# Chapter 10

## Stephen Explores a River

I worried that any time now Mr. Gorin would tell me to return to Bell's Tavern, and that would be the end of my adventures with Stephen. That man was the love of my life. Sally Lively said to cheer up or my face would sour the milk in the kitchen.

A man got off the stagecoach with a small trunk. I carried his trunk to his room that I had just made up fresh. He told me he was Luther Ray from London, England. Several months ago he sailed across the ocean to see the new United States and its wonders. New York was a forest of sailing ships with tall masts. A week later he had sailed up the Hudson River and traveled up the Mohawk River valley on a stagecoach and visited Niagara Falls. At Buffalo he had a choice: He could take a steam boat to Cleveland or buy a ticket on the stagecoach to Pittsburgh. To see more of America, he rode the stagecoach south to Pittsburgh. He shipped by the packet boat "Star of the West" down the Ohio River to Cincinnati, and then to the Falls of the Ohio. He stayed in Louisville, Kentucky, at Locust Grove where the Croghan family lived. He was a relative of the Croghans. John Croghan sent him on the stagecoach to Mammoth Cave.

Mr. Ray was a slim man with a pink smooth face, without whiskers, about Stephen's size. His blue eyes shot around the room as he said in a low voice, "What's it like being a slave?"

Nobody ever asked me this. I thought it might be a trick, so I said, "It is not all bad. They treat me fine. I have a bed of my own and my meals. Most of my work is inside. And I get to meet fine ladies and gentlemen." He seemed in no hurry so I asked him, "Do you have people in Louisville?"

"I have cousins, a lot of them. William Croghan was a famous soldier and then a land surveyor. He died at Locust Grove about seventeen years ago. He and his wife Lucy had eight children. Dr. John Croghan was one of them, who became a medical doctor. But John was an adventurer, like his father and uncle, so he got into the salt business. He asked me to see if there is salt in Mammoth Cave, on my way to New Orleans." Luther Ray went on to say he planned to stay two or three weeks at Mammoth Cave and see everything. I told him Stephen would know whether there was salt or not in the cave.

Mr. Ray handed me a letter. I took it and turned it every which way. "You can read it out loud," he said. I told him I couldn't read, and I didn't know any slave who could read. "That's what they told me at Locust Grove. They have a lot of slaves there, and none can read. When I asked why, they said servants didn't need to know how to read, and if they could they would likely grow rebellious."

Mr. Ray told me that six years ago England abolished slavery everywhere in the English lands. Old William Wilberforce had persuaded the lawmakers after many years of arguing and gathering support that slaves should be freed. Mr. Ray said that Wilberforce gave moral and practical reasons why people shouldn't own people.

When Mr. Ray came to this country he found slavery a normal condition. Here and there some folks spoke out against slave holding, but they were thought to be crazy. He said, "I think keeping slaves in ignorance and not teaching them to read is crazy." He told me that in some states it was against the law to teach slaves to read, but not in Kentucky.

Luther Ray opened his trunk and drew out a book. "This is a new alphabet book. I paid fifteen cents for it from a printer in Cincinnati when my boat stopped there. You can look at it anytime if you want to learn to read."

I wanted to learn to read and write to be able to learn things and answer my curiosity. I watched where he put the book in the chest of drawers. Over the next two weeks I stole paper and pencil and copied ten pages of that book line for line, pictures and all. I did not know how to read words, but maybe Stephen and I could figure it out, unless I was gone. The book was named *THE ECLECTIC PRIMER FOR YOUNG CHILDREN.*

Mr. Ray went into the cave every day with Stephen as his special guide. They became fast friends. When asked about salt, Stephen took him to a place where white crystals grew out of the wall in Main Cave. Stephen had him taste the white stuff. It puckered his mouth, but he said it wasn't salt. Years later a professor from a college said it was Epsom salt, not something you would put on the table. It would give you the runs.

One day Stephen took Mr. Ray into a passage beyond Bottomless Pit. They found a side canyon that was blocked with rocks. There was a missing rock at the top that led upward through a break in the rocks. Stephen said they should stop. The rocks looked loose and might tumble down on them. It was a dangerous place but Luther insisted they climb up. Luther Ray said to Stephen, "Does it end?"

Stephen said, "I don't know."

"Then we must keep going until we find out. That's the way to explore this cave." Luther was right, Stephen said. As they climbed, some rocks shifted so they had to watch where they put their feet and hands. After a hundred feet of climbing up over big rocks they came to a closed room where the passage stopped. "Now we know. It ends."

Luther told Stephen to smoke his initials on the ceiling. "Make the letter L and the letter R. Here, I'll show you." Luther traced the letter forms with his finger on the wall. Stephen used a candle to smoke the letters LR on the ceiling, with the date.

Stephen knew the letters by name, and he knew that each stood for a sound. But he always asked visitors how their initial letters went so he could mark them correctly on the wall or ceiling. When Stephen told me this, I showed him my papers where I had copied the pages of Luther Ray's new alphabet book.

A is for ax. B is for box. C is for cat. D is for dog. I still remember that much of it.

Stephen confessed to me that Franklin Gorin had taught him to read and write back in Glasgow, Kentucky. Stephen still had his first alphabet book, *THE NEW ENGLAND PRIMER."*

It was very old, but it showed how all the letters are made, how letters together make syllables or sounds, and those sounds make up words," Stephen said. "Mr. Gorin made me copy and say words. He would ask me to tell a little story and write my own words on a slate. I remember my first story: OUR MILK COW IS BROWN AND EATS GRASS. After about a week everything made sense and I could read most things: 'A In Adam's fall we sinned all, B Heaven to find; the Bible mind, C

Christ crucify'd, for sinners dy'd.' Those are the A, B, Cs in my reading book," Stephen said.

In the years that followed, Stephen taught me to read and write, first in Roman letters and then in cursive. I loved to hear Stephen read out loud. I owe it to Luther Ray who gave me my first book.

In a few weeks I could sound out names, like SHAR-LOT-BROWN. Later I caught on to how to make a supplies list. A little picture of a potato and letters PO-TA-TO could call to mind what we needed. APLS was apples. The names of things came easier than the words for what to do with those things. Stephen spent an hour with me and Luther Ray some days working out letters, sounds, and words. Stephen taught me some of the letters and short words. I could read JON for John, but Croghan was CRAWN. I did not understand how that word did not sound like it was spelled. "It just is," said Stephen. "Some words sound different from the way they are spelled, so you just have to learn and remember them."

A few visitors left newspapers behind and I could read some of the big letters: HORSES WANTED. WILL PAY CASH FOR SOUND HORSES. It wasn't long before I could read most things and even write some. It took me several years to read everything, and longer to write passably about what I was doing and had done. Of course, I didn't tell anyone.

I knew that if somebody showed me how numbers worked, I was sure I could learn that too.

Near the end of Luther Ray's stay at the cave, he told Stephen that Dr. John Croghan had asked him to report back if the cave was a likely business. Stephen told him it was doing poorly, but if more visitors came, it could be a moneymaker. However, it was no place to get rich mining salt.

Mr. Ray gave Stephen a parting gift. It was *MC-GUFFEY'S FIRST READER*. Stephen slipped that book into his coat pocket. He thanked Mr. Ray for it, and said he had tears in his eyes he was so happy to get it. Stephen said he could teach me to read so I could find out things from books. What visitors said wasn't always right, even though Stephen could remember their stories word for word.

On Mr. Ray's last day I saw a dispatch letter at the counter. It had Luther Ray's name on it. But the main name was Dr. John Croghan, M.D. in Louisville. The northbound stagecoach driver took the letter the day after Luther Ray left on the stagecoach heading south.

Mr. Gorin came with news I didn't want to hear. "Charlotte, we have passed the time for which I rented you. You'll have to go back whenever Mr. Bell sends for you. I wish I could rent you for a year, but the money is so tight I can't do it." He said he'd wait to hear from Bell.

I asked Mr. Gorin what about the law. Didn't he say it was against the law to bring slaves into Kentucky? He said there was talk about changing the law back to where you could bring in slaves again, but there wasn't anybody who would enforce the law, and property was property. He was sorry.

I made it my job to look over the dispatch letters that came two or three a week. If I had seen Mr. Bell's name I could make sure that letter never got to Mr. Gorin. But no letter came from Bell.

Stephen went to Mr. Gorin with a trade. If Mr. Gorin would keep me, he would find more big cave passages and wonderful places. Mr. Gorin just shook his head. He said it was Stephen's job to find big cave, and if he didn't find some more, he would send me and everybody else away. Big discoveries wouldn't pay for the money owed. Only paying guests and visitors would bring money.

When the leaves on the trees turned green, the stagecoach from Louisville brought a guest who signed the big book J. R. Underwood. He looked to be about fifty, built solid. Mr. Underwood went on one cave trip with Stephen. He spent most of two days in Mr. Gorin's house, but took his meals at the hotel. I asked if he would stay long. He said no, he was leaving for Louisville the next day. Mr. Underwood was Mr. Gorin's brother-in-law. I tell this because Mr. Gorin seemed to cheer up after Mr. Underwood's visit and Gorin didn't bring up money for a few weeks after that.

Stephen told me that Joseph Rogers Underwood was a lawyer from Bowling Green, Kentucky, a Representative to Congress in Washington City. He and Mr. Gorin conducted Dr. Croghan's land sales for fifteen years or more. Dr. Croghan sent him to investigate Luther Ray's report about the cave. He was asking questions like, Was it true that money was tight? Was the salt too poor to use on food?

Stephen asked if he held slaves. Underwood said he did, but was thinking of freeing them. He told Stephen about the new colony in Liberia, Africa where freed slaves could settle. Underwood didn't know if there were caves in Liberia.

A little time later two new slaves arrived from Glasgow. Mr. Gorin rented Mat Bransford and his young brother Nick from Thomas Bransford, a white man. Where did Mr. Gorin find the money? I did pay a little notice to Nick the first time I saw him.

Nick was average size, dark brown, and with a springy step. Materson Bransford was older, a head taller, solidly built, and a light shade of brown. I asked Nick, "You two are brothers? How come you look so different from each other?"

Nick said," Yes, we *are* brothers. Each of us had a different mother and a different father." I could see Nick was having some fun with me. He'd make a good cave guide. But my eye was on Stephen.

Stephen told me the water in the underground river was low and he wanted to go back there now that guiding had slacked off. I told him to forget about me going with him. I'd gotten so wet and cold from his last river trip that I didn't want to do it again. He told me that Mat, Nick, Seth, and Aiken were to carry the boat lumber into the cave and to the underground river, that I could carry the paddles. He would carry the lantern. "With that boat I can explore the river and see where it goes," Stephen begged me. I told him to go right ahead without me because I didn't want to be wet, miserable, and cold again. It would be all right if I stayed out.

Stephen lowered his voice, like he didn't want anyone to hear him, and said, "That river will take us to some big cave. I want you to see it first." Stephen could charm the whiskers off a cat. I did wonder where the river would take us. I did agree to help and packed a lunch. But this time I left my other dress in my cabin. Archibald Miller, the former cave manager, was sent with us to help carry the load. He wasn't happy about that, since he had done his share of the work by helping to carry in the lumber to build the bridge over the Bottomless Pit. That first day they carried that lumber to the Giant's Coffin. It was too heavy to carry for long, so they put it down and switched off. It was easier to carry when we put the food basket on the wood and four of us took hold of the boards. The next day we hefted the lumber across the new bridge over Bottomless Pit. We moved it into Pensacola Avenue, and down Winding Way to River Hall.

The Bransfords knew carpenter work and had brought a keg of nails and tools with them from Glasgow.

Mr. Gorin set Mat and Nick to building a little boat in River Hall. They used sawmill boards and square nails to fasten the wood together. They used a maul to pound hemp rope pieces between the board cracks. "The hemp will expand when it gets wet and keep the water out," said Mat. The boat was about three feet wide and eight feet long with flat ends and a flat bottom. It looked more like a wagon bed than a boat.

They launched the boat and Archie took Mat, Nick, Seth, and Aiken out of the cave, leaving me with Stephen. I hoped Stephen would kiss me, but he didn't. He climbed into the boat with his lantern in the front and pushed off with the paddle. "Floating is better than wading," he said. I said to myself, floating is better than waiting.

Stephen began to sing a song. His song echoed. He stopped singing and sounded a low note. The walls seemed to vibrate and the sound tickled my ears. He sang a higher note and then a note that was higher still. The echo of those three notes filled the cave a short time after he stopped singing. "Got big cave here! Big, big cave!" The sound of his paddle grew faint and he was gone.

I sat on a rock, one of the few in this damp part of the cave. I blew out the lantern and watched the glowing ember of the wick fade and die. I figured that would let me see Stephen coming back. It was scary sitting there in the dark so I held up my hand before my face, but couldn't see anything. I sat there a long time. I grew less frightened and began to hear things I had missed before. I heard a drip of water falling into the lake. One, two, three, four–drip. One, two, three, four–drip, One, two, three, four–drip. When I put my hand up near my head I still couldn't see anything, but I could hear my hand. It sounded different as I moved it around. I tried closing my eyes on the darkness and the small change in sound let me imagine where my hand was. I spent a long time waiting in the dark and getting used to listening to the sounds of my hands near and far away. Years later I learned that closing my eyes in a dark passage when the flame was out felt friendlier than staring at black nothing with my eyes open. When I told Stephen about sitting in the dark, he said he asked visitors on most tours to sit down and get used to pitch black. Some of those visitors made scary noises, so Stephen would shush them. One woman said she could not tell the niggers from the visitors in the dark. One visitor fired off his pistol into the water and the shot and its echo scared everyone.

Stephen was away a long time. I got cold and struck a match to light my lantern. I climbed the bank and sat down some more. Soon I was up again and moved around to keep warm. Stephen's echoing voice drifted from down the river passageway. I was starting to wonder if he would come back.

Finally Stephen returned, climbing out of the boat to set a rock on the rope to hold the boat fast. He said the river went on and on. He floated under a low arch at one spot, then came to a Y. He floated the right fork for a thousand feet, to a place where the ceiling lowered and met the top of the water. All along he saw small white cave fish. Once he saw a crayfish scooting along in the water, just like the ones he had seen in Beaver Creek near Glasgow when he was a boy. Only this crayfish was pure white. There wasn't room to turn the boat around at the end. He turned himself around and paddled back out to the Y. He could not touch the bottom of the river, even when he pushed the paddle down a long way.

At the Y again he took the left fork. It was a grand gallery with the finest echoes, and it went on for a long way to a sandbank. He had decided to turn around since it was late and his lamp oil can was nearly empty. He paddled fast so that the front of the boat dipped down and some water came into the boat. He took it easy after that and sang more songs on his return trip.

I didn't get my wish to kiss him because he was too excited talking about the river. He could see big rocks underwater. The fish didn't seem scared and he thought he could catch some if he had a jug to put them in. We walked and he talked. He said we must tell Mr. Gorin about the river right away. No telling where it might go. I asked Stephen if he'd take me in the boat next time. He said No. The boat was too tippy with one in it. With two in it, it might sink.

It hurt me to hear that. Was he trying to keep his river to himself? Since that was all he'd talk about, I got mad. He paid no attention to me and he cared more about that cave and what was around the next corner than me. What was worse, when we got back to the hotel, Mr. Gorin had to hear the story over three times. I scolded Stephen for not telling how far he traveled and how big the passages were. How deep was the river? I went to bed still mad, and tired from that long cave trip.

I felt lost not knowing what was going on around me. Was Stephen so busy with his new discovery that I didn't matter? Was Mr. Gorin so broke he would have to return me to Bell? How could Gorin rent two more slaves if he could not afford to rent me? Was Stephen thinking of running to Liberia? Maybe I had been a fool to put off Cato as I did. At least he was interested in me.

Next day I set off on a long run to turn these questions over in my mind and maybe lose them. The crunching sound of my feet in the dead leaves drowned my confusion. I saw the trees and sloping land as a pathway that pulled me on into a world of my own. My path took me past the spring where we loved each other and down, down, down over rocks jutting out. The bushes in the bottom of the valley glowed a bright green where the land flattened. I trotted around the rims of sinkholes and through high grass.

Sally Lively was fierce and angry when I got back because there was kitchen work not done. "Try not to get blood on you," she said as I tied on a white apron.

# Chapter 11

# Separation is Sad

Cato found me chopping the heads off chickens behind the hotel kitchen. "Looks like Stephen dumped you for a cave. He won't shut up about his river."

"Are you jealous?" I said. "Cato, have you ever found anything wonderful in your whole life?" Cato blinked his eyes and scowled.

"Finding cave passages isn't important. What is important is how a man — me — can take care of a woman like you. Charlotte, you're wasting your time looking after Stephen. He'll turn you into a mule carrying food baskets and boats. If he had a whip he'd make a good overseer. That man lives for the cave, not for you."

Cato told me all his reasons why I should care for him. I'd always know where Cato was. Stephen, you never know where he might be. Maybe lost and never return. Cato was strong and bigger than Stephen. Cato could protect me. Cato could love me good and give me lots of babies. Cato this and Cato that.

My last chop sprayed blood all over Cato and I

tossed the chicken into the old whiskey barrel to flop around.

He wiped blood off his face with his sleeve and said, "Please, won't you be nice to me and let me be your man?"

Before I could answer, Stephen walked out of the kitchen door. "Cato, let me tell you about the river I found. It goes over a thousand feet and leads to big cave."

Cato said, "Me and Charlotte have decided to go together. You can find all the cave you want. It won't matter to us. Stephen, you are out of luck."

Stephen looked wide eyed and serious. His mouth dropped open. It was the first time I saw him without words. "Is that right, Charlotte? Is Cato telling the truth?"

I said, "The only true part is this: Stephen does care for the cave more than for me." I thought to myself that it wasn't true that I would go with Cato. Cato might be a friend to somebody, but I wasn't his girl and I tried my best to avoid him, as I had others who tried to take advantage of me. I said I wouldn't go with Cato.

Cato interrupted, "Stephen, go back in that cave of yours where you belong. This girl is mine. We decided." Cato took the bloody ax from my hand and marched slowly toward Stephen making a chopping motion. Stephen stood his ground. Cato looked down at Stephen from almost on top of him.

Suddenly Stephen brought his right knee up with a mighty strike to Cato's crotch. I thought the force would split Cato in two. Cato dropped to the ground like a sack of meal. He groaned and rolled back and forth. Cato whispered in pain, "I'll kill you. Kill you dead."

Stephen said, "Charlotte said she would not go with you. Cato, sometimes you do not listen. Listen better after this."

Stephen turned and went back into the kitchen. Cato gasped, "You're a dead man, Stephen Bishop."

I felt like running, but I had to pluck the chickens and cook them for Sally. I was afraid Sally would come out and kick Cato. We did not need a dead slave or a crippled one.

When the evening meal was cleaned up I found Stephen. I asked him why he didn't try to reason with Cato, or push him away. Stephen said, "Cato meant to use that ax on me, so I had to shift his attention. He also meant to speak for you, so I had to shift his attention."

I warned Stephen to look out for Cato. A blow like that might be answered. Stephen promised to be careful. "I want to stay in one piece for you." He slipped his hand in mine and pulled me to him. He planted a big kiss on my forehead and another on my lips. I answered back.

The stagecoach brought two passengers and two dispatch letters. I could not read one of the envelopes. On the other I saw the word GORIN. Franklin Gorin opened his envelope. He studied the letter, and then folded it. He called the servants together and said: "I have received good news. Mr. Underwood persuaded John Croghan to lend me some money to operate the hotel and cave. There is enough to rent Mat and Nick for another year, and Charlotte." He said he would talk to Mr. Bell tomorrow and try to agree on a rent price for me.

When Mr. Gorin returned from Bell's Tavern, he pulled me aside. I feared Mr. Bell would demand my return. Gorin said, "Mr. Bell won't rent you to me." My hopes dropped and I felt tears welling in my eyes. "No, but he will sell you to me. He wanted $350."

Mr. Gorin said that during their conversation a new young tavern servant girl with a pretty smile brought them a demijohn of whiskey and two glasses. Gorin thought Mr. Bell's fingers lingered a few seconds too long on the girl's hand. He caught the girl winking at Bell. "Bell's wife, my daughter Maria, came into the room. Robert Bell jumped to his feet.

"I acted fast and said, 'I accept the $330 price for Charlotte. Shall we drink to it?'" Before Bell could protest, or demand $20 more, or sit down, Maria Bell accepted the offer. "I do believe she wanted to be rid of you, Charlotte."

Stephen jumped up and down at the news that I would not be going away after all. He said Mr. Gorin had driven a smart bargain. He bought somebody who could help cook, clean and make up rooms, carry food and boats into the cave, and wet her underpants wading in Echo River.

Stephen and Mat Bransford hitched a team of horses to the wagon and set off for Bowling Green with Mr. Gorin to buy lumber at the sawmill. The lumber was to build a bigger boat for the cave and to patch the hotel. They took sour-faced Cato along. Since it was about thirty miles away, I didn't expect them back for several days. Archibald Miller, Jr. was in charge while they were gone.

The wagon pulled around to the back of the hotel four days later. Stephen and Mr. Gorin were on the front seat. Mat Bransford was sitting on top of the boards, but I didn't see Cato.

"Where's Cato?" I said to Stephen. Stephen said they arrived at the sawmill in Bowling Green, near the Barren River. Mr. Gorin went into the mill to deal for the lumber. Stephen said to Cato he was sorry he kicked him so hard. Cato repeated that he would kill Stephen first chance. Mr. Gorin came out and told them to pull the wagon into the yard. He pointed to a pile of boards and ordered them to load the boards on the wagon. Cato told Mr. Gorin to load the boards himself. Gorin asked again. Cato said, "You heard me. Load your own damn boards."

Mr. Gorin rolled up his sleeves and pitched in with Stephen and Mat to load the wagon while Cato looked sour and angry. They drove the loaded wagon into town and stopped at the slave market. Mr. Gorin went into the office of a slave trader. He came out with three men. The slave trader had a white man and a slave who carried chains. They took hold of Cato and snapped the shackles on his wrists and ankles. Cato began to thrash and jump around when he saw what was happening. He let out a cry. "Don't leave me! Let me loose! I'll be good!"

Mr. Gorin said, "Goodbye, Cato." Stephen begged Mr. Gorin to change his mind and give Cato another chance. Gorin said it was a $500 lesson neither of them would forget. Gorin got $500 for Cato, and Cato was facing an unknown future for being uppity. That is why they returned to Mammoth Cave without Cato.

I thought about the first time when Stephen saved Cato from a beating by the miller. Then about how Cato ran away right into the arms of a slave catcher. Stephen had gotten Cato's attention with a painful strike. But Cato said he would kill Stephen. Rage like Cato's wouldn't die. Yet, I had felt pity for Cato because he did care for me the only way he knew how. White folks have to settle one way or another, even if it costs an ear. But if an owner and his slave disagree, the slave always loses. Mildred was right. There are takers and there are a few givers. Most of us are givers and takers.

Early on I saw Stephen was a giver when Mildred hoped he might be one. Did he really try to talk Mr. Gorin out of selling Cato? Or was that for my ears? Stephen had no reason to like Cato. It could even be that Stephen wanted to be rid of Cato.

Mat settled the question for me. I asked him, "Did Stephen really try to save Cato from being sold?"

Mat said, "I saw it with my own eyes. Stephen pleaded with Master Gorin. Stephen got on one knee and begged him with tears in his eyes not to sell Cato." Mat was too scared to add his voice to the pleading. On the way back home Mat and Stephen talked about separation. Mr. Gorin agreed with them that separation was mostly bad. But sometimes it was good, as when Charlotte was separated from Robert Bell. I have thought about separation since I was a little girl. Wasn't my love of running mostly separation? Running away from a man who wanted me? I decided what mattered most was what you were separated from. If it was from love, that was bad. If it was from hate and greed, that was good. I also decided that running was finding freedom by sorting out confusion and getting to the me inside of me. Maybe cave exploring was like that for Stephen. Underground is separate from everything else, where you are free to explore and enjoy your world.

That journey to Bowling Green put a cloud over Stephen. We talked together every chance we could about separation, selling people, and dividing people. Could you sell your own children? What if they were mean and hateful? If you could sell an evil child because you owned him, could you sell a good child? We agreed that owning and selling people was evil. If you had children, would you own them or just rent them until they got big enough to own themselves? If we had a child, we agreed we'd love him and let him be free to make small mistakes. Then one day our child would be free to experience the results of his good and bad choices.

Mr. Gorin set Mat and Nick to work building a larger boat for the cave. Stephen had taken Gorin for a boat ride in the little boat. Just as Stephen said, they paddled the boat only about eight feet from shore before it started to rock back and forth. Water spilled over the side and they fell out. They looked funny, like wet dogs, when they came to the kitchen door to dry out. They agreed that to take visitors on a boat ride they would need a larger boat.

Mat had learned how to build a boat from an old slave from Nashville. The plan was to make all the pieces of the boat and take them into the cave. They would nail the pieces together on the bank. The boat bottom would curve up to each flat end. There would be five seats, one on each end and three in the middle. Up to ten people could fit in the boat, although four to six was the size of most cave parties. The boat would be about twelve feet long and four feet wide. The men spent most of two weeks sawing boards and fitting pieces. Then it was time to carry the pieces into the cave.

Mr. Gorin turned everybody out early in the morning. One visitor said he'd like to help when he learned no guides would be available that day. My job was to carry one of three baskets of food. Hannah and Sally each carried a basket. The men were Mr. Gorin, John Wigglesworth, Casey Dunn, Archie Miller, Stephen, Mat, Nick, Alfred, Joseph, Seth, Aiken, and the visitor whose name I have forgotten. Every other person carried a lantern in addition to the boards and tools.

At the two small places we fed the boards down the Snake Hole steps from the Wooden Bowl Room and passed them hand to hand in the tight passage in Winding Way. Mr. Gorin and Mat scouted ahead and came back with the advice that the boat yard would be on flat ground near Charon's Cascade.

After that first day of work on the boat I went back to the hotel kitchen and maid work. Stephen returned to guiding the few visitors. The boat builders, Mat, Nick, and Alfred went into the cave every day with their own dinner. Mr. Gorin kept track of the boat by asking how it was coming. Mat said, "Three more days," a few times within my hearing. I wondered if they were stretching the job out by laying out or exploring. Stephen wondered the same thing, but figured they were exploring when Nick asked him about a passage. Nick wanted to know about a muddy passage to the left in River Hall that went to the bottom of some deep pits. Stephen said one of the pits might have been the Bottomless Pit. Nick said he could not see far enough with his light to tell if there was a bridge up there in the darkness.

Stephen asked Mat about their exploring. Mat said, "Boat building is slave labor, like carrying boards and building steps. We'd rather spend time exploring than working. It's a big cave and we'll follow it wherever it goes, so you can't stop us." Stephen said that proved the Bransfords spent more time exploring than being carpenters. They didn't deny their explorations. They just switched the subject when asked. Stephen doubted that Mr. Gorin was fooled.

One winter day Franklin Gorin sent for Stephen to come by his house. Stephen said Mr. Gorin was upset. He had run to the end of his loan money and had no way to pay back John Croghan. Besides, he was several months behind on his payment to Mr. Gratz for the hotel and cave. John Croghan was coming to inspect the property. One of the loan terms was that Croghan would have first right to buy the cave from Gorin in case Gorin could not pay. Mr. Gorin said he proposed to try to ask Dr. Croghan to be his equal partner.

Stephen said that selling the cave would be tragic. In just a few more years paying visitors would flock to the cave. Gorin himself said the visitors had picked up since Stephen had discovered Gorin's Dome. The new Echo River trip would attract more people. Patching the roof on the hotel had stopped the leaks and it was certain that other improvements would keep tourists staying longer. Couldn't Mr. Gorin hold out and not sell?

Gorin said business is business. He'd have to sell the cave, hotel, and the servants as a going business unless they could agree on a partnership. Stephen asked, "Would you sell me, too?"

Mr Gorin said, "You are almost like a son to me. Since you were a tiny baby on Lowry Bishop's farm, I have seen you grow into a fine young man. You are the best explorer and the best story teller. Without you the cave would be just a black hole in the ground miles from anywhere."

Stephen asked Mr. Gorin why he had taught him to read and write. Gorin said there was no law against it, and slaves who learned to read and write were smarter than most people and they could think for themselves.

Stephen said what about the rumors that Franklin Gorin is his father? Gorin looked straight ahead for a long time before he answered Stephen. "I do not know. Your mother was a wonderful woman. She was so smart for a slave. We were a few years apart in age. We played together. We grew up together. Just before she and Lowry took up, we loved each other once. You were born the same year your mother and father got together."

That made Stephen start to cry. "You mean you could sell your own son?"

"What would you do if you knew you were my son?" Gorin's hard question struck Stephen's heart. Blood or not, Stephen's love for Mr. Gorin caused him to cry like a baby. Gorin wrapped an arm around Stephen. "What would you do if you knew?"

# Chapter 12

# John Croghan Buys Mammoth Cave

We tidied up the hotel. John Croghan was coming to inspect the place and we had to make a good impression. Mr. Gorin told us John Croghan was a well-to-do medical doctor. He was about fifty years old. He had inherited money and practiced medicine. But mostly his early money had come from setting up a salt works on his eight hundred acres along the Cumberland River in eastern Kentucky. His brothers, Nicholas and George, had urged him to visit Mammoth Cave. Even his father, William Croghan, knew about Mammoth Cave from his surveying trips.

On his stay in Europe people asked Dr. Croghan about the wonderful Mammoth Cave in his own state. His answer to them was based on stories in newspapers. Gorin's printed stories about Stephen's discoveries set London to talking.

After he returned to Louisville, Croghan sent his cousin Luther Ray to look over the cave. Later he told his land-buying lawyer, Joseph Underwood, to report on the cave. Gorin's desire to borrow money, along with

Underwood's report, had led him to advance $500 as a loan to Gorin. Now Croghan was coming to see for himself.

On his first visit the servants and guides outdid themselves. I made brandied peaches two days straight. We served roast pig one night and roast beef the next. Stephen took Dr. Croghan on the Main Cave short tour the first day, and into Indian Avenue and over Bottomless Pit into Pensacola Avenue and to Echo River the second day. Stephen said he told every story he knew and made up some new ones.

Dr. Croghan kept brushing his thin hair over bald spots on his head. We all noticed that Dr. Croghan had red-rimmed eyes and often used his handkerchief. Almost immediately after entering Mammoth Cave his nose wiping stopped and he said he blinked less. Two days after he arrived he left the hotel with high praise for the effect of the cave air on his sniffles.

Dr. Croghan visited the cave again a few weeks later. He asked about the health of the saltpetre miners. He wanted to know if the guides were healthy. Did visitors complain of sickness? Everybody from Mr. Gorin to Sally Lively, to Stephen, to Archie said the cave was an uncommonly healthy place. Dr. Croghan spent many hours walking around the 2,000 acres of grounds, fields, and woods, sometimes with Mr. Gorin and sometimes alone.

Master Gorin called us servants together one day. He said Dr. Croghan had declined his offer to become a partner. Instead he offered $10,000 for the place. That included the hotel, the cave, and all the servants. Gorin said he accepted the offer, but would have to pay back the $500 loan that Croghan had advanced. Also, he still owed several thousands of dollars to Mr. Gratz back when he bought the place for $5,000. We'd all carry on. Nothing would be different. Mr. Gorin said that he'd build a house for himself on a little piece of land nearby so he could see that nothing bad happened to us.

Stephen, Mat, Nick, Seth, Aiken, John, and Casey had been running regular boat ride tours for cave visitors. Our new tours would give tired visitors a couple of days to recover from their stagecoach or wagon ride. The first day trip would take them through Main Cave, past the saltpetre works, up into the Haunted Chambers. There were pretty formations there, and the tour went to that end of the cave passage. The second day they would see Indian Avenue out to where it got too narrow and low. That wasn't a long trip, so visitors could rest up and eat good. Then on the third day they just had to stay and go on a wonderful boat ride. The guides sang songs on Echo River. Visitors trailed their fingers in the cold clear water. They drank water that had never seen daylight, so they were told. If they gave the guide some money, he would dip out a white cave fish for them to see up close. Our main idea was to keep visitors eating and touring and paying for as many days as possible. The boat ride was so popular that some visitors stayed another day just to do it again.

One visitor knew about the boat ride. He brought an empty bottle. He told Stephen if he caught a white cave fish, he would give Stephen a compass. He had seen one that belonged to Mr. Gorin that he used in his land sales business. Mr. Gorin had shown how the needle points north and points the direction to measure boundaries. Would it work inside the cave?

The man showed how the compass would point north just as well underground as in the road by the hotel. Stephen said, "It took most of an hour to catch that fish and put it through the narrow bottle neck. It squirted out of my hand once." Up close the fish had no eyes. Stephen said the man was satisfied but the rest of the visitors were ready to kill him because they got cold waiting. Outside the cave the man taught Stephen how to read the compass and pace off a line toward a big tree.

Stephen was curious about that compass. He would pull it out of his pocket now and then. Once he stood on the front porch of the hotel with the compass held in his hand. "That way is north," he said, and pointed into the entrance of the hotel. He told me that to go in a beeline from the hotel to the cave entrance you would walk north-northeast. He took the compass with him into the cave. "Guess which direction you go from the Mammoth Cave entrance to the Rotunda?" Stephen said. Might as well ask what number he was thinking of. I had no idea. "Southeast, the same direction as Main Cave goes." Guides who explored with Stephen said he would look at the compass once in a while.

On a run one day through the chestnut trees and past our spring I asked Stephen what direction I had gone. He said I ran southeast from the hotel. On the way back I ran northwest. It never seemed important to me, but Stephen said he got a good idea of the lay of the cave under the land from looking at his compass.

On winter days we gave visitors extra service and food. The cave tours lasted a little longer. But the problem was there weren't enough visitors to keep us busy. Stephen told Mr. Gorin he wanted to explore when there were no visitors. Mr. Gorin said he could go, but not to go alone. I told Stephen he owed me a promised boat ride. He agreed and we set off on the snow-covered path to the cave.

Archie Miller's father, who managed the cave many years before, told him the story of the miners and the saltpetre manufactory. In the Rotunda, Stephen told me a longer story about the seventy slaves that mined saltpetre here in 1812. I will set down the details here because I didn't remember the whole story when I first heard it. First thing when slaves arrived they felled large trees. Then they used an iron auger about twelve feet long to bore a round hole from one end of a Tulip tree log to about the middle. They would switch to the other end of the log and bore out the soft center until the holes lined up. This twenty-foot log pipe could carry water. One end of each pipe was cut sharp so it would fit in the next pipe. They fitted these pipes together with an iron band at the joint to make a pipeline from the spring at the entrance to the log vats in the Rotunda and another pipeline back out. Slaves drove ox carts in the cave and miners loaded cave dirt into the cart to be delivered and unloaded in the vats. Water from the pipeline trickled into the vats. It would leach through the dirt and drain the niter-liquor out through a trough at the bottom of the vat.

To send the liquor out of the cave the slaves built a tall tower that had a pump at the top wedged into a groove in the ceiling. Two slaves on the top of the tower pumped the liquor out of the cave through another pipeline to the entrance. At the entrance, slaves had set up iron cooking kettles for boiling the liquor. They skimmed off the crystals of saltpetre and loaded them in bags. When the bags of saltpetre made a wagonload, teamsters drove the wagon to Wilmington, Delaware where they made it into gunpowder. That saltpetre brought seventy-five cents a pound. It was said the Americans fought the British with gunpowder made from Mammoth Cave saltpetre. It was so profitable that the owners built more vats at Gothic Avenue to increase production. After the war the price of saltpetre sank to twenty cents a pound. The mining continued, but it wasn't much.

Stephen told me the story just as he told it to visitors,

only he was better at describing how spooky the mining was. Heavy smoke hung in the air from the oil lamps. Oxen would appear from pitch dark passages with loaded carts. Miners slowed down their work to explore after the overseer left them. Those who operated the pump developed big muscles in their arms and chests and their skin glistened from sweat in the flickering lamplight.

"One day there was a terrible tragedy," said Stephen. "Just terrible! They had started to lay the pipelines at the entrance when they came to the Narrows. The passage was partly blocked with a large fallen rock. It was too heavy to move. They decided to blast it into smaller pieces with black powder. One man held the steel drill bit to make a powder hole. Another had a sledgehammer. That's when the tragedy happened. The drill holder said to the sledge man, 'When I nod my head, you hit it.'"

We came to the underground river where the small and large boats were tied. "Which boat shall we take?"

"The one that won't tip," I said, because I had not brought an extra dress. Stephen paddled the long boat with the lamp on the front seat. I shielded my eyes from the flame and could see the walls and ceiling magically sliding by. We glided beneath an arch and over an endless lake of still water. Stephen began to sing in the most beautiful voice I had ever heard. He sang several verses of "A King Came Riding" with echoes that were haunting and beautiful. After that he sang a song that he made up:

> *Charlotte Brown, she came to town,*
> *Fancy dressed in orange and green.*
> *Charlotte be my own true love,*
> *You are my black-haired queen.*

*Charlotte waded in the water,*
*Looked like Pharaoh's daughter,*
*Her dress was soaked, she took it off,*
*But thought to bring another.*

I was struck with astonishment while the echoing melody lingered. And it was just like Stephen to make fun of my embarrassment! In song he had asked me to be his love. I certainly didn't miss that part. I asked if he sang like that for all the visitors.

"Mostly I do, but not *that* song." He said some of the ladies with pretty names brought to mind a song. "Almost anything I sing in here sounds good."

Our boat nosed into the far bank where we climbed out and walked on the sandy trail. The passage grew larger and we came to a waterfall. Beyond it the passage became narrow and tall, curving this way and that. We walked for about an hour. The top of the passage was in blackness. I was hungry, "When do we eat?"

Stephen stopped at a muddy place where the walls were wet and a jumble of rocks blocked our way straight ahead. "Want to eat here?" he laughed.

"No. Let's go back to a wide place where it is dry," I said. We did, and spread the lunch on a cloth. I said, "Is this the end of the cave? We've been going a long time."

"It's probably not the end. We're stopped by a wall of broken rocks. I want to look around to see if I can get through the rocks." Stephen was off poking among the rocks in the breakdown. I sat down to wait for him.

I tore off a piece of bread and chewed it. He didn't return, so I ate my share of the lunch and began to worry about him. I could never find my way out of the cave from here.

Stephen poked his head down through a muddy hole in the ceiling and said, "A little way beyond the dig through the broken rocks is a passage to the right. It took me back and up to more cave, but it will wait. Right up here there are stone grapes, like a vineyard." Stephen accused me of eating half of his lunch, as if I hadn't measured carefully.

We returned to River Hall, where we started our boat journey. He'd tied the boat. At the boat yard where they built the new boat, Stephen went to the left instead of the right. It was a muddy way and the wrong way. He poked at some large rocks that filled the passage. One tumbled down as he stepped aside. "I don't believe this is the end. With a little work it should continue." Stephen kept these promising places in his head for the time a visitor wanted to explore where nobody had been before. In Pensacola Avenue we stopped where a large rock had dropped from the ceiling. "I want to put our names here." He picked up a sharp rock and used it like a pencil to scratch *Stephen and Charlotte*. Later, when we were married, I saw he had improved those white scratched names to *Stephen and Mrs. Charlotte Bishop, Flower of Mammoth Cave*, and he had drawn a heart around it.

We rested. "We should get married," I told him. "I want to live with you and never be without you."

Stephen agreed. "I'll ask Mr. Gorin. He told Alfred that he and Hannah could marry next fall after the tourist business slacked off, but the cave will be sold by then. Nobody knows what Mr. Croghan will allow."

We held each other a long time and kissed. He pulled back, "You taste like fried chicken." That wasn't the romantic singer on the river. That was a cave guide getting familiar. My feelings were so strong for that guide I thought I would just give myself to him and let him take the choice pieces.

We climbed the steps at the entrance. Those stars were bright in the dark sky, and a big full moon fell on the fresh blanket of snow. Our footsteps left a trail behind us, the only tracks in the world in the new snow. We headed south-southwest.

At the guide house Stephen bent over and scooped up a handful of snow. He squeezed it into a ball, turned and threw it at me. It struck me full on my chest. I put down my lamp and made a snowball. He began to run, but I ran faster. As I drew up I threw it and hit him in the back of his neck. Snow showered all over his head and down his back. Our fight continued. Some of my snowballs struck the back of the guide house. A few of his hit me, but most missed. I hadn't seen snowballs before, but I found I was a pretty good shot.

Stephen asked Mr. Gorin if we could marry. Gorin said it would be up to Dr. John Croghan when he came to take over the cave. He was happy we had found each other, but property is property. "The decision is out of my hands."

It still worried me that Stephen seemed to care more about where the cave went than about me. Could I live with that? I said to him, "I know you want to marry, but I am afraid the cave will come first." He said that I knew him pretty well by now. The cave was important in his life but it was not the only thing.

He questioned me, "Do you suppose you'll give up running when you marry me?" Stephen knew I fancied running. I felt alive and free like a bird when I could fly over the ground.

I said, "I can live with cave exploring if you can live with running." We spent some time together looking at the books, my new alphabet book and his new *FIRST READER*. *See Charlotte. See Charlotte run. Run, Charlotte, run. Run, run, run.* On page seventeen, I poked Stephen: *I see a pig. How fat it is! Can the pig run? It can not run. It is too fat.*

"You calling me fat?" Stephen raised his eyebrows showing the whites of his eyes. He wiggled his hair. "Oink oink." Reading was hard work, but we got the hang of it when we weren't kissing.

John Croghan arrived in a carriage and team, followed by a wagon loaded with furniture and trunks. It looked like he was here to stay. He moved into Franklin Gorin's house, and Gorin and his wife moved to a smaller place. Stephen and the other servants helped move.

Dr. Croghan had a bright pink face and rosy cheeks. His eyes were no longer red and he kept his kerchief in his pocket. His thin hair was dun colored. He stood about a hand taller than Mr. Gorin. In his frock coat he had a gold chain from one pocket to his watch, a fancier chain than Mr. Gorin's. He took charge like he was used to giving orders. He didn't seem to be a mean man, and asked several times if loads were too heavy. He had a lot of books of all sizes and no shelves to put them on. Dr. Croghan set Mat Bransford to work building shelves. Stephen carried in Dr. Croghan's doctor bag, but didn't look in it. Stephen could read people well, but he didn't know what kind of master Dr. Croghan would be. We watched that man and his every move.

John Croghan called Franklin Gorin, Archibald Miller, and Stephen to meet in his front room. He announced big plans. "We'll make the hotel larger and patch the holes and we'll improve the cave trails to make walking easier. We need better roads so people can come here easier."

"Not too easy," Stephen said. "We want visitors to set a spell, rest up, and spend a lot of time taking cave tours." Croghan smiled and nodded. Stephen understood what it would take to make Mammoth Cave a going concern.

Dr. Croghan divided the work. Joe Shackelford, Mat,

and Nick were to add a new dining room to the hotel with a ballroom upstairs, patch the roof, add a long porch and some rooms, and build some new slave cabins. They also built fifteen or sixteen cottages.

Archie Miller and Stephen were told to go over the routes in the cave, fix the steps where they needed repairs, dig out the high spots and fill in the low ones. Dr.Croghan headed on horseback to the capital at Frankfort to see if he could persuade the legislators to build better roads.

Dr. Croghan had a new cast iron cook stove delivered. It was better than the hearth for cooking. Sally and I decided we could cook up more tasty meals to help keep visitors staying longer and growing fatter. Sally seemed to tire more easily than last year. She gave me more work to do than back a few months before. We spent weeks doing these tasks. When guests arrived we'd stop and attend to them, but the minute they left we ran back to work on the improvements.

Dr. Croghan must have convinced the legislators to help with the new roads because in a few months a road building crew came to Mammoth Cave. There were twenty men and half a dozen mules, and many wagons. They pitched tents and made camp in the side yard of the hotel. When they were not out building the road they sharpened their axes on a grindstone and bedded down the mules with straw. Stephen asked one of the slaves how they built a road.

He said they were working on a seven-mile road from the Louisville-Nashville road to Mammoth Cave and it was a little over halfway done. Two surveyors selected the path of the road, generally following old trails. Woodmen felled trees in the blazed way and then mule teams hooked chains on the trees and dragged them away. Axmen chopped the stumps away. They dug ditches along the sides of the new road to carry rainwater away to nearby gullies. They kept the route as level and straight as possible, but sometimes they had to take the road up or down a slope. To dig dirt they had a couple of pans pulled by four-mule teams. To cut down the high spots the team would scoop off the dirt. They would drag the pan to a low spot where they would dump it and smooth it out. The new road was higher than the land nearby, so it would drain. They placed large rocks for a foundation and small rocks on top. The new road was smoother than the old trails and in dry weather it was good. When it rained, the lowest parts of the road turned to red mud and wagon wheels made ruts. So it wasn't a good idea to travel in wet weather. Some visitors to the hotel tracked in red mud on their boots when it rained.

There were other road building crews. One started twenty-five miles north at Grayson Springs and worked south to ford the Nolin River and then the Green River at Mammoth Cave. One headed overland from Rowletts Station thirteen miles west to Mammoth Cave and another crew built a road between Bowling Green and Mammoth Cave, about thirty-two miles. Fewer visitors came by way of Bell's Tavern because the shortcut roads now passed by the place. Bell's Tavern was stranded. Every day two four-horse stagecoaches would stop at Mammoth Cave, one headed to Louisville the other headed to Nashville.

We became so busy with visitors that Dr. Croghan sent for some more slaves to come down from Locust Grove. There was so much work I had to rise before daylight and wash dishes until after dark. I longed to run and I longed for Stephen. Then two things happened that changed my hopes and made me gloomy. Sally Lively turned sickly and my work increased. The other thing was worse.

# Chapter 13

# Dr. Croghan's Grand Plans

Stephen and Archibald Miller traveled all the routes in the cave, and they crawled many places. Nick joined them on most explorations. When visitors arrived they stopped exploring and conducted tours. Stephen said one of the favorite visitor sites was Haunted Chambers, up a stairway to the right off Main Cave. The passage had a most pleasing shape, like a squashed circle. It was a place where visitors would pay money to have the guide tie a candle on a pole and smoke their initials on the ceiling. Stephen was told Haunted Chambers once contained a dried Indian mummy that was shown to visitors thirty years ago. Before Mr. Gorin came, it was sold to a museum. Several large stalactites, stalagmites, and pillars grew from the ceiling and floor in this room. One place was called the Armchair, where visitors liked to sit in it until they felt the wet stone soaking through their pants. Some guides called the place Gothic Avenue adding to the growing confusion of place names.

Over several months and between tours they dug the

passage deeper between the Giant's Coffin and Wooden Bowl room so nobody had to stoop. They cleared away loose rocks in the Church room and spread sand from banks in the cave over the floor. Guides smoothed trails by tossing rocks aside and making some of the steep hills into steps using big rocks from along the way.

Archie and Stephen had worked out seven tours in the cave that would keep travelers there a week. Most of the routes took visitors in one way and back out the same way, or where the passage widened, they built a trail leading in on one side and back out on the other side. If Stephen could place candles in certain places on the way in, and different places on the way out, it convinced most visitors they were seeing new parts of the cave for the whole trip. Now and then they found a circular route, in one way and out another without retracing steps.

Dr. Croghan wanted to go on the longest route in the cave, to a place called The Temple. It would only be worthwhile if a large group went with many lamps. The Temple was so large it looked like outdoors on a moonless night, but if everybody had candles or lamps they could see the room. They asked me to trail along behind a tour of ten people, carrying a food basket. Nick carried another food basket. We set off after lunch. Stephen handed out all the lanterns we had. Dr. Croghan reminded Archie to order more lanterns.

I knew the route to the Coffin. Stephen told stories I had heard about saltpetre mining. He repeated how Charles Harvey's hair turned white when he lost his way. Stephen pointed the way behind the Coffin and said that was a trip for another day. A visitor asked Stephen where that route went. "It leads to Gorin's Dome, largest pit in the cave, and then over a pit called Bottomless, then you come to an underground river. We have explored that river for two miles and we do not know how far it goes." He lowered his voice as if to tell a secret, "It may go to Louisville and another branch to Nashville."

I heard "ooo"s and "ah"s from the tour. One woman asked, "You mean we might take a steamboat from Louisville to Nashville and not see daylight? Not get rained on?"

Stephen said, "It's a possibility."

We moved on to a place where Stephen stopped the tour. "Sit on the rocks and look up. This is the only place in the cave where you can see stars in the daylight." The ceiling in that room was as black as any night. There were many white spots in the black sky. I thought it looked like real stars on a dark night except the stars didn't twinkle. A man asked why we could see the stars when it was still afternoon. Stephen repeated the question so all the tour could hear it. Then he said, "When well diggers sink a well more than twenty feet and look up from the bottom, they can see stars in daylight. Now we are more than one hundred twenty feet below the surface, so we can see the entire Milky Way from this deep." He waited for that to sink in.

A voice on the end of the tour said, "Is that the truth?"

"It is true only in Mammoth Cave. Everyone else will deny it, but you have seen it with your own eyes," said Stephen.

Another man spoke up, "If we extinguish all our lights we can see if it is true."

Stephen asked everyone to blow out the lamps, When the wicks stopped glowing it was pitch black and there were no stars. The man who suggested the test said, "See, it is a humbug. There are no stars."

Stephen's clear voice rang out, "Only in Mammoth Cave can you blow out your lamp and not see stars. Am I not right? You can't see the stars without light anyplace in Mammoth Cave." Some of the ladies and gentlemen groaned.

We walked for hours through a large passage that was mostly forty feet wide and twenty to thirty feet high. It was rough walking over the rocks strewn on the floor. We came to a vast room that opened in all directions. Passages led off several ways. The place looked to me to be one hundred feet across, two hundred feet long, and fifty feet high. We moved on another half mile or less to a place where we heard the sound of falling water. Closer to it, water poured out of a hole in the passage ceiling and fell fifty feet into a deep pit. Archie called it the Cataracts. By this time my basket was getting heavy and I switched it from one hand to the other. Shifting the load had helped at first, but now my shoulders ached. So much of this part of the cave looked the same I would gladly have turned around — I had seen enough.

The path ahead was climbing. I could see the lights of the whole tour moving single file up through a hole in the ceiling. When I caught up to where the tour was stopped I was struck with astonishment. That room was far larger than the last big room we had passed through. Truth be told, I could not see the far wall or the wall across the room. Stephen mounted a large rock to address the tour. "We are in the biggest single room in Mammoth Cave. It is called The Temple or Chief City. Between all the rocks in this two-acre room are burnt torches discarded by ancient Indians. We found woven slippers, pieces of cloth, stone tools, clamshells, and flint chips. It is as if the Indian chief and his tribe made this their city."

Stephen ordered the baskets of food to be unpacked and bid the visitors to sit on rocks large enough to make a table. We served each visitor a plate of cold fried chicken, yam custard, sliced apples, bread with jam, and cider or wine in small glasses. One of the visitors complained there was no place to wash his hands or relieve himself. Stephen sent the gents back the way we had come and the ladies ahead. I led some of them over and around the rocks out of the way. Washing was out of the question, which was too bad as soot and ashes covered everything. Indians had built fires from wood they had carried in. A few of my ladies returned to the food badly smudged.

"You're lucky," said one woman. "You don't have to wash because you are black to begin with."

After the lunch we packed away the leftovers. Stephen passed out candles and he handed the biggest taper to Dr. Croghan. "We'll be the first people to see how large the Temple is. Please spread out by walking to the walls of the room. Light your candle from your lamp, and then look around you." We did as we were told. Dr. Croghan climbed to the center of the room and stood on a rock.

I found a spot on top of a rock as big as a kitchen table near the far wall. When I lit the candle and looked I could see a circle of lights. The lights were one hundred fifty to two hundred feet apart. The room was oblong, maybe three hundred feet wide and six hundred feet long. The ceiling was sixty feet above us. Dr. Croghan was below most of us. The spectacle took my breath away and made me wonder if the Indians had lighted the Temple in this way.

I heard a voice begin to sing, and others joined, "Rock of ages, cleft for me, Let me hide myself in Thee; Let the water and the blood, from Thy riven side which flowed, Be of sin the double cure, Save me from its grip and power." Toward the end of it I could hear Stephen's strong voice. They sang it again, this time with a little more force but the sound still failed to fill the room. Later I asked Stephen how he came to know this song. He said a lady sang it on Echo River and he had joined in the second time. It sounded better on Echo River, he said. Chief City might be the most impressive sight in Mammoth Cave, but it soaked up the sound of singing.

We turned around and left the cave following the same route. Stephen placed some candles in different places, but I recognized all the turns. We came to the entrance stairs. A woman asked how far we had walked. Stephen said twelve miles. I knew better. Stephen said the refreshing and healthful air of the cave made a long walk seem short, but I knew this was a story. I was blowing black snot from my nose hours later from breathing dusty air from smoke and ashes. The visitors all turned in, leaving Nick and me to clean up the baskets and leavings back in the kitchen.

Nick said it was a shame that many passages in the cave had no name and some had several names. The Temple was also named Chief City. Stephen thought it was fine if the names got mixed up. Then it would take a guide to straighten it out, but Nick said he would speak to Dr. Croghan about naming passages.

Nick was the second cause of my gloom. I felt bad because we were overrun by visitors and that meant more hard work and long hours. Now Nick sank my spirits lower, "Dr. Croghan wants to build a hotel in the Temple. He says with more slaves we could clean out all the rocks from the passage floors and haul visitors to the underground hotel in carriages."

"No!" I cried. I imagined gangs of seventy slaves, teamsters, road builders, carpenters, and overseers with whips. There would be washing, cooking, cleaning up horse droppings, emptying chamber pots, drudgery, and toil. No!

Stephen said Dr. Croghan seemed to be in earnest because he was a man of big plans. We thought few people would want to stay at an underground hotel. And it would be a shame to spoil the grandeur of the Temple as it appeared with our lights. It was an altogether wonderful place like no other. Part of the appeal of the place was it was hard to get there. The other servants agreed with us. It would be a bad move to turn a spooky cave into an ordinary hotel.

Stephen was bolder than the rest of us. He asked Franklin Gorin what he thought about the idea of an underground hotel. Gorin said it was a poor one and that Dr. Croghan would be smarter to put the money into improving the hotel we had. But Gorin warned Stephen that Dr. Croghan owned the place now and could do whatever he wanted.

Everyone talked about the big plans for a couple of weeks. New visitors thought the idea made no sense.

Stephen said to Dr. Croghan, "If you built a couple of rooms underground, you could try out the idea without building a big place. Visitors will tell you if they like the accommodations. If they do not like them, you'll hear it from them." Dr. Croghan said that was practical advice and he would think about it some more.

Stephen also told Dr. Croghan that we wanted to marry if we could gain his permission. Croghan asked if Charlotte was willing, or was that just Stephen's say-so? Dr. Croghan said that when slaves up at Locust Grove in Louisville asked to marry, he and his brothers always asked each of the parties if that was their wish. When it was just one servant's idea and not the other, they said no. If they both wanted to marry, they would have to work hard for one year and show that they were not lazy or disloyal. Then they might marry.

"Franklin Gorin said you two wanted to marry, and that you promised him you would find a wonderful discovery." Dr. Croghan remembered that Stephen was told that making discoveries was his job, which he owed in exchange for having a kind master. Any guide could lead tours through the cave, but not just any guide could make big discoveries as Stephen was doing." We will see," was Dr. Croghan's final word.

Stephen was always looking for likely places to find more cave. I reminded him of the breakdowns of rocks in River Hall and at the end of the miles-long passage beyond the boat ride.

Christmas came to the hotel. The only Christmases I knew were at Bell's Tavern. Mrs. Bell had cut green branches and bittersweet berries for decorations. There were sweet smells of lavender and cider heating on the hearth. Mostly the guests drank more wine and brandy than usual. Mr. Bell gave Mildred and me an orange on Christmas Day, the first I'd seen. I didn't know what to do with it. Did you bite into it like an apple? Mildred showed me how to peel the thick skin and suck the sweet juice from the sections inside. That Christmas Mrs. Bell got a new shell comb for her hair and she gave Mr. Bell a gold chain for his watch. Beyond that, Christmases were just a heap of extra work.

Some of the guests at the hotel sang songs around the fireplace. The public rooms smelled of evergreen boughs and beeswax candles. I helped Sally roast a magnificent round of beef. She made Yorkshire pudding, but it fell flat. We worked long hours at the hotel and Dr. Croghan reminded all the servants to smile because it was good for business. I saw Stephen only now and then, but guests would return from cave tours marveling at Stephen the guide. His knowledge and entertaining stories stuck with them throughout their visit, as when they repeated "Water that never saw the light of day," and "When I nod my head, you hit it."

A couple of days after Christmas we were down to six guests. One of them, Charles Sparks, slipped Stephen a silver dollar. He wanted to go on a cave trip that nobody else had taken. Stephen hunted down Dr. Croghan and told him what the visitor wanted. Dr. Croghan said he could take such a trip, but Stephen required a tour of six. Was Sparks willing to pay six times the regular ticket price? Sparks reached deep in his pocket and flipped out a $20 gold piece. Croghan acted like it happened every day. He reached in the cash box and laid down two dollars in change. And he handed the man a ticket. Dr. Croghan and Mr. Sparks walked to the guide house to meet Stephen.

Many hours later Mr. Sparks returned to the hotel with his clothes covered with mud. I fixed him a late supper and asked if he enjoyed the trip.

Mr. Sparks said the trip was the finest thing he had ever done. They had discovered a new avenue in the cave. They moved large rocks that blocked their way and walked a long distance, crouched over in a stoopwalk, and crawled on hands and knees. In another place they lay on their bellies in the mud and pushed into a low passage with their feet. The food basket was too big to fit.

They passed by a side passage that had never been explored. "We came to another tumbledown of rocks, very wet and drippy." Sparks was wide awake now, waving his hands. His words poured out.

Stephen had pulled a large rock out of a jam and a blast of air poured out of the black hole putting out their lamps. Stephen fired his lamp again, and shielded it from the wind. He told Mr. Sparks to go through the hole, then handed him his own lamp. Sparks said, "I was on a precipice looking over a deep pit. I feared for my life but Stephen joined me and lit my lamp. We edged around the pit on a narrow ledge."

I tried to fight back a yawn. I was too weary from a long day. Mr. Sparks continued. "We climbed up a muddy pile of rocks into an immense room, a dome so high I could not see the ceiling. There were three giant

columns on one wall. It looked like a Greek temple."
Stephen said they were the first persons to see this new
discovery.

"I sure got my money's worth," said Mr. Sparks as
he picked up his muddy coat from the floor of the dining room and headed for his room.

What had Stephen found? Had he taken Sparks on a
new route into Gorin's Dome? It would not surprise me
if Stephen rediscovered a fancy place and told the visitor he was the first to see it.

Next morning I ran to Stephen the minute I put the
corn pone pan on the iron stove and the biscuits in the
oven. Sally was cutting bacon. I told her I'd be back
soon.

"You look pleased, Mr. Guide."

"We went to River Hall. There's a wall of rocks, a
breakdown there. We worked about an hour and a half
moving rocks and digging our way. Mr. Sparks is a
natural digger, so we opened the blocked passage and
went on and on." Stephen described the breeze as stopping and starting. They walked and crawled through a
passage with a ceiling that became shaped like the letter
A. The walls were black and they glistened with wet-
ness. Stephen and Mr. Sparks climbed up into a dome
higher than Gorin's Dome. His description of the place
matched that of Mr. Sparks.

Stephen said they needed new names for the new
discoveries.

"Did it go on?" I asked. He didn't know. However
they'd passed up several promising unexplored passages. Dr. Croghan would be most pleased at this new
find, but would Stephen's newest discovery convince
Dr. Croghan to let us marry?

# Chapter 14

# Mammoth Dome

Archibald Miller, Jr. and Dr. Croghan called the new discovery Mammoth Dome. Nick and Mat said they knew exactly where it was, because they had poked around in that same River Hall breakdown when they were building the big boat. "In fact, we told Stephen where to look," said Nick. This wasn't the first time a guide claimed to beat another in finding something wonderful. I was sure it would not be the last time, either.

I asked Stephen where Mammoth Dome was. Is it under the hotel? Under the guide house? Under the privy? Stephen said, "How should I know?"

"You have your compass. You should know," I said. Stephen scratched his head.

"I'll find out," he said finally, after one of his long silences.

Sally Lively's energy continued to slip away. Her weakness nearly doubled the workload for Hannah and me. Hannah and I grew closer as we worked harder than before in the kitchen. I asked Hannah if she and Alfred would marry. She said yes, they wanted to marry, but there was always the risk they would be separated if Dr. Croghan decided not to give permission for their marriage. There was some bad blood between Alfred and Dr. Croghan's family, and maybe Alfred would be punished more beyond his banishment to Mammoth Cave.

I told Hannah my ideas about separation. If she wanted to marry and Alfred was willing, then they should. No matter what the risk, being with one you love was worth it. Hannah spent hours at Sally's cabin putting cool washrags on her brow and helping her dress for cooking.

Several weeks went by before Stephen spoke of Mammoth Dome. It was after supper in the hotel that he appeared at the kitchen door where I was washing dishes. "Are you going to be done soon?" he said.

"Why?"

"I thought I'd show you where Mammoth Dome is. If you jump up and down hard, you will bust through the ground and see it all the way down to the bottom as you fall."

His remark was mysterious to me as I put the clean dishes on the shelf "Should I dress warm?"

"A sweater or light coat would be desirable. Some of the refined ladies prefer a shawl." Stephen was giving me the talk he usually saved for visitors.

"How about a light wrap—like this!" I knocked him on the head with my fist. He pretended to be injured and doubled over in fake pain.

"Ooow, lady, that wasn't refined. Somebody needs to teach you manners." Stephen led the way outside with his lantern and compass. We were walking away from the front of the hotel into the woods. My lantern hardly lighted the dead leaves. The forest floor sloped downward and we came to a cliff. We walked around the rim of the cliff and descended a narrow valley. After several minutes walking I could see all sides of the valley. It was a big sinkhole, shaped like a giant slop basin with a small bottom. We were uphill from the lowest part.

"Now we are on top of Mammoth Dome and where we are standing must be just above the top of it. If the rocks are thin enough we can jump up and down and go down to the bottom of it quick." Stephen's smile told me he wasn't serious. Still, we'd come down a long way from the hotel.

"I'll just cling to you, Mr. Guide. We can jump together and you can explain it all as we go down. Fall down far enough and you can sing to me." Stephen reached for me and pulled me to him. I threw my arms around him, taking care not to burn him with my lantern. We kissed for a long time. My oh my, that man was sweet.

"You are my dearest darling," he said. "I am yours. I want to marry you first chance."

"We'll jump up and down and you'll bury me!" I said, and I loved him too, and that I was his. We kissed some more.

"Want to see Mammoth Dome from inside the cave? We can't see anything of it here," Stephen picked terrible times for cave exploring trips. But of course I would go with him anywhere. I told him I'd go, but not all night. Morning will come too soon.

I borrowed some food from the pantry and tied it in a bandana. We went into the cave and stopped at the saltpetre vats in the Rotunda. "Where is it?" I asked.

"Mammoth Dome? Just a minute." Stephen had counted our steps and glanced at his compass now and then. I knew he was seeing the cave in his head. He thought and thought. Finally he pointed west, toward the small passage, Little Bat Avenue, we had entered the first time he took me into the cave. "It is about 500 paces that way."

"Then let's go see it." I was up for anything. We left the Main Cave and turned left into the round passage that finally came to a mud slope. We stopped. The crack I had squeezed into to hear the waterfall was still noisy with the sound of falling water. Joe Shackelford had named the crack and its pit Crevice Pit. Joe said there was probably a lantern or two in its bottom and he had been told that a slave was lowered into it on a short hay rope, but screamed to be pulled back up. Stephen said he didn't believe the story.

I asked, "Do you think Mammoth Dome is around here someplace?"

Stephen picked up a couple of loose rocks. He squeezed into the crack as far back as he could go. "I'm going to drop these rocks in the pit and see if we can find them in Mammoth Dome. If we do, we'll know the two passages are connected." He let loose of the rocks one after the other. We could not hear them hit anything. I asked him how he would tell if the rocks on the floor of Mammoth Dome were the same ones he threw into the pit.

"I don't know. They all look alike."

I unwrapped the bandana and handed the food to Stephen. Then I picked up some more rocks and put them into the bandana and tied the corners together to make a bundle of rocks. "Throw this in. If you find the bandana below you will know." Stephen squeezed back into the crack as far as he could go. He dropped the bundle into the pit.

We ate the food and retraced our steps to the Rotunda where we continued along Main Cave, behind the Coffin and through the Wooden Bowl Room. I knew the route to the bridge across Bottomless Pit and through Winding Way to River Hall, where Stephen showed me how he and Sparks had dug out the rocks.

Rock walls in the A-shaped passage were black and beads of water clinging to the walls sparkled in our lights. We climbed through a small opening and onto a scary ledge, Stephen holding my hand. One look into the deep pit on the left made me shiver. Water fell from the blackness above into the blackness below as we climbed to a flat place where three giant columns lined one wall. The ceiling was still out of sight. We looked around the floor among the rocks. I spotted a flash of red, the bandana tied around the rocks. Nearby was a battered rusty lantern. We knew then exactly where Mammoth Dome was: right under that crevice off the passage in Little Bat Avenue where we ate. And Stephen reminded me we had been outdoors directly above that place in the narrow valley.

Stephen could not shut up about what a wonderful discovery we had made. I wanted to return to my cabin to get a few hours sleep. Part of me wanted to kiss Stephen but none of Stephen wanted to kiss me, or go back, or shut up — he was probably planning where to go next. I was so tired I began to cry.

Stephen saw me sobbing. He put his arm around me, "Just let me explore a little bit."

"No! Take me back. Take me back right now." I was hot. Hadn't we found enough for one night? And with Sally ailing, I would have to start breakfast cooking the minute I got back to the hotel. We did go back, but Stephen was silent most of the way.

"I'm sorry," said Stephen when we got back to the hotel. I didn't wait for his words, but ran to the kitchen, still wiping tears from my eyes.

I lighted a new fire in the cook stove and shook up the hearth fire. Meal preparations were easier without

the cook and helper getting in the way. Hannah and
Sally would arrive any minute. Only they didn't.

I mixed the hotcake batter and patted the biscuit
dough in a pan, and then I set off to find Hannah. She
wasn't in her cabin. Was she with Alfred? I looked in
Sally's cabin. Both Hannah and Sally were there. Hannah sat on a chair beside the bed where Sally lay. Hannah cried softly. I told her to awaken Sally and come to
the kitchen.

"Sally is dead. I sat with her all night. I tried to find
you to help, but you were gone." She said that Sally's fever got stronger. She sweated, shivered, and breathed in
gasps. Earlier in the night she had moaned and groaned.
Sally cried out that she was coming home to mama.
Then she grew quiet and her breathing became harder
and harder until it stopped in silent and permanent
sleep. I put my arms around Hannah and rocked her.
The candle lighted the rim of the basin of water and the
wet rag Hannah had used to cool Sally's fever.

"Did you fetch Dr. Croghan?" I asked Hannah.

Hannah looked up in alarm, her eyes wide open.
"No. I didn't think about it. When I couldn't find you,
Charlotte, I didn't know what to do."

I knocked on Dr. Croghan's door and he opened it
wearing his night shirt. I told him Sally had taken a fever and had died in the night. Hannah had tried her best
to cool her sweating head with water.

Dr. Croghan said he wasn't surprised. He had seen
Sally's symptoms of pneumonia for several days and
knew she was dying. He had given her medicine to
reduce the fever, but pneumonia like that was almost
always fatal. "I am so sorry," he said, "She was a good
cook and those are not easy to find."

He asked me and Hannah to take over and fill in as
cooks.

Sally was buried the next day in a board coffin that

Mat nailed together. The servants all gathered. Dr. Croghan said that life is hard and always uncertain. We should pray that God would give Sally rest and take her soul to heaven. Mr. Gorin said that Sally was the best cook he had ever known. She could cook for big and small crowds and she had a keen sense of duty and loyalty. We would miss her and always remember her.

*Separation by death.* I had not thought of that before, and now I dearly missed Sally Lively and wished I had known her better. I had known Mildred pretty good—why not Sally? It was because Mildred treated me like a friend and told me what was on her mind. Sally was just as demanding, but Sally kept her feelings to herself and seemed only interested in working me hard. Hannah's tears told me that she had felt close to Sally. Perhaps she knew Sally longer than I did and maybe she told Sally about the plans that she and Alfred had to get married. Come to think of it, I had not made much effort to get to know Hannah, so I decided to change that.

A couple of days later Dr. Croghan came to me. "Charlotte, I want you to be the chief cook. You and Hannah can run the kitchen. I will get some of the others to be cook part time." That was *not* welcome news. I protested that I wasn't the cook Sally was. Croghan said anyone that could make brandied peaches could cook. I worried that I didn't have the experience and know-how to cook for our big hotel.

Hannah wasn't the helper I had hoped, either. Her mind was on getting married to Alfred, who seemed to appear at the kitchen door just when I needed her most. Her dreamy moods made me angry. I had to tell her every least little thing.

Spring came early. More guests arrived on the stagecoaches, and when I needed Hannah most I would find she had walked off with Alfred. We were cooking for twenty-five to thirty-five guests every day.

Alfred and Hannah married one Sunday, with Dr. Croghan's permission. One of the hotel guests was a preacher and he agreed to hold a wedding ceremony for them outside in back of the guide house. Most of the servants were there, except for the guides who had taken tours into the cave. Hannah wore a borrowed calico red and white dress. Alfred wore a clean pair of brown trousers and a white shirt. Mat wore a brown jacket and striped pants. It was the first wedding I had seen and it was short.

Reverend McCracken said we were gathered before God and witnesses to marry Alfred and Hannah. "Would Alfred take Hannah to be his wife?" Yes. "Would Hannah take Alfred to be her husband?" Yes. "Then you are husband and wife," he said.

"Let us pray," he said. He then prayed for the better part of half an hour. If the wedding took two minutes, the prayer took twenty. He prayed for blessings and happiness, many children, faithful service, harmony, obedience, dutiful service, humility, protection, wisdom, and abundant service. Slaves had not much choice about service.

Alfred and Hannah went back to work right after their wedding. Alfred headed down the cave with a tour of eight visitors. Hannah joined me in the kitchen, still dreamy.

Dr. Croghan announced that he'd build the first rooms of the underground hotel. It would not be built in Chief City just yet. Rather, he'd build two rooms a little way beyond Giant's Coffin in Main Cave. He had sent for stonecutters and masons from Louisville. The rooms would be as fine as any above ground. Since the rooms would be close to the entrance, we'd not need a separate kitchen. Guest meals would be cooked in our kitchen and carried into the cave by our servants. I wasn't able to do a good job as cook with the hotel we had, so how could I cook for underground guests as well?

I complained to Stephen. "Can't you talk him out of his underground hotel?" Stephen said we were lucky it wasn't a forty-room hotel back in The Temple.

A wagon arrived from Louisville with four slaves and their stonecutting tools. Dr. Croghan and Stephen took the four into the cave. At a flat spot in the floor between the Coffin and Star Chamber, Dr. Croghan stopped. "We need two fine hotel rooms with stone walls," said Dr. Croghan.

They spent some time discussing details of room size, how many doors and windows, whether to make a stone roof, and where to cut the stones. Rocks were all over the floor, so no additional rocks would be needed to trim the stones. The rooms would have one doorway and one window. The boss of the stonecutters said, "Why do you need a window? It will always be dark out the window."

"Because all hotel rooms have a window," was all Croghan said. They originally wanted to make the rooms ten feet by ten feet. Stephen pointed out that they could use the cave wall as a long wall, and only build three stone walls. That way, for the same amount of labor they could make the rooms a little larger. The masons said they didn't need mortar to lay up the walls. They would lay them dry, like the retaining wall around Locust Grove. Alfred could bring them rocks to trim. Since it didn't rain in the cave the rooms would stay dry, and for a roof they could stretch canvas. Mat and Nick could nail together a wooden floor.

Work on the stone hotel rooms went on for three weeks. Alfred convinced Dr. Croghan that he could lay masonry as well as the stonemasons from Louisville, and that he could build the second hut at less cost. The masons left, but Alfred's stonework was sloppy compared to the experts, and some guides said it was because he was drinking too much.

During that time the kitchen went from bad to worse. It took us too long to prepare meals. Dr. Croghan received complaints from guests who said the food was not worth the price and the service was poor. I did the best I could, and urged Hannah to give her best, but it was a losing battle.

Dr. Croghan came to me. "I am disappointed with you. I made you chief cook because I thought you could handle the work, but I see you can't. So I have sent to Locust Grove for them to hasten Charles Haney down here. He's the chief cook at Locust Grove. My sister can't spare him, so I'm sending you up to Locust Grove to replace him. You'll have fewer people to cook for there."

No! I could not leave Stephen. "Can't you give me another chance?" I pleaded.

"I wish I could, but you have had two months to prove yourself."

"But Stephen and I want to marry. Can't I stay here and do other jobs? I will be the chamber maid for all forty rooms."

"And who will cook at Locust Grove? My family would disown me if I don't send you up there. When Charles arrives, you'll go back on the same wagon."

"Stephen and I love each other. You said we could marry in a year. That was three months ago."

"It can't be helped." Dr. Croghan turned and left me with a cracked heart and tears welling up in my eyes.

# Chapter 15

## Locust Grove

I had been sadder in my life, but I had never been madder. How could Dr. Croghan send me away from Mammoth Cave to a strange house far away? He knew Stephen and I wanted to marry. Hannah and I were doing the work of four slaves. Clearly we needed more help because the number of visitors had picked up. The construction mess was everywhere and we had to sweep up piles of sawdust and shavings. There were not enough hours in the day for two people to cook for the dining room, and we fixed cave lunches on top of regular meals. Of course we couldn't keep up.

But his disappointment was unfair. Sending for my replacement was more punishment than anything else. I understood even better why George had set fire to Bell's Tavern. My anger told me to burn the hotel and then run. But I thought of the poor chances of a fugitive slave getting away after burning his master's business, and Stephen would certainly suffer. Dr. Croghan would have to shackle him to keep him from coming after me.

Dinner or no dinner, I needed to run if only for a little while. I circled around the hotel and off through the trees toward the Mammoth Dome sinkhole. I hit the bottom on a dead run then angled toward the Green River. Rain fell from low dark clouds. The land flattened as I ran along the river downstream. The tall grass was covered with mud from a recent flood. A small stream stopped me, so I ran up that stream a few hundred feet to where it started as a big spring. I ran around the spring and back toward Green River. The rain beat faster, making a loud crackling noise on the leaves. I came to the road and turned down toward the water. In low water it was easy to ford the Green River.

I waded the river to the far side and headed up the stagecoach road. Up and up I ran, curving through the tall trees. I passed a house where smoke rose from the chimney, but I saw nobody. Rain soaked me to my skin and it ran down my head over my face. I must have run for an hour before I grew tired. I saw that I needed to talk to Dr. Croghan, to tell him of my anger and maybe he would change his mind. Or maybe he would act mean and punish me good. Slaves had to be careful and not be too frank with their masters. The risk of wrath was too great. I returned to the hotel like a muddy drowned rat to find Hannah at her wit's end.

Dr. Croghan banged through the door to the kitchen. "Charlotte! Where is dinner? I ought to whip you bloody. Look at you, dripping wet! Hannah said you just took off running. I am furious."

"I'm pretty mad myself. I have worked myself half to death to do a good job cooking for you. Then you tell me you are sending me away. It is a punishment I do not deserve. I need more help, that is what."

I was afraid I had gone too far. Croghan spoke: "You are angry because I am sending you away from Stephen. I know you want to marry, but I demand a year of hard work and loyalty. I am not getting it from you."

"Listen, hear me and hear me good," I was getting

hotter. "My loyalty is to the success of Mammoth Cave. That is where your loyalty should be and ours too. You want me to work twice as hard as one person can do but I need help. You give me no help. You pile on the work like to break my back. Sally had two helpers and I have one, and I ain't a cook. I am a human being and I am angry." I hit a wooden spoon on the meat block and splintered it.

"Fix dinner fast. I'll deal with you later." Dr. Croghan headed for the dining room. Hannah looked frightened. She held her face in her hands.

"I fried a mess of ham. It is in a pan in the oven. I didn't know when you would return," Hannah stammered. Earlier in the day I had put beans to soak, so now I drained them and poured them into a big skillet with a little molasses and slid it over the stove top to heat. In a little time we loaded the serving dishes and had the girls take them to the tables. Dr. Croghan rang the dinner bell.

Stephen returned with the long tour. He poked his head in the kitchen door. I told him to get in here and help. Maybe washing pots and pans was hateful work for a celebrated cave guide, but I needed help. He scrubbed pots cheerfully.

I told Stephen the bad news that I would be sent to Locust Grove in Louisville and their cook would come here. I told him of my strong words with our master. Stephen wondered if Dr. Croghan couldn't bring down more slaves to help since we were busier than ever before.

It was late and the rain had stopped when we finished putting up the kitchen. Stephen was quiet during these chores. As we walked to the slave cabins we paid no attention to the puddles. To hear Dr. Croghan talk, he was a man of action. Sometimes he did what he said he would do. Sometimes he did nothing. He said he was going to send me away but he might or might not do it

If I went away, Stephen said we had to find a way to send messages to each other. Then we had to think about how to get together again. At the door to his cabin we lingered and kissed. He took my hand and drew me inside. We kissed some more. I wanted him more than ever, but mostly I wanted his strong arms around me to hold me and protect me. We loved that night, but the main thing that stuck in my mind was that our lives and plans together were at risk. I returned to my cabin turning over in my head what we could do.

It was still dark in the early morning when I wrapped a shawl around my shoulders and hurried to the kitchen. Hannah was making biscuits and cornbread. Stephen poked his head in the door. "How did you sleep?" he said.

"Not much," I said, and continued, "Stephen, can you draw a map of the cave from the entrance to Mammoth Dome?"

"Maybe. I draw maps on the cave floor for visitors who want to know where they are. But a real map? I don't know."

I told him if he could make a good map it would impress Dr. Croghan. Maybe that would change his mind about sending me away.

Several days later Stephen said he had paced off distances from the hotel to the cave entrance. He knew how many paces in which compass direction were some of the places in the cave. That is how he took me to the sinkhole over Mammoth Dome beyond the hotel. He had made a list of those numbers and directions, but he was puzzled about what to do next. I told him to talk to the slave in charge of one of the road building crews.

The road gang boss pointed Stephen to Moses Short, the surveyor. Moses was ebony black, about six feet tall, and wore a slouch hat. The two got on famously and talked through part of several nights. He told Stephen how to make a map by laying the compass on the paper and extending lines along the compass bearings. The length of the lines represented how many paces it was from place to place. Stephen had done that in his head on the ground above the cave to locate the Mammoth Dome sinkhole. So now he could draw a map of what he had done on the ground. Moses showed him how to draw the cave walls, just like a road, along the lines.

In the end Stephen's map showed part of the cave from the entrance to the Giant's Coffin and the passage over Bottomless Pit, through River Hall and Sparks Avenue to Mammoth Dome. Branching off from the Rotunda was the Main Cave to the left and another great hall to the right. Branching off of that was the passage to Crevice Pit at the top of Mammoth Dome. Moses had Stephen draw the hotel and the sinkhole valley nearby.

"You draw a north arrow on every map," said Moses. The map I saw was messy but it looked like parts of the cave I had seen. Stephen showed the map to Dr. Croghan. He was fascinated and spent a long time asking questions about where things were. He wanted to know how Stephen had made the map.

Dr. Croghan said that he had a map made by a surveyor, Ed Lee, in 1835. "Lee claimed the map showed eight miles of cave, and Archibald Miller said it was twenty miles of cave but I never trusted the thing," Croghan said without looking up from Stephen's map. He reached into a cabinet and pulled out a rolled map. Stephen was fascinated by the Lee map that looked similar to the one he had made, but neater and with proper lettering and names. It didn't show the new discoveries, Stephen noted.

Dr. Croghan said, "I'll give you a list of names for passages in the cave. Go over these with Nick and Mat. Where we have two names for the same place, I'll pick one." Nick had told Dr. Croghan about his concern about names.

Stephen guessed that Dr. Croghan was delighted, and asked if he would change his mind about sending me away. Croghan said it wasn't punishment, but the only way his sister Ann at Locust Grove would stand for their cook to come to Mammoth Cave was if they got a replacement. He would be sorry to see me go, although he was angry with me for running off before a meal as I did. He needed me and would try to find a way to bring me back. But the business problem was getting a regular cook as fast as possible. "I'll take Charlotte with me when I return to Locust Grove day after tomorrow," Dr. Croghan said.

Charles Haney, the cook from Locust Grove, arrived the next day in a wagon with his assistant, a young slave, Albert, who appeared to be twelve or thirteen. He brought an assortment of pots and pans, and a lot of food. The driver would take Dr. Croghan and me back the day after. I showed Charles Haney and his boy the kitchen, smokehouse, store rooms, and wash house. Archie Miller took him to his cabin. Charles set his boy to sweeping the cabin.

In the meantime Stephen spoke to the wagon driver. They talked in low voices and I saw Stephen draw some money out of his pocket and count it into the driver's hand. The driver nodded. Later I found Stephen had paid the driver to carry messages between us or to pass the messages to other drivers.

We said our goodbyes the last night and agreed to send messages. I wished Hannah happiness in her marriage to Alfred. At dawn I climbed into the wagon with a bundle of my clothes, the pages I had copied out of the ECLECTIC PRIMER, and a silver dollar that Stephen pressed into my hand. Dr. Croghan sat beside the driver as we headed down into Eaton Valley on the new road toward Rowletts Station.

New sights and deep longing for Stephen came and went in my mind. I couldn't think about the one but what the other got my attention. Forests gave way to fields and a big cloud reminded me of Stephen's face. We stopped for a drink and I was happy, then I was sad thinking of Stephen spilling water on his chest in Bell's storage cave. I just knew we would be together one day, but what would the road be like around the next corner?

Our trip to Louisville and Locust Grove took three days. We crossed the Green River at the old Big Buffalo Crossing, at Munfordville, on a ferry drawn by a mule. I saw how it worked. The ferry was tied to an iron ring that slid along a thick tight rope stretched across the river. That tether kept the ferry from being carried downstream. We drove the wagon and team onto the boat. The mule on the far side was driven by a slave to pull the ferry upstream along the big rope. When they crossed the river coming back the other way the current would carry the boat downstream. So they didn't need a mule on the downstream side of the river.

Munfordville had a toll booth on the Louisville Nashville Turnpike that cost ten cents. We rolled through a creek ford, and north up some steep hills. We came to an upland and then we came to Elizabethtown, a bigger town than the few houses at Munfordville. There was a large courthouse in the center. North of Elizabethtown we came to a long downhill and from there we drove past knobs. We had knobs back at Bell's Tavern at Three Forks, but these hills were more pointy with steep sides like a haystack. All along the road were farms and tobacco barns.

Dr. Croghan took a room at the two inns where we stayed, but the driver and I bedded down in the wagon.

I was glad it didn't rain, but I was not glad the driver snored.

Locust Grove was a new world for me. Our wagon pulled along a country road, up a hill with a large brick house on it. The big house was two stories high, solid red brick on the outside, with a fine long front porch. It had four big chimneys, two on each end of the house. It looked about a hundred feet long on the front with five windows upstairs and four on the first floor. Each window had shutters. The front porch had stone steps up from the ground. We pulled past the main house where I could see four windows on the side.

We turned off the road and pulled into a hitching yard and large stable with a barn beyond that. An orchard lay beyond the barn. I saw many outbuildings beside the house. There was a separate building with a chimney, a kitchen and pantry with cook's quarters, and a smokehouse. The overseer's house was part stone, part logs.

There were several storerooms, and a stone ice house. A well was near the kitchen. I could see a grand privy for the owners and a slave privy. Beyond, back the road we had come from and up the other side of a little valley, were six slave cabins. Farther down in the valley bottom was a spring house. I could see several vegetable gardens, but it was too cold for garden work. Fields stretched in all directions. Compared to the Red Rose Hall in Mississippi, it was most grand.

Dr. Croghan introduced me to the overseer, George Williams. He showed me to a slave room next to the kitchen, and introduced me to the kitchen slaves. They were mostly younger than me, some darker, some lighter. An old slave woman with only a few teeth and white hair took my hand in both of hers. She pumped it up and down and said she was happy to welcome me. The rest of the help looked fearful. I wondered what kind of a cook Charles Haney was, and whether he took the good pots with him to Mammoth Cave.

"You will be cooking the evening meal for ten people," said Mr. Williams. "They will be Mrs. Ann Jesop, Dr. Croghan, his brother George, and me in the dining room, and six house servants including yourself in the kitchen." I looked over the help and asked each person what service they had been doing, and how they liked it. They told me who carried food and served the big table, who helped the cook, and who washed the dishes and pots. The fetch slave, Isaac, was a little boy who had the job of bringing whatever I asked for. Since I was new, I would need all their help.

I marveled at the kitchen, pantry, and smokehouse. There was a new iron ten-plate cook stove, like the new one at Mammoth Cave. There was more variety of food than at Mammoth Cave or at Bell's Tavern. They had crocks of fruit preserved in sugar water. There was plenty of flour, lard, and sugar for baking sweet bread, cake, muffins, and biscuits. I asked about their storage cave. They didn't know what I was talking about. Where did they keep the milk? They pointed to a dairy house out back.

If I had this much help at Mammoth Cave and so many supplies, I know I could have been a better cook. It is one thing to cook for ten and another to cook for forty or fifty.

We finished the meal and cleaned up the kitchen by 7:00 in the evening. The boy Isaac would lay the fires in the stove and bake oven first thing in the morning and we'd aim to have breakfast ready at 7:00.

I found the wagon driver in the stable brushing down a chestnut horse. "If I give you a message for Stephen Bishop, will you take it to him?

"Either I will, or one of the other drivers. Stephen

told me to take care of you and I said we'd carry any messages you wanted. We don't go regular. Just now and then," he said. He introduced me to another driver, a tall thin black man with features that looked a little like my own.

"I'm Jim Brown," he said.

"My name's Charlotte Brown."

"Where are you from? You grow up around here?" Jim Brown seemed friendly enough.

"I came from Mammoth Cave and before that I was at Three Forks, Kentucky, and before that I was sold in Nashville. I grew up at Red Rose Hall near Columbus, Mississippi."

"Red Rose Hall? Me and mama came from there! We was sold to a dealer from Lexington and then bought by the Croghans." He wondered if I was Charlotte, his little sister who was left at Red Rose Hall. I said I was the only Charlotte there, so it must be me, but I was raised by Addie and Tom Wells.

"Tom Wells? Then you are my left-behind sister."

We reached for each other, our eyes flooding with tears and a hundred memories of Red Rose Hall filling our heads. He told me mama had married again. He had four younger brothers at another farm on the 694-acre estate. They are James, Gibson, Stephen, and David. My Mama had died two years earlier. My mind spun around. Was he really my brother? Did I have other brothers I never knew? We spent a couple of hours talking about what had happened to us over the years, the bad times and good times.

Late that night I wrote a message to Stephen with a pencil on borrowed paper:

> Dear Stephen,
> I hope this finds you in good health. When
> I arrived at Locust Grove I found Jim. He is

*my brother from back home. He is a driver. I
have help as cook and am well. Take care of
yourself. Love,*
                    *Charlotte*

I gave it to Jim next morning. He folded it and said
he would see that it got to Stephen within a week or
two.

I wrote Stephen that we had some excitement at
Locust Grove. Lizzy Williams, the overseer's daughter,
told me all about it. Two politicians and their friends
arrived one day because one had insulted the other. The
other was so angry he challenged the first man to a duel
with pistols. They met in a field beside the Locust Grove
grist mill. Each man had a few friends to stand by and
encourage him, and mostly they tried to talk one or another to settle their differences peaceably. But honor had
to be satisfied.

The two men stood back to back with pistols cocked
and at the ready. On command, each walked ten paces
away from each other. They turned to face each other
then they leveled their pistols and fired. When the
smoke cleared, both men were standing. Their shots had
missed! The friends rushed to them and took away their
pistols. Dr. Croghan invited everyone to the house for a
drink and a meal, saying that Providence had prevailed.
God wanted both of them to live.

Those fellows put down a great deal of liquor and
kept toasting each other as servants brought in the food.
Lizzy thought some of them had started drinking early
in the day. It didn't surprise her that their shots missed!
George Croghan matched them drink for drink until
he passed out. It took four servants to carry him to his
bed. John Croghan was embarrassed. He said goodbye
to most of the guests who hurried off before we served
after-dinner drinks.

It was only later that I learned of the strange happenings at Mammoth Cave that would change Stephen's life forever.

# Chapter 16

# Exploring

A couple of weeks passed without word from Stephen, so I got the hang of the new kitchen at Locust Grove and what folks liked to eat and didn't like. Toward the end of that time I asked Mr. Williams if I could run if I got my work done. He said I could run, walk, or creep. But stay on the estate. He pointed which way was north, which south, east, and west. Locust Grove was about a mile wide east and west and a little more than a mile deep from the south bank of the Ohio River.

One afternoon after dinner I ran south a half mile to the Muddy Fork of Beargrass Creek. Our small grist mill sat on the bank by a sharp bend of that stream. The mill was two stories tall, like a barn, and a black man sat in the wagon doorway. I asked him if he was a slave and he said he was a free man and had the paper to prove it.

He was the miller, so I asked him about the mill. He said they built a dam upstream. Water from the pond behind the dam ran in a ditch and a trough made of boards and spilled out on top of a twenty-foot water-wheel of buckets. The weight of the water in the buckets turned the waterwheel slowly. We went inside the mill.

The drive shaft of the waterwheel drove two cogged wheels. One was driving a bucket elevator that would raise grain dumped from a farm wagon up to a bin on the second floor. Grain flowed down a chute to the millstones that were driven by the other cogged wheel. Ground cornmeal or wheat flour in the bin could be raised by another elevator to a bin on the first floor where the miller bagged the cornmeal and flour.

I asked the miller how he came to be free and he said his former owner rented him out to Lucy Croghan, but paid him a dollar a week. He saved his money and bought his freedom after ten years. "There's a lot of free Negroes in Louisville, but they all work like slaves." I planned to write this to Stephen about how the grist mill worked, because he had told me about the floating mill at Goose Spring.

I ran following the stream that angled northwest to where it cut a notch through the limestone cliff along the river. The sight from the high edge of that cliff was wonderful to behold with the wide river stretched along the bottom land and three steamboats moving upstream and down. I saw some buildings and church steeples along the bank to the left. That was Louisville, I learned later. I ran northeast for about a mile, then south to the mansion. Fresh spring breezes kept me cool. Lanes separated the fields and I figured I could run down some of them when I knew my way around better. I felt free when I was running although I knew better.

Dr. Croghan treated a few patients in a room that was added to the side of the mansion, where his mother lived before her death. His patients mostly came on horseback or in buggies and some looked pretty sick to me. Dr. Croghan's medical diploma hung on the wall and it had a name on the bottom, Benjamin Rush. Occasionally he rode out on his horse to visit the sick, and once he was gone all night. He returned with red eyes and sniffles. I think he didn't like doctoring much, but if you have family money and land, maybe you have to work hard, even if you have about twenty slaves to do the hardest work.

Ann Jesop was Dr. Croghan's sister. She was married to General T. S. Jesop. When the General was off soldiering, Ann Jesop often visited the home where she and her brothers grew up. I asked her once why Dr. Croghan didn't have a wife and she said he would probably always be a bachelor.

Ann Jesop also went on to say he had courted Mary Bullitt, but never got around to asking her to marry him, and when he returned from Europe, Mary had married somebody else.

Mrs. Jesop also said that he had an eye for Mary's younger sister Eloise. "He thought she should want him, but he was too proud. He was a procrastinator."

"What's a procrastinator?" I asked.

"A procrastinator is a vain man who does not strike while the iron is hot. He worried more about what she would think of his bald head than whether he could be a loving husband to her."

Eloise married another man. Ann was pretty and smart and friendly to me, but she only stayed a few weeks at Locust Grove.

The third week I was there Jim handed me a letter from Stephen.

> *Darling Charlotte.*
> *Yours finds me cheerful and busy. But I miss you. For 3 wks we tried to rent rooms in the cave. Visitors took one look and return to the hotel. One couple stayed one night, but*

*complained of damp bed clothes. I found a big*
*cave passage where we had our picnic. I guess*
*that is all for now.*
     *Your loving friend, Stephen.*

I learned later the underground hotel rooms were a big failure. Few visitors even thought twice about it when offered a chance to stay there. Too spooky. Those that agreed to look mostly decided against staying there overnight. As Stephen said, the bedclothes were always damp. They had to give those visitors their money back. They complained of cold food, too, when the servants carried it in. Thank goodness, Dr. Croghan soon gave up the idea of the underground hotel.

His next idea was to use the underground rooms for consumption patients to live to recover from their disease. He more or less got talked into Mammoth Cave as a sanatorium by some of his doctor friends. Dr. William McDowell wrote that a cave would offer constant temperature, pure air, and would be an ideal place to cure consumptive invalids.

Dr. Nathan Gaither came to visit Dr. Croghan. They had dinner together, a nice leg of mutton, and wine afterward. I entered the parlor where they talked and waited quietly for a chance to ask if Dr. Gaither would stay the night. Dr. Gaither told Dr. Croghan reasons why Mammoth Cave would be a good place to cure consumption and other breathing ailments. He said that Dr. Bird agreed with him. Bird had written that saltpetre miners twenty-five years before had stayed in the cave for weeks at a time and found it a healthful place. Dr. Croghan said the cave air had helped his red eyes and sniffles, and asked Dr. Gaither if he would stay over so the next day they could talk with other doctors. Dr. Gaither said yes, so I went upstairs to prepare his room.

The doctors left the mansion the following morning to make their medical visits. Mr. Williams said Dr. Croghan might be gone as long as a week. About a week later, when master Croghan returned, I asked if he went to Mammoth Cave. He said only briefly. He and Dr. Gaither visited Dr. William Mitchell in Glasgow where Mitchell had some patients with consumption. He was distressed because nothing seemed to make their condition better. Doctor Mitchell was starting to cough and feel weaker himself. He pleaded to be allowed to spend some time in Mammoth Cave to see if it would help his worsening condition. Dr. Croghan said he would think about it. He also said Stephen made another big discovery in the cave, but he didn't hear any details.

I ran to the stable to see if Jim had a message from Stephen. He said another servant had driven the buggy but he relayed that driver's report. At Mammoth Cave the doctors had talked for a short time with Archibald Miller, the manager, Mr. Underwood, and Franklin Gorin. They had eaten a noon dinner at the hotel and left immediately but they didn't see Stephen. Stephen had entered the cave early with a short tour but had not returned when the Croghan tour left.

It made me damn mad that Stephen had not sent me a letter. He didn't know that Dr. Croghan was coming. Well, I had not sent a letter either because I did not know Dr. Croghan was going to Mammoth Cave. A bad thing about being a slave is you don't know what is happening and you can't find out like white people can. Love at a distance is worse than that. I thought I would die of curiosity wondering what Stephen discovered beyond Echo River where we ate our picnic in the cave.

One wonderful thing we had at Locust Grove was our ice house. In the winter slaves would go to the Ohio River or to Beargrass Creek whenever they froze over.

They sawed ice cakes and stacked them in wagons. They unloaded the wagons into the ice house out back. Slaves sprinkled the high pile of ice blocks with sawdust from the mill. We kept some of the ice in the dairy house to keep milk and butter cool until the ice was gone late in summer and then we used the spring house for storing milk and butter.

The ice house was made of stone, but the big house was made of red bricks that were made here and fired in a kiln. The overseer said that slaves had made bricks for two years before they had enough to build the three story house with a full basement. Stephen had described the brick kiln at Goose Spring Farm where he and Cato got bricks, so I wanted to see the kiln for myself.

Down by the Muddy Fork of Beargrass Creek is a clay bank where two slaves dug the clay and loaded it into a wagon and took it to the kiln. There they packed the wet clay into loose wood boxes that had no top or bottom, but rested on a board. They scraped off the top of the brick to make it smooth. Then they pushed each wet brick out of its box. They let the bricks dry for several days. When they had a pile of dry bricks they stacked them inside a beehive kiln of brick and closed the iron door. The next few days they kept a fire going under the kiln day and night and baked the bricks just like bread in the oven. At the right time they would let the fire die down and then open the door. They piled the red fired bricks with layers of straw between them. Now and then masons would haul away a load of bricks to build something.

Isaac would bring food from the spring house. When I went there myself I saw the spring of water trickling out from a ledge of limestone into a trough. As I stood there a breeze of air picked up and cool air gushed out from a small hole in the rock where the spring water flowed. I thought of Stephen and our questions in the cave at Bell's Tavern—where does the water come from and go? If Stephen were here, he would surely look into that.

Many of my thoughts when not cooking were on how to get back to Mammoth Cave or get Stephen sent to Locust Grove. I had more time to think because our workload wasn't so heavy and help was plentiful. Sarah, about fourteen, was the best baker I knew. Her mama taught her to make biscuits, muffins, bread, and cake. I encouraged her to try new things. She found that vanilla extract made good tea cookies that smelled delicious.

She figured out peach cobbler and I showed her how heavy cream would make it taste better. Tom, a shy boy who always looked down at the floor, learned fast and could cook greens, turnips, parsnips, beans, and vegetables. I showed him the dried herbs from our herb garden. I made him try each kind with different vegetables, salt, and bacon pieces. Soon he had a taste for what would be good to eat. The test was whether the people we served wanted seconds.

My pride and joy was Lizzy Williams. I thought she was white, but learned she was the daughter of our overseer and her mulatto mama. She was eighteen, a year younger than me. She was very smart. I taught her everything I knew about cooking and she taught me new recipes. I caught her reading from a cooking book one day. When I said I could read a little too, she told me her mama had taught her to read and write. We made a bargain. She would help me learn to write better and I would help her become a better cook. In one corner of my room next to the kitchen we set up a little school. She told me the best way to write was to think about what I wanted to say. Then ask the question, "What are you talking about?" Next, ask the question, "What about it?" Learning to write better cut into my running time. Lizzy turned into a better cook than I ever will be because she always knew how things would taste.

Lizzy opened the New England Primer, picked out a verse, and had me write it over and over.

*Have communication with few,*
*Be intimate with ONE,*
*Deal justly with all,*
*Speak evil of none.*

I hated writing with the pen and ink, copying the same words over and over. But Lizzy's corrections made my handwriting better until it looked pretty good. We also got better at reading to each other.

That summer Dr. Croghan spent more time away from Locust Grove. He was guiding the improvements at Mammoth Cave. Charles Haney had turned Hannah into a real cook instead of just a helper, and he had trained other helpers. Complaints about the hotel food and service stopped. Stagecoach traffic increased to four a day. Twice that summer I got letters from Stephen, and I sent three messages of my own back with the drivers.

Stephen's letters were short. One told about how Dr. William Mitchell had moved into the stone hotel room in Mammoth Cave to see if his health would improve. My letters were longer. I told about Locust Grove, what I had seen on my runs. On one run I came across the farm where my four younger brothers lived. I found two of them, James and Gibson. They looked nothing like me or my brother Jim. They said they had only met Jim once or twice. They never knew about me. They said they had to get back to work. I wondered if they really were my brothers or not.

Dr. Croghan returned from his second long tour to Mammoth Cave. I asked him if he had seen Stephen. He said yes, he talked with him almost every day. Stephen's popularity as a guide increased with every trip he led. Dr. Croghan said Stephen proposed that I be sent down for the summer to be the chief chamber maid and supervisor of the hotel wash house.

"I would send you down tomorrow, but we can't spare you here. Everyone is pleased with the meals you fix, especially the bread and cobbler. The cobbler is my favorite," said Dr. Croghan.

I told Dr. Croghan I had a good solution for that problem—a remedy, you might say. I confessed I had been training Lizzy to take over as chief cook, and Tom as the vegetable cook. Sarah had made my reputation as the best baker in Louisville. She was my cobbler secret. "But I added the cream!"

I never saw Dr. Croghan so dumbfounded. He stood with his mouth open. "I see," he said. "You really love Stephen so much that you trained up the kitchen staff to replace you?" He said he would think about it some and give me an answer soon.

Soon came about a week later. He had patients who called on certain days. They mostly coughed and looked pale. He went to Louisville to collect rents. Twice we had to hold dinner for an hour and several times we were told to delay the evening meal. I felt sorry for the doctor and told him he was working too hard. He sighed and said, "My patients are so ill and I can't cure many of them. Some will die of consumption, just like Sally died of pneumonia. Other doctors tell me the same. They are urging me to build a sanatorium, a consumption hospital in Mammoth Cave."

I saw opportunity. "Stephen and I can help you. You can't do it by yourself."

"Alas, no. But you had better go to Mammoth Cave and do what you can to help me." Then he added, "But only for the summer!" Inside I jumped for joy.

I spent the next few days getting Lizzy to think like a chief cook, to give orders to Tom and Sarah. She must send Isaac for things instead of going herself.

"I'm depending on you," I said, "You can work together." Mildred's words came to mind, "Some people in this world are takers. Some are givers and takers. Some are givers. I expect all of you to be givers that I can count on and be proud of." My heart soared high like a bird when I heard the magic word from Dr. Croghan.

"Pack."

Days later our wagon loaded with garden truck pulled into the back of the Mammoth Cave Hotel. Dozens of visitors strolled over the lawn. The stable was full of horses with buggies and wagons parked nearby. I looked for Stephen but didn't see him. I was desperate to find him.

Dr. Croghan took me to Archibald Miller. He wore a striped shirt with sleeve garters, a manager in appearance at last. Croghan explained that I was there to help for the summer busy season. Miller said it was high time, the chamber maids were frantic trying to keep up with the crowds and the wash house overload was causing the servants to grow surly. I went off to organize things better after putting my dresses in my cabin.

At the wash house three slaves plunged the dirty sheets and towels into the boiling wash water. Steam rolled out all over them and they glistened as they lifted the wet sheets into the next tub, ran in some cold water, then scrubbed the dirty spots with soap on wash boards. From there they hoisted the wet linens into another tub and two servants rung out the water. Every hour or so they carried the wet wash outside to dry on clothes lines. They said guests would have to sleep in dirty sheets if it rained. I thought they could do a better job if they had another hand.

Every time I caught a minute to look for Stephen, he was gone in the cave or I was asked to do something by Archibald or a guest.

I watched the chamber maids next. They mostly loafed between breakfast and dinner. I asked why. They said the clean linen would not be ready until after dinner. They wanted to clean a room and change the linen all at one time, room by room. When the dinner bell rang for evening meal they would be finishing the last rooms if they were lucky.

It wasn't right to spend time loafing when they could start sweeping the rooms when guests left, then return when the clean sheets were ready to make up the beds. I could see that the girls spent too much time going back and forth. First they carried a piece of soap. Then they brought new candles. Next they emptied the slop jar.

I saw Stephen outside the window, but when I ran out, he was gone.

I saw some boards outside, and asked Mat to make me three boxes with carry handles. A couple of days later I filled the boxes with soap, candles, towels, and writing paper. I sent the youngest chamber maid to the wash house where they needed help, then went with the other two down the hall, leaving a box by every fourth room door. The three of us entered each room one by one and cleaned it in a few minutes, all but the bedding. We moved to the next room and cleaned it.

Having the supplies outside in the hall meant no long trips to get supplies, and we had all the rooms cleaned by noon. After dinner in the kitchen we went to the wash house and folded sheets and towels that were dry, and then returned to the hotel with clean linen to make the fresh beds. I could keep my eye on the servants when we worked better together than as one person alone.

Toward the end of my third busy day I looked out

and saw Stephen climb the hill slowly. He looked tired. I just dropped everything and ran to him. If he had been avoiding me, I would find out. "What's wrong?" I said.

He said, "I am so tired I am dying. Dr. Mitchell from Glasgow is staying in one of the stone huts in the cave. He has been living there day and night for three weeks. Every third day I am his personal slave. Nick and Alfred trade off with me."

Stephen said that he could not guide every day, and there was no time for exploring. He went on to say that Dr. Mitchell was a grumpy man who complained about everything. Nothing satisfied him, not the food, not the service. He smoked cigars and blew the smoke out his nose. When he was bored he demanded that Stephen read the newspaper to him or play cards with him.

I asked if Dr. Mitchell's health was improving. Stephen shrugged and said, "Who knows?" and he added, "Who cares?" He described Mitchell as coughing regularly and spitting into his chamber pot. The patient's eyes were red. Stephen said, "I am turning into a crabby old man's nursemaid, not a great cave guide and explorer."

I tried to talk some more. But Stephen picked up the lanterns and headed to the guide house. I had to get back to the rooms because the clean bed linen had arrived. This was almost worse than being separated from Stephen at Locust Grove. So near, yet so far away. And I thought he'd be glad to see me!

# Chapter 17

## A Burden Too Heavy to Bear

Dr. Croghan thought the consumption experiment was worth doing. If Mammoth Cave could cure consumption, thousands of people would be saved from death. The doctor said it would be a blessing that would be remembered long after we had forgotten the trouble it caused us.

I waited for Stephen's second short tour to return late that same afternoon. He was more cheerful, and asked to talk with me after he cleaned and put away the lanterns. I hoped he would suggest a walk or run, or anything to get us away from the work for a time.

Stephen told me what he and a couple of guests had discovered in the cave. They had wanted to find a place where nobody had been before. Mr. Patton was from Louisville and Mr. Craig was from Philadelphia. They'd packed enough food for two meals and set off for Echo River in the cave. They had climbed out of the boat and walked a long way through a wide passage that narrowed to a canyon. Stephen had taken me there back when we had eaten a picnic lunch near the end of the cave.

They climbed through a crawlway leading upward to where Stephen saw stone formations that looked like grapes on an arbor. The vineyard was a pit that rained down water. They were in a big passage that went both ways. The passage to the right split: one fork went to the right, the other to the left. The ceiling of the low passage heading to the left was covered with white stone snowballs. Reflected light from the white crystals dazzled their eyes. Stephen said this was the prettiest part of the whole cave.

They went along and the passage opened up higher. Delicate stone flowers and crystal crusts of white, yellow, orange, and tan covered the walls and ceiling of this passage. The shape of the passage was like the squashed circle in Haunted Chambers. Stephen said they walked more than a mile until they came to a mountain of rocks. The passage to the right wasn't decorated with flowers and crystals, but had red sand on the floor and bare tan limestone walls. Back at the vineyard with the stone grapes, the passage also went to the left. This canyon wasn't as large as the other two passages, and it connected to where we had eaten our picnic.

Stephen waved his hands around with excitement. He described the beautiful crystal flowers and the unexplored passages that branched off on the left and right.

"It goes for miles, Charlotte! You must see it." Given how busy we both were, I didn't see how I would get to see the wonders. I also felt left out of his excitement. I felt the cave had a stronger grip on Stephen than I did. If that was true, then my only hope for our future was to go into the cave with Stephen, to understand what he found, no matter what.

Stephen was already planning tours into this area. He told Archibald Miller he wanted to carry four cans of lamp oil to the room with snowballs, and beyond. Then tours could go all the way into the newest part of the cave and be sure to have enough light to return. Archibald said, "I can't spare a guide to help you. You will have to find your own mule."

Now was my chance to get away. I told Archibald Miller I wanted to improve our service to visitors, and he said to go ahead.

I called a meeting of the chamber maids and wash house help. "You're doing a good job and together we have solved the big problems. Things now run smoothly at the hotel and wash house, but we will get busier. Certainly we'll get more help." I told them I wanted us to do our jobs even if some got sick, or if I wasn't there. Tomorrow I expected everyone to work without me. I told them I would be helping Stephen, but I didn't say where we were going or what we were doing.

Early in the morning I met Stephen at the guide house. He had filled four big oil cans and two small ones, and I had packed a lunch. We hoisted the cans by the shoulder straps and slung them against our hips, and went into Mammoth Cave where we passed by the Giant's Coffin, over Bottomless Pit, and took the boat on the far side of Echo River. The straps of the heavy cans cut into our shoulders and I wanted to rest, but Stephen said we must press on. I carried the oil cans up through the small side passage to Stephen in the vineyard.

I was astonished at the white ceiling in the snowball room. It looked like the back wall of the guide house after our snowball fight, except that every piece of the ceiling was covered with white balls. We decided to eat dinner there.

Once we were relaxing, I decided to speak to the heart of my concerns. I asked Stephen why he cared about me. He said, "I like your curiosity, your storytelling, and the way you solve problems. I love how you tell me what you are feeling. Even when you feel bad you follow me, and you're not afraid of me. You're honest and I can depend on what you say. And you have a nice smile."

Nobody had said anything like that to me in all my life. I felt like a queen with a crown on my head. I told Stephen why I admired him. First, he showed courage in exploring dangerous places where he could get lost or killed. He wasn't afraid to tell me how he felt, especially when he was scared or angry. He had the picture or map of the cave in his mind and knew where to look to find more new cave places. He could stick to hard work when it wasn't pleasant. Most of all I felt he loved me with his mind as well as his body. Stephen was a passionate man.

We kissed a lot, then Stephen jumped up. "There is so much to see!" We left the lamp oil cans in the snowball room and set out. We came to a wide place in the passage. Large gypsum crystal flowers dangled from the ceiling. Some were opened to show the whitest crystals, and some showed clear crystals in the center. A few looked like big white feathers that curled and branched. He said he'd name that place Charlotte's Grotto after me.

We walked onward passing side passages on the left and right. Each turn showed more gypsum flowers and crystal crusts. We walked for a mile or more when we came to a big rock tumbledown.

Stephen took my basket and set it on the floor. "This is as far as we have explored, the end of the cave." He started climbing upward over rocks as big as travel trunks, and around some as big as chicken coops. We left the passage behind and climbed up into the darkness.

"It is the mountains," Stephen yelled. "We are mountain climbers." The openings pinched closed one by one. Stephen peered up in the gloom where the fallen rock met the solid ceiling or wall. We moved sideways, sometimes looking up while moving. Stephen stiffened and said, "A black hole! I see a way to go!"

He squeezed through the hole and I followed. We were in a large room, larger than the Rotunda but not as large as Chief City. The room was above the passage we had just come through. It stretched to the left and right. It was ninety feet from the deepest part straight ahead to the flat ceiling. We climbed a high pile of rocks to the left and were in a passage six feet high by fifty feet wide. We picked our way over large blocks of rock on the floor, to the end of the passage. To the right was a deep pit. We threw in rocks that crashed far below. A solid rock wall blocked the passage.

We turned around and walked and climbed down the way we had come. We stuck to the right wall and walked until the passage floor became muddy. We heard water dripping and saw it splashing on huge wet boulders that blocked our way. Back in the center of the new big room we found a passage straight ahead from the way we entered the place. We squeezed through some loose rocks to get down into the passage. Then we walked several hundred paces to a place where water dripped from a dome into a pit. There were beautiful stalactites and rock drapery that hung in folds. Stephen struck some stalactites that made a musical sound.

Stephen drew out a pencil and wrote our names on a flat wall. On our way back Stephen said we must name something wonderful after Dr. Croghan. "How about Croghan Hall for this big room?"

"How about Charlotte Brown Hall and Croghan Lane off of that?" I said.

"Can't do that," he said. "Maybe Charlotte Bishop Hall, but you got to be nice to the guide and give him a little something." I gave him a big kiss on the lips. "Not enough," he said.

On our way back Stephen said, "That's a lot of cave

to discover on one trip. Sometimes you work for days to find a tiny passage. Other days you walk or crawl for miles and find nothing." Stephen was patient and had plenty of strength. I didn't know if I would make a good explorer. I would want to find something wonderful every time. Still I wondered what was down at the bottom of that new deep pit or beyond the pretty stalactites.

We held hands part of the way back, but it was hard to walk over rocks without having my hands free. We reached the snowball room where we left the oil cans. Stephen said, "Come on. We'll go a little ways up this way before we turn around." It was late. Tomorrow I would be tired and need sleep. But I followed that man for hundreds of paces in a passage that was forty feet wide and eight feet high.

Finally I said, "Mr. Bishop, this is ugly cave. I wants to see them flowers. They's so purty, and I am too tired. You will have to carry me back before I swoon." Stephen stopped. He pulled out a pencil and wrote our names on the wall.

He turned, hands on his hips, and pretended to glare at me, saying, "Lady, it all depends on how much money you got. If you don't have money, I can take it in trade." I choked back a laugh and slapped his face.

On the long trip back we talked about how we could get together and marry. Dr. Croghan had promised we could marry in a year and we were nearly half way through that year. We had survived so far through separation. I told him that Dr. Croghan said I would have to go back to Locust Grove when the summer business slacked off. Our letter writing was sure no substitute for being together. That man was too sweet to leave alone. I had seen some of the other servants trying to get on his good side.

Stephen had some ideas about us, but he went back

to talking about the side caves we had passed. Where would they go? Next time in here he would take visitors into those new passages. If I was curious, Stephen was King Curious.

Hannah hailed me at dawn as I climbed the hill. I left Stephen behind to clean up the lamps. She said, "Charlotte, I need to talk to you about Alfred." I told her I would listen as soon as I changed into my chamber maid dress.

She told me that Alfred was a rough man. He was a good guide in the cave, but he wanted to be treated like an overseer or slaveholder, not like a husband. She hated to be ordered around. Now that she was pregnant, she felt sick some of the time. When she felt the sickest was when he wanted her to fix dinner, chop firewood, or lie down to make love. "How can I tell him sometimes I just want him to hold me? Can't he be kind sometimes? I feel like a cow or just property and I'm miserable!" Hannah was sobbing while the other chamber maids were waiting for me to join them. I pulled her to me and let my arms slip around her. We held each other tight. Her tears trickled down my neck. I told her I had some ideas and would find her later that day when I finished my work.

Stephen went in and out of the cave that day, doing and fetching for Dr. Mitchell. Once I caught him for a few minutes and told him about Hannah's problem. I asked him to think about what to tell her.

Stephen said he decided to talk to Dr. Mitchell in his stone room about Hannah's grief. He wasn't on good terms with the doctor because the gruff man complained so much. Also, Stephen hated the stink of the doctor's cigar smoke. But maybe he could learn something. He didn't tell Dr. Mitchell Hannah's or Alfred's name but started by saying, "You're a doctor and have seen a lot of people. Could I get some advice about a woman I know who has a serious problem?"

The doctor perked up. He stopped thinking of himself and his discomfort. "What seems to be the problem?" Stephen explained that the woman was pregnant with her husband's child but he treated her like dirt. He ordered her around and never spoke kindly or tenderly to her. How could she get her husband to change?

"I've seen that," said Dr. Mitchell. "I've been that man, sad to say, but maybe I can help." He said women who are newly pregnant often get sick and their feelings bust out. That may pass as weeks go by. Then, the wife should go out of her way to be a giver, to be especially nice to her husband. She shouldn't act mean or spiteful but be as loving and tender as possible. Also, the wife should tell her husband what she needs, not what he should or shouldn't do. She might say, "I need for you to hold me in your arms," instead of "You should hold me in your arms." If you remind some men of their duty it just makes them mad. Telling them what you need lets them take charge and think it was their idea. I squeezed Stephen's hand for this good advice. Stephen said that after this advice something changed in the way Dr. Mitchell and Stephen got along. They listened to each other better and tried to be more friendly to each other.

Hannah said she would try the advice and let me know what happened. A few days later she said, "Things are improving with Alfred and me." She told Alfred that pregnant women feel on edge sometimes. She asked forgiveness for any bad things she said. Alfred said he was angry, but would try to do better as a husband. Hannah explained how comforting it was to be held and cuddled, how she needed a lot of that. Alfred said he was just the man to hold her good. He actually thanked her for her courage in telling him that. Hannah and I grew closer after that.

Dr. Croghan had made a list of passage and place names in the cave. Stephen said it included some old familiar names, and names of the Doctor's relatives and friends. Stephen had read off the names to Mat and Nick. They discussed each one, and decided that the man who owned the cave could name anything he wanted to. Stephen said that the names should be put on a map of the passages. They agreed, and urged Dr. Croghan to make a map.

Dr. Croghan called the heads of the hotel and cave guides together. Archibald Miller was there. Stephen was chief guide. Charles Haney, the cook, was there in his white coat and I came as the head chamber maid and wash house superintendent. Dr. Croghan said that Dr. Mitchell's experimental residence in Mammoth Cave was a failure. Dr. Mitchell probably didn't have consumption. He was addicted to tobacco and it was poisoning him. Dr. Croghan had taken away his cigars. Mitchell protested for a while that tobacco was a medicine. When Dr. Croghan would not give him back his cigars, the patient announced he felt a great deal more relief from his condition since he had moved into the cave. He still coughed and spat, but not so much. In his opinion living in the cave would benefit consumptive patients and perhaps cure them.

Dr. Croghan said, "I still think the cave is a healthful place for consumptives. But Dr. Mitchell's problem is smoking, and not consumption." He said that his medical school teacher, Dr. Rush, had discovered the poisonous effect of tobacco. However, pleas from other doctors had persuaded Dr. Croghan to open a sanatorium, and he would need all of us for this new endeavor.

Archibald Miller asked if showing Mammoth Cave to visitors would cease. Dr. Croghan said no. The tours would carry on as usual. Stephen asked if stone huts would be built for the patients. Dr. Croghan said no. He would have Mat Bransford buy lumber and canvas. They would build more huts with wood floors and canvas walls. I asked about the chamber maid and wash house work. Dr. Croghan said the other servants would handle that, "All except you, Charlotte. You will return to Locust Grove."

Stephen asked how he could serve ten or fifteen patients every third day and still lead cave tours. Dr. Croghan said Stephen would have to spend two days serving patients and one guiding cave tours. And maybe Stephen would become the sanatorium superintendent.

Stephen's eyes widened in panic. He looked at me as if he had seen a ghost. Then he looked at the floor. I asked him afterward what he thought. His hands shook as he replied, "I'm destroyed. I'm a cave guide, not a nursemaid. I have some money saved and I may run away. This is a burden too heavy to bear." I had not seen Stephen so angry and so defeated.

# Chapter 18

# A Consumption Sanatorium

Stephen thought it was a bad idea to build a sanatorium in the cave for disease sufferers. And the plan of Dr. Croghan to put him at the service of sick people was worse. He had $300 saved from contributions grateful visitors had given him after tours. If Mr. Underwood's account of the new colony in Africa for slaves was right, maybe Stephen could buy his freedom and buy a passage there. However, Stephen had not learned any more details. The hospital idea wasn't the only thing that made Stephen angry.

Alfred, Joseph, and Mat were telling lies about Stephen. He overheard Alfred tell a tour, "Stephen was the first to cross Bottomless Pit on a slender cedar sapling." A visitor asked Stephen if it was true that he threw a ladder over Bottomless Pit and crossed over carrying his lantern in his teeth. One visitor asked if he had jumped across. "Ha ha, I bet it would take two jumps." Stephen was described as the one to find Charles Harvey when he was lost. Stephen spoke to each guide individually. He asked them to not tell false stories about him.

One of them said, "We tell those stories because visitors believe them. Then they ask for you. That's one more cave trip we don't have to take."

Another responded, "Hell, Stephen, that's just part of the entertainment. Nobody believes anything we say."

Dr. Croghan said if he heard a visitor complain he'd stop the practice. But he smiled when he heard some of the lies.

One summer day Dr. Mitchell told Stephen that he was leaving the cave. Five weeks was long enough. He was a nervous wreck without his cigars and the guides thought he looked worse than when he came. His complaints about the food and service made no one want him to stay. A visitor brought him a bottle of whiskey that he drank in a couple of days. He insisted his condition was very much relieved and he wanted to go home, and the sooner the better. He had sent for his people from Glasgow to come and get him. Dr. Croghan examined him and shook his head as if to say Dr. Mitchell's end was near. Stephen and I thought Dr. Croghan wanted to get rid of him before he gave Mammoth Cave a bad name.

That same afternoon Mat and old Ben turned into the stable area with two wagons pulled by two teams of horses. New lumber filled the wagons and there were several bolts of canvas cloth. This was the start of the new underground rooms. Over the next several days guides and servants carried boards and framing lumber into the cave. They built three huts beyond the two stone huts in Main Cave's Grand Avenue. They laid out two-by six-inch floor frames in a ten-by-twelve-foot shape. They nailed boards across these and a couple of feet up each side. For the rest of the walls and ceiling they built a light framework of two-by-fours. They nailed canvas on the frames. It made a total of five cottages for the sanatorium.

Sick patients began to arrive. Dr. Croghan said several doctors had sent them when they failed to respond to treatment at home. One of the visitors said that one hundred invalids were headed toward Mammoth Cave, and a man named John Harper was the first to arrive. He climbed off the Nashville stagecoach. His home in South Carolina was three hundred eighty five miles away. He was a frail man with thin cheeks and watery eyes. He stayed in a hotel room until his room in the cave was fitted with a bed, a bench, a clothes chest, table, slop basin and pitcher, and chamber pot. Dr. Croghan had ordered some fancy candle lanterns with reflectors from Louisville. They would burn eight or ten hours.

After I carried his trunk to his room and wished him a pleasant stay, I asked Mr. Harper how he enjoyed the journey.

He said the long stagecoach ride had nearly finished him. His fever had come on strong in Nashville and he had to stay over for a week. Cold wet cloths on his head had quieted the fever, but he felt weak and he coughed a lot. Mr. Harper's doctor had written a letter to Dr. Croghan as a result of reading an article by Dr. Bird that cave air should cure consumption. Croghan had written back that he would not take in any users of tobacco or alcohol.

Mr. Harper checked out of the hotel and walked down into the cave room on September 15, 1842. I know because I saw the hotel register myself. That was several weeks before Dr. Croghan and I were to leave for Locust Grove. Two other patients arrived. One was from Alabama. Another was Oliver Anderson who moved into the fifth room in Grand Avenue. Anderson was talkative, Stephen said.

The slaves carried in food twice a day, once in the

middle of the morning and once in the middle of the afternoon. Stephen carried provisions two days then went back to guiding on the third day. Harper asked Stephen many questions about the strange surroundings. Since winter was coming, would he have to use a fireplace to keep warm? Stephen told them the cave temperature stayed the same throughout the year. It was 55 degrees winter and summer. Mr. Harper kept bundled up.

Stephen said Mr. Harper was the loneliest man he had met. His family had drawn away from him when his doctor said he had consumption. They had moved him to the country where they thought the air was fresher. At first they visited him every day. Then they came once a week. Before sending him to Mammoth Cave on his doctor's orders, they had him draw up his last will and testament.

"The whole world is against me," Harper told Stephen. "God is sentencing me to die, but I've done nothing wrong." Harper blamed his doctor for not curing him. His energy was draining away and his fevers were coming more often. He wished his doctor and family could experience the discomfort he felt. Just before he arrived on the stagecoach he had coughed up some blood.

Harper said the chamber maid woke him up too early each morning. She was responsible for his fatigue. The meals in the cave were not to his liking. It was depressing to lie awake in the cave surrounded by darkness, not knowing if it was day or night. An inconsiderate patient's coughing had awakened him. Then Stephen had brought him a meal that wasn't warm enough. Did Stephen have something against him?

Harper more and more blamed Stephen for his unfortunate situation. Each day made Harper more bitter against God, his doctor back home, and his family. He hated those at the hotel, he despised his fellow patients with consumption, and was unhappy with Stephen himself. "You've put me here and condemned me to die," he said pointing a bony finger at Stephen.

Stephen tried to be friendly with Mr. Harper. Stephen reminded himself that he was the celebrated cave guide who can get along with anyone. Plainly, being cordial didn't work. Stephen asked several guides and me if we had any ideas for handling Mr. Harper. Joe Shackelford told him to be more polite. Pepper his statements with, "Yes sir, no sir. I'm sorry sir." Joe said that some southerners and other men measured a slave's value by how low he could grovel in word and deed. "They like a slave that knows his place."

Oliver Anderson was a different patient. He asked many questions. Is the air in the cave good to breathe? What is the air temperature in degrees Fahrenheit? How long are the avenues in Mammoth Cave? What caused the black stain on the walls and ceiling of the cave? Stephen accompanied Mr. Anderson's relatives when they came to visit. "They come from a long line of question-askers," said Stephen. The best thing was they brought books for Anderson to read.

Mr. Anderson said he wanted good answers to his questions. Stephen started at the beginning. Yes, air in the cave was good to breathe. The temperature was 55 degrees Fahrenheit and stayed that even in summer and winter, night and day. The length of the cave was twenty miles, except it was more than that because of discoveries Stephen had made. How much more, he didn't know. The black stain on the walls and ceiling was from soot and smoke, just like the black stain on a fireplace hearth. If you rub against it, it stains your skin.

"Looks like you rubbed against it extra hard," he said to Stephen. He invited Stephen to walk with him down the Main Cave. "Tell me what made all of this."

Mr. Anderson waved his arms in all directions, pointing at the flat ceiling and the curving walls. "And where did these big rocks come from?" Many of the rocks on the floor were the size of travel trunks.

Stephen told him an underground river made it. The river started up high, back in the Haunted Chambers, then it dropped lower to make Main Cave. It continued to drop, and it was now flowing several cave levels down as Echo River.

Anderson asked if the water came from Noah's flood of forty days and nights, as the Bible described. Stephen said there are five levels of Mammoth Cave. That would mean eight days of flood for each level. And since the bottom level was still flowing, it probably wasn't Noah's flood. It probably took longer than that.

"Most rivers flow on the surface of the earth. Why would there be underground rivers here? What was different?" Mr. Anderson asked questions that stretched Stephen beyond what most visitors asked.

Stephen said the rocks around Mammoth Cave are cracked. Where the water can get into a crack, it does. It is like a cracked roof on a house. When it rains the water leaks through the cracks. Get enough leaks and enough rain and water flows out the door. They continued their walk.

Anderson became the teacher and Stephen became the student. "I brought a book by an Englishman, Dr. Lyell. He is a geologist. He says that carbon dioxide gas in the air and rainwater make an acid that dissolves lime rock. So if the water that leaks into the cracks is acid, it will dissolve the sides of the cracks to make cave passages."

Stephen told Mr. Anderson that if you can remove rocks, as streams and rivers do, then you can make a cave. Mr. Anderson asked, "But what would happen if the cave roof fell in?" Stephen remembered the stream in the storage cave at Bell's Tavern. He remembered my question, why would we be under water if the stream didn't have someplace to go? If the water could not get out it would fill to the top and spill over the sides like a horse trough.

Stephen said it was like a clap of thunder in his head when Anderson asked such tough questions. All of a sudden Stephen saw the answer. Those old underground rivers *did* go on before the passage roof collapsed. *Beyond every breakdown of rocks there is a cave passage.* Mr. Anderson was asking more questions, but Stephen cut him off.

"If you block the flowing water in a cave, it rises to flood through other openings. I think the underground stream in Main Cave got blocked when the ceiling caved in. So the water flowed out the Narrows and past the entrance and through Dixon Cave."

"What is Dixon Cave?" demanded Anderson.

Stephen told Mr. Anderson that Dixon Cave is a short section of large passage, just as big as Main Cave, that continues a few feet beyond the entrance toward Green River. It was mined for saltpetre. But because it didn't lead to more cave, nobody had looked at it for many years. The idea that cave passages continued had occurred to Stephen before, but this time it suddenly made sense. There were hundreds of places like that in Mammoth Cave. Each was a possible place to discover hidden cave.

Anderson asked, "Is a ceiling breakdown the only thing that can stop a passage?"

"No. A passage can fill with sand or mud. A passage can go under water, like Echo River." Stephen was so excited he took Mr. Anderson's hand and they turned around. They walked fast the way they had come, past the stone huts and through the Rotunda. Mr. Anderson ordered Stephen to slow down as he was out of breath.

They came to Little Bat Avenue and to the end of it near Crevice Pit. "There, look at that mud slope filling the passage," Stephen pointed.

"What about it?"

"Beyond that mud is White Cave. It is a short cave with fine decorations of stalactites and stalagmites. It has every kind of bug, too. That was once part of Mammoth Cave!"

Stephen and Mr. Anderson got on splendidly because they gave each other good ideas. Mr. Anderson said he would let Stephen read his geology book by Dr. Lyell. Stephen liked the picture in the front of the book. It showed three columns standing at the shore of the Nile River in Egypt. There was a high water mark on the columns showing that the river level had changed several times. Also, the columns looked like those in Mammoth Dome. Stephen found that book longer and more difficult to understand than his *McGuffey's First Reader*, so he gave up trying to puzzle through it.

What was Stephen to do with crabby Mr. John Harper? He asked all of us. Everyone had some ideas. Alfred's idea of pushing him into Bottomless Pit seemed good, but Stephen pointed out that Dr. Croghan would miss the money.

It was Stephen's turn with Mr. Harper a couple of days later. "You again? Why doesn't Dr. Croghan hire some decent help?" said Mr. Harper.

Stephen laid out his dinner and said, "I want you to know three things. First, you are angry and bitter because you have a disease you didn't ask for and that you can't cure yourself. I, too, have a disease. It's called slavery. I did not ask for it and I can't free myself. It's really my owner's disease.

"Second, you have choice. You can try to make others miserable at no benefit to yourself. Or you can try to comfort those around you who suffer as you do. I also have a choice. I can blame you or my owner or my parents or God for me being a slave. Or I can try my best to do a good job to help you and show you a wonderful cave.

"Third, you could ask Mr. Anderson some questions and listen to his answers. He is sick, just like you, but he made me feel better. So I think he can make you feel better, too."

Mr. Harper was quiet. Then he said, "Are you a preacher?" Stephen said he wasn't. Mr. Harper said, "Maybe you should get into that line of work." Stephen said his aim was to make Mr. Harper as comfortable as possible and treat him like a human being, and not as a sick and bitter invalid with no hope. Mr. Harper never again yelled at Stephen.

I heard later when I was at Locust Grove that Mr. Harper died in the cave in January. He was lucky to have Stephen as a friend.

Stephen's idea that all passages and places should be named and shown on a cave map bothered Nick. "I know you like to draw maps, but you forget something," Nick said. "Us guides are the only people who know their way around in here. We are the only ones who can tell what a place is called or the story of it. You put that all on a map and anybody can find their way. They won't need us and won't worry about getting lost."

When Stephen spoke to Dr. Croghan, he said maybe a cave map was a poor idea. Dr. Croghan said that was nonsense. In the winter, when tourists stopped coming, he was thinking of asking Stephen to draw a detailed cave map. He could put it into a book he planned to write. Many visitors had asked for a book describing the cave.

Drawing a map seemed to me a way to get Stephen

to come to Locust Grove where I would be cooking. I told Stephen he should teach the other guides to take care of the consumption patients, and if he could teach his replacement, he might get a trip north. In the few days before I was to leave we arranged to send letters back and forth.

Dr. Croghan looked troubled on the eve of our trip to Locust Grove. He said in a low voice that his brother George had been drinking and gambling. He'd been accused of embezzling money from the Army. Unless Dr. Croghan could repair the damage, his brother could ruin the family name. He said he'd have to go to Washington City. He would not be at Locust Grove for some time and I'd take orders from the overseer, Mr. Williams, while he was gone.

I said goodbye to an overworked Stephen. We may have been pledged to each other, but being owned beats being pledged. My eyes poured tears and my heart cracked once again as our wagon set off for Locust Grove.

# Chapter 19

## Absence and Crises

Ihated to leave Mammoth Cave. Part of it was I needed Stephen and he needed me. The other part was that the whole world seemed to be falling apart. Stephen was growing bitter at fetching and doing for patients in the cave. He made a few friends but mostly the patients treated him like dirt and ordered him about like a personal slave. Mat, Nick, Alfred, and the other guides tried to avoid the patients. Guides called them prisoners.

Dr. Croghan was spending more time looking in mirrors and combing his thin hair over his bald spot than managing the cave. He seemed to forget that Mammoth Cave depended on a stream of satisfied visitors and hotel guests. He saw getting more patients as the way to get more money. When a new patient arrived Dr. Croghan talked about room and board payment in advance before he discussed the man's medical condition. I learned more about what happened after I left to go north. Stephen told me about events four months later.

Stephen was still vexed by Mr. Harper between when I left and before Harper died. The two got on better after their talk, but Harper was still irritable and touchy. Stephen sought out Franklin Gorin for his ideas. Gorin was smooth with people who were being difficult. Mr. Gorin told Stephen there are some people in this world that will hate you no matter what you do. The problem may have nothing to do with Stephen and everything to do with the fix they are in. Only a conceited man could hope to get along with everyone. Wise people do the best they can and stop fretting over the vexing ones.

Stephen did his best to puzzle out Charles Lyell's book about geology. It described pipes in England and things that made little sense. What made sense to Stephen was that underground rivers carved cave passages. The limestone rocks had so many cracks that when the water flowed in a passage it filled all the cracks. Cracks that were below the river would be full of water, too. Stephen and Oliver Anderson talked about what Stephen was reading. Mr. Anderson said that what Stephen saw was more important than what he read. When Stephen was on Echo River, had he ever seen a crack full of water?

Stephen had seen lots of them. From the boat you could look down and see large blocks of limestone and between the blocks were cracks full of water. Beyond the last place where the boat could dock in Echo River was a low crack in the wall. Stephen waded into it and found a flooded passage that continued wet and muddy for a long way. He did not go to the end, as Luther Ray had urged him to do. Stephen got cold and miserable. "I'll leave that to others," Stephen said.

Anderson asked if Stephen had seen pipes. Stephen said he had seen smoking pipes, but not the kind Lyell wrote about. "Are you sure?" Anderson said.

Stephen said Sidesaddle Pit and Bottomless Pit were large rock pipes. But they were not quite round like the log pipe sections in Main Cave near the old saltpetre works. Mr. Anderson said, "Forget what they look like or how big they are. What do pipes do?"

"They carry water," said Anderson. Stephen had seen such pipes many places in Mammoth Cave, only they were called pits or domes. Yes, most did carry water. But Charles Lyell's pipes were plugged with chalk. What about that?

Mr. Anderson said, "Haven't you seen plugged pipes?" Stephen thought, while Mr. Anderson continued, "There are some wooden pipes in the Rotunda. Some are whole pipes and some are half pipes. Some plugged with petre dirt when the saltpetre mining stopped." Stephen knew of passages that were plugged with dirt. Wasn't a passage a kind of pipe? Stephen got the idea at once that maybe Lyell's book did have something important to say.

Lyell said that natural forces today, such as water and wind, are sufficient to create the landscapes we see today. If that was true, it meant that the rivers that flowed deep in Mammoth Cave were just like the rivers that carved the upper levels. It didn't need strong earthquakes or Noah's flood or intense rains bigger than anyone has seen to make the cave passages.

Anderson said, "Think about what you read and compare it with what you see. You may see things in a different way. You may see that things are indeed as they are described. Or you may see they are not. Believe in what you see. Think about new information you get. That's natural science."

Later Mr. Anderson talked with Stephen about experimental science. "Can Mammoth Cave air cure consumption?" Stephen said he didn't know. "Yes or no?" Anderson demanded, "Which is it?"

Stephen was ready to shout back, "I don't know!" Anderson explained that Dr. Croghan was running an experiment in medical science. An experiment always starts with a question to which the answer is yes or no. Then you test the question by putting consumptive patients in Mammoth Cave for a while. If they all get better and are cured, the answer is Yes, Mammoth Cave air can cure consumption. If they all get sicker and die, the answer is No.

When Stephen came to Locust Grove months later he told me the answer was No.

Of the thirteen consumption patients, most grew sicker and five died in the cave. The rest left the cave looking more dead than alive. He said Dr. Croghan was disappointed his experiment didn't help patients recover. But at least it showed what not to do. A No answer is better than ignorance. Stephen said that Luther Ray had taught him that valuable lesson when he asked the question of Stephen, "Does it go?" Stephen said that in cave exploring "Yes" or "No" is always a better answer than "I don't know."

Stephen thought the smoke from fires in the huts made the patients worse. He said it might have killed some of the weaker ones. Some days the smoke was so thick that cave visitors coughed and choked. A few wanted their money back. He told Dr. Croghan the smoke would kill the cave tour business, if not the patients and guides.

Our letter writing wasn't much better the second time than my first stay at Locust Grove. Only two letters from me made it to Stephen. Stephen sent one letter to me. His letter was mainly a complaint about the smoke from the patients' heating and cooking fires in the cave. "It is like living in a chimney," he said.

Early in my stay, Dr. Croghan and his brother George left for Washington City. Immediately Mr. Williams called all the slaves together in the barn. He said that Dr

Croghan and his brother would be gone for two months. In the meantime he expected all us servants to follow his orders. His daughter, Lizzy, would be the chief cook and I would work for her as second cook. There was a lot of work to get ready for winter. Produce had to be harvested, pumpkins picked, corn shucked and shelled, potatoes and turnips dug and put away. After the first freeze we'd butcher hogs and fill the smokehouse again. The overseer droned on about all the work to be done and who was assigned to do it.

My face got hot at Lizzy's promotion over me. I had taught the overseer's daughter everything she knew, but not everything I know. It paid to be the overseer's daughter. That was for sure!

My anger boiled pretty hot when I heard Mr. Williams say, "Dr. John and Mr. George are about disgusted with how lazy you servants have become. They authorized me to whip anyone caught laying out or slacking in their duties."

The reputation of Locust Grove and the Croghan family was to treat slaves kindly and to seldom punish bad behavior. On the other hand, I knew servants whose silent protest to slavery was to do as little work as possible. But his threat of the lash was stupid and brutal. It was a kind of defiance he could only get away with if the owners were gone.

Lizzy said she had taken over as cook when I had left to go to Mammoth Cave. She moved from her parents' cabin to the room next to the kitchen, the quarters I stayed in when I was the cook. She said I could live in slave cabin number 3, about a hundred yards east of the kitchen. After I settled there I wrote a letter to Stephen.

> *Dearest Stephen.*
> *I am settled in cabin no. 3. It is not as*
> *fancy as my old room next to the kitchen. It*

*has better light for writing letters. Lizzy Wil-
liams, the overseer's daughter, has been made
chief cook and I am second. Lizzy has heard
that you are to be brought here to help with
Dr. Croghan's book after the New Year and
business is slack at Mammoth Cave.*

*Lizzy has heard a great deal about you and
she thinks it odd that you are not married, so
she must not know everything. She asked if
you are tall or handsome. It sounds like she
has her eye on you. I would tell her you are
spoken for, but I don't want to be third cook
or slop slave. Yours with all my love,*
          *Charlotte.*

Lizzy's questions about Stephen told me to beware. I
told her that Stephen's heart and soul was in Mammoth
Cave. He could be gone for days at a time and come
back with his clothes muddy and torn. I didn't know
what she had heard about Stephen from Dr. Croghan,
but I didn't want her to expect too much. On other sub-
jects, such as cooking, Lizzy and I got on fine. We had
only a few people to feed since the brothers were away
in Washington City, so we took turns cooking meals.

One day I asked Lizzy about Liberia. "Why do you
want to know?" she said. I told her Stephen had said he
wanted to go to Liberia if he could buy his freedom. I
knew nothing of Liberia.

Lizzy told me the story: "Many years ago some men
formed the American Colonization Society. Some of
these men were slavers and some didn't believe in slavery. They bought some land in Africa, in Liberia. Their
idea was to convince slave owners to free their slaves
and the Society would pay for their passage back to Africa. Slaves could live there as free men and start their
lives over." She said she was against the program.

Lizzy surprised me by knowing so much, and knowing that Liberia was a bad plan to be rid of Negroes. It didn't have any benefit for slaves and it sent them back to Africa where many of them no longer had relatives. The slavers who captured them would still be in Africa.

"Remember that duel last year?" said Lizzy. "One of the men was Cassius Marcellus Clay, a political hothead. He was forming the Kentucky Colonization Society to send freed slaves back to Africa. If any owner is going to free his slaves, they should become free men right here." She gave me a pamphlet to read.

A man named Garrison wrote that slaves should be freed, not sent back to slavers. Those people who wanted to send Negroes away simply didn't want black people around. It seemed to me there were four kinds of people: Those who owned slaves mostly thought it was good and profitable to force others to do their work for free. A few slave owners enjoyed the money but felt it was wrong to own black people. They wanted to be rid of Negroes altogether, and Cassius Clay was one of these. A third group were white people and freemen who wanted slaves to be free from their owners because slavery was wrong. A few of those were helping slaves escape from their owners or encouraging slaves to rise up and kill their owners.

I thought about these things and about Stephen's curiosity about Liberia. That is when I saw there is a fourth group: Slaves.

No matter what slaves think, their opinion does not matter and they will get the worst of it. Cato was upset. He tried to run and got caught. Then he resisted and he got sold. Others had got themselves beaten, cut bad, branded, or killed. Most slaves tried to get along and get what they could. Some slaves were takers, some givers and takers, and a few were givers. Which was Lizzy?

Back when I was teaching her cooking and she was

teaching me to read and write better, I thought she was a giver. When she was made chief cook, I thought she must be a taker. What was her interest in Stephen? And why did she tell me about Liberia and give me the pamphlet?

If her father, white Overseer George Williams, caught me with that pamphlet, I could be in big trouble. So I gave the pamphlet back to her and told her I had a hard time understanding it. It was as if a door closed in my heart about what I could share with her after this.

Dr. Croghan, George Croghan and his wife, and Ann Jesop returned to Locust Grove after the first snow. Busy servants felt more relaxed when the owner's family was around. We had preparations for winter well in hand. Stacks of firewood stood outside most doors, and a great load of meat had been curing in the smokehouse for about two weeks. Dr. Croghan had ordered a sleigh from the east that was a sort of horse buggy without wheels, but there wasn't enough snow to put it to use. For an English harvest festival we cooked a larger feast than the usual Sunday dinner because the Croghans always had hungry guests, many of whom stayed for several days.

One day Dr. Croghan received a letter from Seldon Throckmorton, a new manager he had hired for Mammoth Cave. In the letter Throckmorton reported that money receipts were up and expenses down. He was having the hospital huts in the cave torn down as the residents died or moved out. The problem of smoke in the cave was much better than it had been because some storms had passed through the area creating a wind in the cave. Also, owing to fewer patients, there were fewer fires. He said that Stephen was perfecting his guiding skills so that many visitors were extending their stay in the hotel to go on more tours.

The new manager complained that visitors were asking for a guidebook of the cave and they had none to sell, so he urged Dr. Croghan to print a guidebook to meet the demand.

Dr. Croghan told me this because he knew I wanted to know about Stephen. "Throckmorton is right. We do need a guidebook and we do need a map of the cave in it. I'm sending for Stephen to come to Locust Grove so we can put the guidebook together after the holidays. We are too busy for the next few weeks, but after that we will start writing." Croghan seemed to gain a new spirit. My heart pounded faster.

I wrote to Stephen at once to tell him the news, but the letter never arrived. There wasn't any snow either, so the new red sleigh stayed in the stable where the neighbors all came to see it. My brother Jim said any horse pulling that sleigh on snow or ice would probably fall down.

# Chapter 20

## Stephen at Locust Grove

Holiday preparations were lively because Ann Jesop's two boys loved to play tag. They raced up and down the stairs and through the basement. Their laughter and taunts amused the adults rather than annoyed them. With the two Croghan brothers and their sister Ann at home, a steady stream of callers visited, some of whom the family invited to stay for several days, and we had to prepare rooms for them. Twice, a Negro band set up in the large room upstairs and played music for Mrs. Jesop to give dancing lessons for her boys and several other children. She had learned dancing in Washington City.

Two of the neighbors, a couple who joined the dancing class, planned to marry after Christmas. They asked Ann Jesop if they could hold the wedding at Locust Grove instead of at a nearby house that was too small. They had started the Beargrass Preparatory Friends Meeting under the care of the Indiana Yearly Meeting of Quakers and a committee of oversight was going to visit them. If that committee approved and recommended it to the Friends business meeting, they would need a larger place for their family and friends, so they wanted to hold the wedding at Locust Grove. Ann scheduled the wedding for the middle of January. "I don't know what to expect of Quakers," said Mrs. Jesop, "I've only attended Gentile weddings before."

I kept watching the stable for the arrival of a wagon or carriage from Mammoth Cave. There had to be a reason why Stephen hadn't answered my letters.

Mrs. Jesop, Lizzy, and I planned to serve a goose for the Harvest Dinner. We didn't raise geese at Locust Grove, but our neighbor George Gwathmey had a flock. Ann Jesop and I rode over to the Gwathmey farm and picked out a plump goose. Mrs. Gwathmey said we must cook two geese for as many as we planned to feed. I asked her cook how to prepare geese for a holiday dinner.

"It is different from chicken because the goose is very fat. After you kill a goose and scald it to pluck the feathers, you must remove the insides and boil it good in a large pot." She said we'd need to prepare a lot of dressing to stuff the bird. When the skin is good and tight and dry, the fat comes out in the bottom of the pan. It is a mess trying to carve the roast goose at the table. That's why we needed two geese. We should carve one in the kitchen before the meal and then parade the other one around the table so everyone can admire it, and set it on the sideboard. Bring in the carved goose and let Dr. Croghan serve that first, then take the fancy goose to the kitchen and carve it while folks eat.

We drove the buggy back to Locust Grove with two fine geese honking in their cage. We decided on a sausage and apple bread stuffing for the first goose, and a chestnut and dried fruit bread stuffing for the second, giblet gravy, mashed potatoes with butter and garlic, greens, baked beans, and fresh baked bread with preserves, and for dessert we'd have brandied peaches in cobbler with heavy cream (my specialty).

That harvest feast earned high praise from the family, but Lord, it was a lot of work! We decided that for Christmas we'd have a roast beef. It would be easier than fooling around all day with greasy geese.

Dr. Croghan said Stephen would arrive from Mammoth Cave the week after the New Year. Lizzy asked questions about what he would be doing and where he would stay. Did he like anything special to eat? Dr. Croghan said Stephen would stay in the slave quarters, and he would draw a map of the cave for a new guidebook with George. Also, Stephen would describe places in the cave when Dr. Croghan had questions. I told Lizzy that Stephen was a cave man who liked to eat cave crickets and bats. "He mostly drinks brandy and whisky to ward off the cold of the cave," I explained. Lizzy's eyes widened.

Christmas came and went. Our steamship round of beef lasted for several days. We cooked many dishes and nobody complained about not having goose again. Then Stephen arrived in a wagon pulled by two horses. He carried his extra clothes in a bundle and had his coat turned up around his neck, with a white scarf wrapped around his face and tucked in at his throat. I could not wait to get my hands on him! We brought him into the kitchen to warm up. Lizzy introduced herself and took his bundle. She pulled up a chair, had him sit by the big cook stove, and asked about his trip.

Stephen greeted me with some reserve. Lizzy's welcome had brought out the best of Stephen's guide friendliness toward her. "I understand you are the Chief Cook. I have learned to be nice to chief cooks." Lizzy gathered her apron and opened the oven door. She pulled out a steaming beef pie and set it before Stephen. I think Stephen must have come all the way from Mammoth Cave without eating.

Mr. Williams entered the kitchen. "Dr. Croghan said Stephen will be staying in cabin number four while he is here."

Lizzy said, "That's too far from the main house. There's a room upstairs over the kitchen. It is warmer, too." I knew from my previous stay at Locust Grove that next door was the chief cook's quarters. I had lived there myself. I also knew that room had its own stairway and a room above. The upstairs was all one room, handy for Miss Lizzy Williams to visit with Stephen? I had to think of something.

"Cabin number four has a fire laid in the fireplace. It has two windows, so there is better light than upstairs. It is so dark upstairs Stephen would need a candle at all times," I said.

Stephen jumped in, "Yes, I will need light to draw a cave map." Then Stephen lowered his voice as if it were some grave secret, "And to tell the truth, I'm afraid of the dark." I choked a laugh and pretended to cough. The great cave explorer and guide afraid of the dark? But Mr. Williams and Lizzy stood wide-eyed with their mouths open. They nodded as if in sympathy. I moved quick!

I scooped up his clothes bundle and set his empty plate back on the corner of the table. "You just come along with me, Stephen Bishop. I'll fetch you to cabin four, like Mr. Williams says. You can get settled and maybe get a little rest from your journey." I swung the door open wide, letting the winter air in. Stephen jumped to his feet and followed me out the door. He yelled a thank you for the delicious pie, and we were gone.

Cabin four had a small porch like the other slave

quarters. I lighted a fire in the fireplace. When the chimney was drawing good I closed the damper down to keep the heat in. There was a cot in one corner with a calico coverlet and a blanket, a table, a chair, a row of pegs on one wall for hanging clothes and two small windows on either end of the cabin.

First thing, Stephen pulled me to him and wrapped his strong arms around me. I hugged him back and we kissed for a long, long time. I slid my hand down the back of his pants and felt his flat butt. I told him I missed him more than I missed his letters. He said he sent two, but they never reached me. I'm sure we'd have loved for hours, but the others would expect me back. I didn't want to go, but I pulled away. "There'll be time later," I said.

I walked back the road to the kitchen near the main house, which was framed in the winter western sun.

"I think Stephen hasn't slept for a week. He was snoring when I left," I said to Lizzy and her father. We cooked the evening meal, served it, and cleaned up the dishes.

Two events kept us busy. We prepared for the Quaker wedding. And George Croghan met with Stephen to talk about drawing the map of Mammoth Cave. Stephen said he would need some large sheets of paper, pencils, and the Edmund Lee map of Mammoth Cave. George asked Dr. Croghan for the Lee map, but it was under lock and key at Mammoth Cave. It would take at least a week to send for it. In the meantime, Stephen unfolded his map of passages from the entrance to Mammoth Dome. He worked several hours each day drawing snakes. That is what the passages looked like on his map.

Preparations for the Quaker wedding were easy. I talked to Mrs. Jesop and to Mary Thurman, the bride, about a wedding dinner. They decided to have the wedding at 11 o'clock in the morning on Saturday and we'd serve a wedding dinner after that. Mary Thurman's family delivered the invitations. Tilford Appleby, the bridegroom, arrived on the ferry from Indiana late that morning. We set up a long bench against the far wall of the ballroom upstairs, where the band had played and we placed straight chairs on either side of a walkway. There weren't enough, so Mrs. Jesop told Stephen and Isaac to take the wagon around to the neighbors to borrow some straight chairs.

Late that afternoon Stephen returned with twenty-five chairs. Stephen stayed for the wedding rehearsal, because Ann Jesop said a rehearsal needs an audience. We took seats, men on one side, women on the other. Us slaves sat in the back. The wedding party of four came down the walkway and sat on the bench facing us. There was Mary Thurman's sister Osie, Mary, Tilford, and Tilford's friend Silas. "Where's the preacher?" I whispered to Ann Jesop in the row ahead.

"Shush," she said, "These Quakers don't have a preacher. They marry themselves." We sat a long time while nothing happened. The tall clock ticking in the corner was the loudest noise in the room.

After fifteen or twenty minutes Mary and Tilford stood up. Tilford took Mary's hand in his and said, "Before God and these our friends, I, Tilford Appleby, take you, Mary, to be my wedded wife. I promise to be to you a loving and faithful husband as long as we both shall live."

Mary Thurman then said, "Before God and these our friends I, Mary Thurman, take you, Tilford, to be my wedded husband. I promise to be to you a loving and faithful wife as long as we both shall live." They put rings on each other's fingers. They kissed in a most polite way and sat down. That old clock ticked off another ten minutes. Then the wedding party stood up and shook hands with everyone, even the slaves. They pretended to sign a witness book.

I was struck dumb at the simplicity of that wedding. In every wedding I had seen, some preacher talked about obedience, duty, servanthood, diligence, and more obedience. It was an excuse for long windy preaching, not for two people marrying.

Afterward I helped Mary change into her regular clothes. I asked her, "Is that how Quakers marry each other?"

She said it was, that a wedding, after all, is a personal matter between the man and woman and God. You don't need a third party to marry the two of you. On the other hand, it was a public testimony and celebration. The silence was for talking to God and listening to God. Sometimes God moved people to speak, but not in a wedding rehearsal.

When I told Stephen of Mary Thurman's explanation, he grinned and said, "We should do that, just marry ourselves. I don't see why we'd have to be Quakers." I agreed. I started to think about how we could marry each other. Didn't Negroes in Africa marry each other when they decided to become husband and wife?

The Appleby wedding guests filled all the chairs on Saturday. We prepared a ham dinner with raisin sauce, sweet potatoes, rice with beans, stewed apples, and a vanilla pudding with whipped cream for dessert. It was lucky we had the extra chairs. We sat ten guests in the formal dining room, eight in the regular dining room, and ten in the hall. It was a more joyful celebration than when Alfred and Hannah married, and there was no preacher to show off his long prayer while the food grew cold.

I asked Lizzy Williams what she knew about

Quakers. She said they were some of the first to be against slavery. Dr. Croghan had met some Quakers when he was studying medicine in Philadelphia. They wanted the slaves to be free right now and they didn't care who knew it. A few Quakers in the south still held slaves, but many of those had plans to free their slaves and send them to Africa. There weren't many Quakers in Kentucky, so they had not yet made a nuisance of themselves among Kentucky slaveholders. Lizzy thought the Quakers would not mind slaves at a wedding, and it would be a new experience for the slaves.

Why had the Croghans hosted a Quaker wedding, since they held twenty slaves? Lizzy said the Croghans were neither very religious nor very political. They knew slavery was on the way out. Back in 1790, when William and Lucy Croghan had built Locust Grove, they had forty slaves and they farmed seven hundred acres then. Now the family was down to twenty slaves and had sold off many acres. The family money came from selling thousands of acres of Kentucky land that William had patented back when he was a surveyor.

Lizzy took me aside and whispered,"George and Dr. John have a low view of slaves. They rented out Alice last year, and the man who hired her sent her back. He said she refused to work and was not worth one dollar. Ann Jesop may be a Croghan sister by blood, but I think she has a Quaker heart."

Lizzy was making things clear to me, and I thought back over many events. Joseph Underwood, Dr. Croghan's land agent in Bowling Green, owned one hundred fifty slaves and was planning to free them and send them to Africa. Mr. Underwood had urged Dr. Croghan to do the same. Franklin Gorin, another of Dr. Croghan's land agents and Stephen's first owner, seemed to see slaves as people, not as a pack of servants. Occasionally visitors at Mammoth Cave would lower their voices and ask slaves how they were treated. Maybe Lizzy was right. Slavery might be failing in Kentucky, but not if you owned a cave and slaves did most of the work.

Lizzy said, "Now that I've answered your questions, tell me about you and Stephen." I said that I had known Stephen for about four years. He was a cave explorer first and a masterful cave guide second. He had made a lot of money for Dr. Croghan by making cave tours so enjoyable for visitors that they would stay over for days to take more tours. And they would tell their friends about wonderful Mammoth Cave and clever Stephen. I told Lizzy that Stephen and I intended to marry soon.

Lizzy said, "Do you have a wedding date?" I told her no. Lizzy looked thoughtful, and added, "Then I think I will give Stephen something to think about." She said that Stephen was clever enough to become the next overseer of Locust Grove.

Her father, Mr. Williams, wasn't getting younger and had recently been offered a position as manager of the Applegate estate in Louisville. If her father left his overseer job, which any white man could do unless he was indentured, then there would be a vacancy at the overseer job. With her help and influence, Stephen could become the new overseer.

I got angry and blurted out, "Do you think Stephen would seize an opportunity like that? Would he marry you to get it?" Lizzy said if Stephen was as clever as Dr. Croghan and George Croghan said he was, then he would jump at the chance.

I said, "In that case, the sooner you ask him, the sooner you will have his answer." I left the room, angry at Lizzy's designs on Stephen. However, part of me was laughing at what kind of a diplomatic answer Stephen would give her. I wanted to be a mouse in the corner listening.

I needed to run to straighten my thoughts. I headed north to the Ohio River. I ran southwest along the edge of the cliff toward Louisville. What if Lizzy could charm Stephen? She was pretty and had powerful friends. Could Stephen be tired of guiding in the cave? Maybe I had guessed wrong about his loyalty. Two passing steamboats hooted mournfully.

Two days later I looked out the window of the regular dining room. I saw Lizzy and Stephen talking. They stood between the kitchen and well. Stephen nodded yes. Lizzy smiled and pointed to the fields and buildings and to the house itself. They talked for about ten minutes, they parted. I left the house by the back door and circled around the house and to the stable. Jim was there. I asked him if he had a horse blanket or anything else that needed mending. He handed me his jacket with one elbow worn through and a piece of thin leather. I folded the bundle and walked briskly to cabin number four.

Stephen was holding a section of his map up against the window. He smiled when I entered and pointed to the chair. "Are you going to be the next overseer?" I said.

"No, I think not. Lizzy told me her father might leave and go to work for a wealthy merchant. If I would agree to marry her, she would see to it that I would be appointed overseer. Then us two slaves would be on top, have a mess of kids, and live happily ever after." Stephen smiled again.

"And you said...?"

"I thanked her kindly for her generous offer. She is indeed very beautiful. But I went on to tell her that there's a problem. Dr. Croghan has agreed to set me free if I show him where the Indian gold bullion is buried in Mammoth Cave. Dr. Croghan also has romantic designs on Charlotte. I told him it would be a blot on the Croghan family name if it were known that he had taken a slave mistress. The solution is for Dr. Croghan to order Charlotte to marry me at once, then to manumit me. In exchange, I would show him where the gold bullion is buried in Mammoth Cave and would buy Charlotte's freedom." Stephen finished spinning this astonishing tale, put his hands on his hips, and smiled innocently at me.

"And Lizzy believed you?" I asked.

"I really don't know how much of it she believed. But I don't see how she can check out my story." Stephen put down the map, and came over to me for a hug. "The sooner we get married, the sooner we can get on with our lives. And Lizzy can get on with her life."

# Chapter 21

# A Map and a Wedding

George Croghan decided that Stephen should draw his map of Mammoth Cave at the house instead of in slave cabin number four. They used the drawing room on the first floor where the Croghans' uncle, General George Rogers Clark, lived before he died in 1818. It had north light that was good for map drawing. Mr. George Croghan, I learned, was really a colonel in the army and we should refer to him as Col. instead of Mr.

Dr. Croghan made a list of names of people to honor with passages or places named after them. Audubon Avenue was named after John James Audubon, a family guest and an artist who drew pictures of birds and visited Locust Grove on his trip down the Ohio River. The Clark family name was on the list. Lucy Rogers Clark Croghan, Dr. Croghan's mother, and George Rogers Clark, the famous General, were to be remembered by the name on a large passage. All told, there were about twenty names. Stephen was to place these names on the map in addition to the seventy or eighty names already given to places in the cave.

One of the drivers brought Edmund Lee's map from Mammoth Cave. I saw it unrolled on a large table they had brought into the room. Col. George Croghan and Stephen were bent over the map with lines on it. Stephen said separate drawings showed the side view of the main passages and how they went down from the entrance. It showed what was known of the cave in 1835, three years before Stephen came to Mammoth Cave. Of course Stephen had discovered many more miles of passage since then, but he'd seen the map at Mammoth Cave.

Stephen told me how the map drawing was going. There were problems. First, George Croghan was drunk part of the time and didn't understand that drawing a cave map is hard work. It takes care and can't be rushed. Second, Col. George said that it was impossible to obtain large enough paper. He accused Stephen of wanting to plot the cave "full size," as large as the cave itself.

Stephen traced the Lee map from the entrance to the end of Main Cave beyond Chief City. It showed the passage from the Entrance to Bottomless Pit where it stopped. Stephen unfolded the sketch map he had made to locate Mammoth Dome and the Hotel and he held it up to the windowpanes to trace it onto his copy of the Lee map. It fit onto the Lee map paper. Now Stephen was puzzled. How can we make the Lee map smaller to fit on the paper?

George Croghan had studied map making in the Army. His father was a surveyor and his two uncles could read and draw maps. He asked Stephen how much more room he would need on the paper to draw the rest of the cave. Stephen didn't know but he guessed it might be three times as much room. Col. Croghan drew small squares on the large tracing Stephen had made. Each square was three inches by three inches. On another sheet of paper he drew one-inch squares.

He told Stephen to draw the cave map, much reduced in size, square for square. It took Stephen three days to make the smaller size map on the large paper. The pencil map was now ready for him to add the many new miles of cave that Stephen had found.

Stephen complained that his map wasn't a true map made from a survey, as the Lee map was. George Croghan told Stephen not to worry: "It's a diagram showing how the passages branch off from each other. Besides, nobody will know the difference when they see it." The map was beginning to look like a pile of pig guts at a butchering.

Stephen told me that it was vexing to draw the map. He drew it in pencil. There was no good way to correct a line if he drew it in the wrong place. He took to drawing lightly first. Then he would draw the line more heavily when he was satisfied. He told me this as he held me in his arms. Several times he fell asleep telling me about the map.

We talked of marrying. It was a year since Dr. Croghan said we could marry after satisfactory work and the year was past. We decided to marry on a Sunday afternoon when many of the slaves would have completed their work. We could have a gathering in the barn and marry each other, just as the Quakers did. I passed the word to Jim to invite the stable hands and our little brothers. I told Sarah, now sixteen and a beautiful woman, to invite the kitchen help and all her family and their friends. She said she would bake cookies for after the wedding. I didn't speak to Lizzy, but knew Sarah would tell her immediately. Isaac had a large family, so I told him to invite all of them.

The Saturday before our wedding Stephen and I told Dr. Croghan we'd be marrying the following afternoon. He looked surprised. "Married? Did you ask my permission to marry? Did you?" He looked hurt and angry.

"Yes, you said we could marry after one year. That time is up, so we are getting married," Stephen said.

"But you've not finished the cave map. I absolutely forbid you to marry until that map is done," he ordered.

Stephen said, "I know you want the map finished and it is coming along well. I will finish it before returning to Mammoth Cave. But you gave your word we could marry in a year. What will people think of the Croghan family if you go back on your word?"

Dr. Croghan frowned. He looked around to see if anyone could hear him. "I'll have to think about it. Of course, Charlotte will have to stay here because Locust Grove can't spare her as our second cook."

Stephen smiled broadly, "Your family has always treated slaves right. Would you want your neighbors and friends to know that you would separate a husband and wife?"

"I'll discuss this with my brother," Dr. Croghan said, leaving.

Stephen and I went to the barn. We found the wooden box the sleigh was shipped in and pushed it against one big door. It was chilly in there, but we worked fast. We piled hay in eight or ten places for folks to sit. We turned a hogshead upside-down to make a place for Sarah's cookies. Then we went back to the kitchen to warm up.

Dr. Croghan entered the kitchen and told us, "George and I agree that you may marry tomorrow. But that won't excuse you from doing your work." We nodded. He asked, "Do you have a preacher who will marry you?"

Stephen said, "We will marry ourselves, just as Mary and Tilford Appleby did."

"But they were Quakers. The Society of Friends is peculiar in many ways. Marriage is one of them. You're not Quakers," Dr. Croghan lectured.

I spoke up. "You're right. But a marriage is a personal thing between Stephen and me and God. Stephen and I will know we're married. You will know, and any of the servants who come will see that we're married." I hit just the right tone of respect and authority.

"Well, then, you have my blessing. May I attend?"

"We'd be honored to have you attend, but you must promise one thing," I said.

"What's that?"

"You will not eat more than two cookies."

On Sunday afternoon the barn was still chilly, but then the sun came out and we opened the big door so our guests could see the woods and rolling fields leading to the river. At two o'clock Stephen and I walked in among the servants sitting on hay piles, and Dr. Croghan who brought his own chair. We wore the best clothes we had. I had a calico skirt of red and orange and I wore a white blouse. Stephen wore a chocolate-colored coat, a white shirt, and striped black pants. We sat on the wooden box facing the guests.

After about ten minutes of silence, Stephen squeezed my hand and we stood up facing each other. I was scared, but never so happy in my life. Stephen looked deep into my eyes and spoke with his rich musical voice, "Before God and these friends I, Stephen, take you Charlotte to be my wedded wife. I promise to be a loving and faithful husband to you as long as we both shall live."

I was sure everyone could see the tears in my eyes. I looked into his eyes with all the affection that flowed from me. "Before God and these friends I, Charlotte, take you Stephen to be my wedded husband. I promise to be a loving and faithful wife to you as long as we both shall live." We kissed for a long time and when I looked up the sun brilliantly lighted up the fields behind us. It was as if God had chased away the clouds and ordered the sunshine. We sat silently facing the guests for a few more minutes.

Jim stood up and said, "Today my sister that I thought I would never see again has married a good man. I hope they will be happy and have a lot of children. May God bless Charlotte and Stephen Bishop." He sat down with a broad smile on his face.

Sarah stood up. She sang forth in the purest, most naturally beautiful voice:

> *Amazing grace! How sweet the sound*
> *That saved a wretch like me!*
> *I once was lost, but now am found;*
> *Was blind, but now I'm free.*

Did anyone else notice? She changed the last line. It really is "Was blind, but now I see." When we were eating cookies, she told me she changed the last line on purpose. She said it was Lizzy's idea.

Dr. Croghan stood up holding a bottle of wine. He pulled some fine glasses from a basket at his feet. He arranged them on the top of the hogshead. "I want us to toast Charlotte and Stephen." He poured wine into the glasses and passed them to all the servants. "To the Bishops, good health and long life! May they remember this day when we gave them our love and best wishes!"

Lizzy raised her glass and said, "To the story tellers!"

I don't know the reason why Col. George wasn't there. He would have finished the wine.

Nobody could stay long because the sun passed behind clouds and the weather grew colder. Stephen and I spoke with those who were the last to leave. We thanked Dr. Croghan for his kind words and the toast and I thanked him for not taking the last cookie. I kissed Stephen and we held each other tightly. I hurried off to the kitchen to help with the evening meal. When that was cleaned up I walked with Stephen back to cabin number three, our own cabin at last.

That night was wonderful. Stephen seemed to glow in the firelight and my heart was excited. We loved for a long time and then drifted to sleep. Stephen awakened me and we loved and whispered some more. I have seen Stephen in the cave pleasing visitors beyond what they expected. But he pleased me even more. Stephen made me feel desired, beautiful, and valuable like that Indian gold bullion. Maybe good eating is a way to a man's heart, but I found another way to Stephen's heart. I knew I had a kind, tender, loving husband. The sweetest man in Kentucky.

Stephen told me every detail of his mapping experience with George Croghan. I was afraid he would forget that we were married, since this was supposed to be a joyful time, not a worrisome labor.

Stephen felt more and more vexed by map drawing. The paper wasn't big enough to show the cave as it is. Col. Croghan said to just fold the cave to make it fit on the paper they had. In some places the passages went under or over other passages. Stephen aimed to draw the junctions properly when the map was nearly finished. Col. George lettered the names of passages where Stephen told him to put them. George turned the map to letter those names near the top of the map, so the names were upside down.

Stephen wanted to draw a north arrow on the map and show the location of the hotel. "No," said George Croghan, "A north arrow is needed on a map, but a diagram doesn't need one. And it will make it more mysterious if people don't know where the hotel is located."

Stephen didn't like to be rushed, but. Col. Croghan was in a hurry to finish. Stephen knew Col. George was drunk when he misspelled some of the names of passages. He lettered *Little ball Room* instead of *Little Bat Avenue*. He spelled it *Simmes Pit* instead of *Symmes Pit*, and *Pensacola avenue* was spelled *Pensico avenue*.

George Croghan announced one morning that he had to ink the map fast because the publisher was coming to pick it up later in the day. He spent most of the day making the lines darker. John Morton of Morton & Griswold Publishers arrived in the middle of the afternoon. George handed him the map without letting Stephen check it. George had written on another piece of paper what the title was to be: *Map of the EXPLORED AVENUES OF MAMMOTH CAVE OF KY. By STEPHEN BISHOP, ONE OF THE GUIDES.*

They spent more time discussing the lettering style for the title of the map than examining anything else. George showed Mr. Morton the map that his uncle, Captain William Clark, had printed in his official report. William Clark and Merriweather Lewis were famous for their expedition to the west. He said, "Make the title just like the title on this 1814 map in Uncle William's report." Mr. Morton made careful notes.

We learned later that Dr. Croghan was furious when he saw the first copy of the lithographed map. He demanded that the publisher replace the upside down lettering. The passage junctions were a mess. Indian Avenue and Preston's Branch were drawn through Main Cave, and you couldn't tell that Indian Avenue lay below Main Cave and that Preston's branched off from Indian Avenue. Gothic Avenue and Pensacola Avenue were shown on Main Cave with a similar confusion

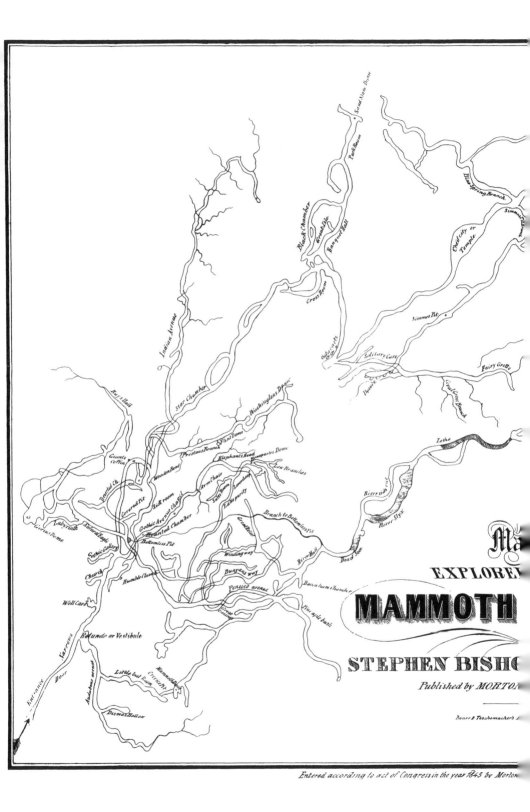

Ma[p]

EXPLORE[D]

**MAMMOTH**

STEPHEN BISH[OP]

*Published by MORTO[N]*

*Bauer & Teschemacher's L[ith.]*

*Entered according to act of Congress in the year 1845 by Morto[n]*

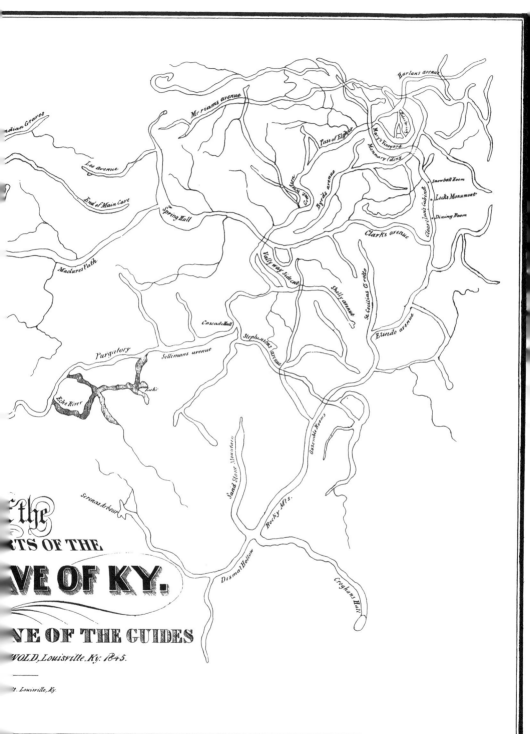

Indian Graves

Harlans avenue

Meriams avenue

Pass of Elghor

Mar's Vineyard

Mummary Gding

Lee avenue

Snowball Room

End of Main Cave

Byrds avenue

Cæsar's Cabinet

Locks Monument

Spring Hall

Dining Room

Clarks avenue

Maclures Path

Valley way Side walk

Shelly avenue

St Cecilias Grotto

Cascade Hall

Elindo avenue

Purgatory

Silimans avenue

Stephensons Avenue

Bushi

Echo River

Assemble Rooms

Sand Stone Mountain

Serenas Arbour

Rocky Mts.

of the

TS OF THE

VE OF KY.

Dismal Hollow

Croghans Hall

NE OF THE GUIDES

WOLD, Louisville, Ky. 1845.

t. Louisville, Ky.

the Clerks office for the district of Kentucky

of junctions. Gothic Avenue should have been on top, Main Cave below that, and Pensacola Avenue below Main Cave. Stephen didn't know if Col. Croghan took the blame for the defects, or whether he accused Stephen. Col. George Croghan had gone back east to soldiering.

Dr. Croghan was trying to write a guide book to go along with the new map. Before Stephen left he saw Dr. Croghan lay out books, pamphlets, and articles by five or six authors. He copied down sections of some of these accounts of the cave. We later heard that Dr. Croghan had written to his friend Alex Bullitt, who was the editor of a New Orleans newspaper. He wanted Bullitt to write the new guide book, since much of what Bullitt had written about Mammoth Cave was easy to read. Bullitt agreed to write the book about the same time that Mr. Audubon said he was too busy to prepare illustrations for the book.

That summer we sold printed copies of Stephen's map of Mammoth Cave at the hotel. Stephen accepted praise for his map, but he wasn't happy with it. There were too many defects to suit him, but I don't think anyone else saw the mistakes.

As for the guide book, Dr. Croghan put it off. He made one excuse after another about why it wasn't written and published. He told Stephen he would place his map in the book, if and when he could get around to it. Dr. Croghan let Stephen read some pages he had written. Stephen said the handwriting was hard to read because Croghan wasn't a penman and there were many smudges on the pages and lines were scratched out. Where it was easier to read it looked like Croghan had copied somebody else's writing because the handwriting was clean.

Later Dr. Croghan's friend from home, Alexander Bullitt, came to the cave and Stephen took him on all the cave routes. Mr. Bullitt said Dr. Croghan was paying him to finish the guide book.

Stephen and I left Locust Grove on a wagon to Mammoth Cave. The Croghans didn't believe in separating married slaves. It was an unseasonably warm day and it stayed mild weather for the next couple of days as we headed south.

# Chapter 22

# Guide in a Showcase

We arrived at Mammoth Cave on a chilly day and the hotel was mostly empty. Nick, Mat, and Alfred had taken the few visitors into the cave and we learned that Archibald Miller, Jr. had moved a few miles away to farm. Mr. Throckmorton was the new manager of the hotel and cave. He asked me to set up a kitchen in the guide house and prepare meals for the guides and I was to make the cave tour lunches. He had us move into Stephen's old cabin.

We restrung the bed with new hemp ropes. I borrowed a coverlet from Hannah and took two blankets from the hotel storeroom. I found Mat and asked him to install pegs in the wall to hang clothes.

When our house was done we looked over the guide house, built to keep the lanterns and guides between tours. There was one big room with a kitchen in one corner. The hotel kitchen had prepared cave meals, so we had to pick up the seven lunch baskets there and take them to the guide house. Mat said he would build a shelf cabinet, like a pie safe, to hold ten baskets.

Until that shelf cabinet came, those baskets cluttered the place. It took about a week to move all the lunch preparation from the hotel kitchen to the guide house, and the kitchen servants were glad to be rid of the job of packing cave lunches.

Nick Bransford and Stephen talked over breakfast one morning. Nick wanted Stephen to teach him how to find more cave passages and I could hear them as I cleaned up breakfast for the guides and started on the cave baskets.

Stephen told Nick, "You know about as much about the cave as I do. But I'll tell you what I look for." Stephen held up his hand and touched his thumb. "Number one, find the water and follow it. Number two, follow blowing air. Three, look behind breakdowns. Four, when the floor drops down but the ceiling stays the same, look for a low passage at the drop." That's all I remember.

I asked Stephen that night about exploring. Was he ever afraid to explore? Did he find it hard to not explore? He said for him exploring was natural. It made no difference if it was the cave, the woods outside, a sinkhole, even me. He said there is pleasure in seeing the shapes of things change as you move. Moving lights cast highlights that move among the shadows. Black shadows shorten and curl around rocks, then the shadows lengthen as you walk onward. Outdoors as you move the sunlight or moonlight shifts and changes how things look as you go along. Look back, and it all looks different. He said looking back kept him from getting lost in new cave. He liked the play of firelight on skin, on the round shapes and hidden places. I shivered thinking of his explorer's hands.

I told Stephen that for me, exploring was finding surprises. I felt surprised the first time I found I had five fingers on one hand and five fingers on the other hand. And to find ten toes was wonderful. I liked to count Stephen's fingers and toes. He asked if he should surprise me and cut off one of his fingers one day. I told him I would rather have all of him.

After that, Stephen told Nick everything he knew about exploring and how to find more cave. He told him, "It's an attitude. You have to keep asking, 'Does it end?'" I don't think Stephen ever forgot anything he had learned.

By late summer of 1843 I was growing a little larger with our baby. I felt sick or dizzy for a few weeks. I was afraid Stephen would find me ugly and swollen. Instead he said I was more beautiful than ever as he cradled me in his arms. When he returned from the last cave tour of the day he would brighten up and smile, as he did for each new cave tour. I kept busy cooking for the guides and making basket lunches for the cave tours.

One day I noticed the wine supply seemed to be shrinking faster than I was putting wine in the cave lunch baskets. Guides came in and out of the guide house all day, and sometimes I had to go to the hotel kitchen for food. That is when I saw that open bottles seemed to lose three or four fingers of wine. I took an empty bottle and filled it half full with lamp oil. I set it beside the full bottles on the shelf. In a couple of days the lamp oil went down by three fingers. After that the shrinking stopped. When Mat held a match up to Alfred's mouth one day after breakfast, all the guides laughed. I figured I had solved the mystery, Alfred had drunk the wine.

Stephen asked if I wanted to see Black Chambers. I said yes, but what was the catch? He wanted to refill the nearly empty lamp oil can at Chief City. None of the guides wanted to carry the load. After months of cooking I was ready for anything. Stephen unrolled a printed copy of his new map with his name on it in big letters.

He pointed to an arrow in the lower left corner, the entrance. He traced his finger diagonally upward through a confusing jumble of passages, past the Star Chamber to the Banquet Hall. He paused and pointed to the Black Chambers.

"I want to show you the blackest place in the cave," he said.

After feeding the guides their evening meal, we shouldered the heavy cans of lamp oil. I wrapped cornbread in a bandana. Entering the cave, we walked a long way without stopping, then the passage widened and the ceiling soared over our heads in a giant rotunda, the Banquet Hall. We placed the cans beside the trail and set off into the Black Chambers. Walls and ceiling were black as midnight. Stephen said it was soot from Indian torches and fires. At a smooth spot on the wall Stephen picked up a sharp rock and wrote both of our names, Stephen L. Bishop and Mrs. Charlotte Bishop. The words stood out in white letters on the black wall. He said, "Looks like I will have to go back and add your new last name to other places where we have written your first name. It will keep Mammoth Cave up to date." He gave me a big kiss. I threw my arms around him.

I whispered in his ear, "What does the L. stand for in your name?"

"Lucky. Lucky I found you!" He stuck his tongue in my ear and made me shiver.

We turned around and returned to the oil cans. I had forgotten how heavy mine was, and switched the rope to my other shoulder. We walked past the Cascades and onward to Chief City. There we poured the lamp oil into the empty can.

"I'll let you in on a little joke," said Stephen. He unrolled his map. "We are at the junction of Blue Spring Branch and Main Cave. See that?" I saw the words snuggled against the passage on the map. "If we keep going this direction in Main Cave, what is the next passage we come to?"

I made out the letters: *Indian Graves*. It was a passage to the left just beyond Blue Spring Branch. We walked toward where it should be, and after several hundred feet came to a breakdown that filled the passage. The trail ended. I looked back the way we had come, and asked, "Did I miss Indian Graves?" I had not seen any passage to the left.

"You didn't see it? Then we'll have to turn back and you'll have to look harder." Stephen's voice had that merry note that told me I was about to be made a fool of.

"Is this really the end of the cave?" I asked. The breakdown was dry and dusty and no water was coming in. I remembered how we had worked our way up and through the Rocky Mountains rock breakdown at the end of Cleaveland Avenue. We found big cave there.

Stephen said, "I've looked hard. There's no way through." We returned through Main Cave. I looked under every ledge and behind every rock for Indian Graves. There was nothing. We came to Blue Spring Branch. I looked again at Stephen's map. He must have made a mistake.

"Can't find it? Too bad. That's where the Indian gold bullion is buried!" Stephen's excuse for turning down Lizzy Williams's proposal was on his map. How many others would come here looking for treasure and not realize the joke Stephen had played? He created a mystery with a few strokes of his pencil. George Croghan had drawn over Stephen's joke passage with his pen and never suspected the prank.

I told Stephen he wouldn't get a kiss from me for his foolish trick. He took matters into his own hands.

I was more tired from that trip than from any other. After all, I was carrying our baby. Stephen didn't ask me on any exploring trips for the rest of the season. It was mostly because he was kept busy guiding cave tours. Visitors from far and wide asked for him to be their guide. Mr. Throckmorton mostly obliged them so there were many days when Stephen had to guide three tours.

My time to deliver our baby was growing close. It kicked me hard enough that I dropped a pan of biscuits one day. Hannah said she would help me when the time came. Stephen helped me prepare cave lunch baskets and wash the dishes after meals. The guides made coarse jokes about Stephen the kitchen slave, but he just laughed and continued helping me.

Hannah and Alfred had a baby of their own, so Hannah knew when I had pains a few minutes apart to get ready. She brought old Mrs. Garvin, who had delivered several babies at Mammoth Cave. I was in hard labor about two hours, and then Thomas Bishop came out all slippery and dark red. He cried when Mrs. Garvin wiped him off. She wrapped him in a small piece of blanket and gave him to me. Stephen was full of smiles and happy songs about his new son. I was glad when the ladies left early in the morning. Stephen climbed into bed beside me and we held little Thomas between us. Stephen said holding something we had made was better than discovering Cleaveland Avenue and Mammoth Dome put together.

It took me about a week to get my strength back. Thomas was nursing well and I had plenty of milk. Stephen filled in for me at the guide house. He endured more coarse jests about doing woman's work but he was good-natured about it. He said that next time he would have the baby and I would cook and guide.

Nick and Rebecca Bransford lived two cabins down

from us. They had one daughter, Hannah, and a baby on the way. Nick looked up to Stephen and tried to learn everything he could about being a successful guide. Rebecca told me one day that Nick said he knew as many stories as Stephen, and that his fame also was spreading. The two had explored together many times and were best friends. Having small babies made Rebecca, Hannah, and me good friends. They told me about their happy times and their troubled times.

They wanted to know why Stephen and I got on so well. I told them it was because we explored life together—not just the cave—but everything. He taught me to read. When Stephen brought home a newspaper left by a visitor, we'd read it out loud to each other. I ran with Stephen, or did before Thomas arrived. I loved to hear about the fascinating visitors on his tours, and some of the vexing ones, too.

Stephen helped me write down the supplies list for cave lunches and food for the guides, and my handwriting was better than my spelling. He read stories to Thomas and me and he would hand me the newspaper for me to read out loud. Stephen received money from some of the visitors for doing a good job guiding. Once he was offered a dollar if he could make change for a twenty dollar gold piece. He didn't have change, but after that he carried twenty dollars in change. Being ready to make change helped him to earn twice as much money as before.

Rebecca Bransford came over one day. She said the old Felix Demunbrun place was for sale. I told Stephen about it that night. "That's where we ran under the chestnut trees. Remember the spring? If the price includes the spring, I would be interested."

Stephen found out that Franklin Gorin was the agent for the land. On a Sunday we took baby Thomas over to see Franklin Gorin. He held the child in his arms and told him his parents were ornery people. They had some uppity ways and didn't always know their place. He winked at Stephen.

Stephen asked Mr. Gorin about the Demunbrun place. Was it for sale?

Mr. Gorin said it was for sale, but didn't know if it could be sold to a slave. The farm had twenty acres, more or less. "In Kentucky, more or less always means less," he warned. The land ran along a ridge top and down into Eaton Valley. The price was $19 an acre, so $380 would take it—if it could be sold to a slave.

"How can we find out?" Stephen asked.

"Three things," said Mr. Gorin. "First, do you know anyone with $380?"

Stephen nodded Yes.

"Second, will the owner sell to a slave?" Mr. Gorin answered this himself, saying he could ask the owner. "Third, would Dr. Croghan, who owns you three, be agreeable?" Once again, Mr. Gorin could ask our master.

Several weeks later on a Sunday night Franklin Gorin sent a slave to our cabin to fetch us. We bundled up Thomas and set off through the fallen leaves. Gorin had a fire burning in his fireplace. He didn't ask us to sit.

Gorin said, "I talked to the land owner and he is willing to sell to anybody for $380, even a slave. But it has to be cash on the barrel head. I also talked to Dr. Croghan. He said that if you bought property, it would become his, since he owns you."

Our hearts sank at this dismal news. We needed a bigger cabin. Our small cabin was too tiny for three of us. What if we had more children?

"But," said Gorin, "I told Dr. Croghan that if he allowed you to buy a farm, it would guarantee that you would stay at Mammoth Cave and not run away. He

said he would have to think about it. I told him not to
think too long because I had another larger farm for sale
on the other side of Green River. I told him you were
interested in that farm."

Stephen began, "But we aren't interested in that. . ."

I interrupted and cut Stephen off. "Yes, we're very
interested in another farm, one that is larger and farther
away!" I said. Gorin nodded and smiled.

I asked Mr. Gorin why he was being so kind to us.
He said he would get fifty cents per acre commission
on whatever he sold. It was business. "Also, I like your
little boy, even if you two try my patience sometimes."

The following Sunday night we learned that we
owned a farm. Dr. Croghan had promised Franklin
Gorin he would honor the sale to his slave because he
agreed it would keep Stephen tied to the cave no matter
what. Then we learned something that stunned us.

Dr. Croghan had told attorney Joseph Underwood
to write in his will that all his slaves were to be manumitted seven years after his death. A child, a farm, and
finally promised freedom one day. That was a reason to
celebrate.

On the way back to our cabin in the light of a full
moon Stephen said, "Do you think if we push Dr.
Croghan into Bottomless Pit we'll still be set free?" I
held Thomas tighter to me and set off running back to
our cabin. I could hear Stephen behind me yelling, "I
didn't mean that! Honest!"

Several times during the winter we explored our
farm. We drank deeply at the spring of water and piled
up rocks to form a larger pool. It was more of a trail
among the chestnut trees than it was a good road. We
found a flat spot near the spring and we decided that
was the place to build a cabin of our own. After all, Stephen still had more than $50 in his money box.

"And don't forget the gold bullion. We'll build a

hotel and find a cave of our own!" Stephen was always a man of vision.

We talked to Mat about helping us build a cabin. He agreed, and Nick said he'd help also. It took many months to build the cabin because they could only work after cave tours. The log cabin was two stories high with a stone chimney at one end and a big fireplace inside. The finish of our new cabin was when Nick found a long piece of rock that looked like a fence post. He dug a hole in the ground and tipped the rock into an upright position. The rock had a two-inch hole in it near the top.

"Now the Bishops have the finest hitching post in Kentucky," said Nick. We celebrated with the families we knew, Alfred and Hannah, Nick and Rebecca, Mat and Parthena. I invited the Gorins, but only Franklin came for a little while. Dr. Croghan was off in Louisville. Alfred brought out a bottle of wine that looked suspiciously like one from our cave lunch supply. Nick asked if he intended to light it for us.

Thomas grew like a weed at our new home and Stephen talked about making a cave guide out of him. I had to remind Stephen, "He's just a little boy!" As a toddler he liked to take his daddy's hand and walk to the spring to fetch water. I took him with me to the guide house most days. Hannah Bransford was getting to be old enough to watch him some days, along with her baby sister, Annie.

"I want to be a cave guide," said Hannah. "My daddy took me into the cave last week and I carried old corn cobs. He said the visitors like to keep one when he tells them it was left over from the oxen in the petre dirt mining days. Some visitors pay money for one." Hannah Bransford squinted her eyes, "I wanted to run down one of those avenues and see where it goes. Daddy said I was too little."

Our life was clouded over one day when Joseph Underwood came to meet with Dr. Croghan. They spent several days together in Dr. Croghan's private quarters in the hotel. Mr. Underwood saw Stephen on the porch and said to him, "How do you think you will like Liberia?"

# Chapter 23

# Liberia

Joseph Underwood seemed serious, but Stephen had learned not to take things he said too seriously until he learned more about them. Plainly, Mr. Underwood acted as if Stephen should be pleased.

"I've decided to free my own slaves and let them earn some money so they can go to Liberia to settle. I've almost persuaded Dr. Croghan to do the same and he wants to think about it." Mr. Underwood smiled as if waiting for Stephen to say something.

"When?" Stephen said.

"In due time. Nothing's settled. You'll have to ask Dr. Croghan." Dr. Croghan had been absent from Mammoth Cave for long periods of time recently. Stephen reported to the manager, Josiah Mosher, who decided which guides would take which parties into the cave. On his last visit to the cave Dr. Croghan had looked tired. Many times recently, before he left Mammoth Cave to attend to business at Locust Grove or in Washington City, he seemed older and weaker. He brushed his wispy hair over his bald spot more often than usual.

Stephen had a good singing voice, especially on Echo River. He would hear a new song from one of the visitors and try to remember it. Dr. Croghan brought musicians down to the cave from Louisville. Stephen said they played new music in the hotel dining room, and sometimes a visitor would hire one or another to travel into the cave and play the fiddle or horn. Stephen asked a horn player, Carlos, how he could remember the new songs. The musician told him to write down the words as best as he could remember, then practice at home. "If you don't get the tune just right, just tell the visitors that's a variation," said Carlos.

Carlos played music at the cave two summers. Stephen practiced singing around the house. I remember "Home Sweet Home," "When Stars are in the Quiet Skies," "Oft in the Stilly Night," and the "Canadian Boat Song." Two gentlemen from Massachusetts taught him the hymn "Old Hundred." Later he picked up "My Old Kentucky Home," but he hated that song. A visitor asked him to sing it on the river. He said, "That will cost you one dollar." She shut up.

Visitors could buy Stephen's map at the hotel. One day a wagon arrived from Louisville with a wooden box full of new books. The books were for sale. It was *Rambles in Mammoth Cave in 1844* by a visitor. Stephen's map was folded up inside each book. Stephen said the book was the same one Dr. Croghan had started to write at Locust Grove. The procrastinator, Stephen's private name for Dr. Croghan, had finally finished the book. Stephen knew that Dr. Croghan's friend Alexander Bullitt really wrote the book since Stephen had taken Mr. Bullitt on tours to all parts of the cave. Bullitt had taken notes in a black book, and was a good story teller. Other guide books came and went, but Dr. Croghan didn't think they were as good as *Rambles*.

The finest music that Stephen heard was played by a visitor from Norway. He was Mr. Ole Bull and he brought his violin. His tour begged him to play in the Main Cave so he tuned his violin and played a song. Stephen told Mr. Bull that in Echo River the sound would be better. Mr. Bull nearly turned back when they came to Fat Man's Misery in Winding Way. The passageway was too tight and Mr. Bull was afraid he would hurt his violin. Stephen wrapped his violin in his coat and carried it through without a scratch.

On the river Mr. Bull played again. The echoes were splendid. But Mr. Bull wasn't satisfied. He asked Stephen if there was any place in the cave where the sound would be halfway between dead with no echo and too much echo. Stephen led the tour to the far shore of Echo River and along Silliman's Avenue to a great bend in the passage. Mr. Bull wiped off his violin with his kerchief and played again.

On the return trip one of the men accompanying Mr. Bull said the musical sound was unearthly and fine, better than any concert hall. They returned the next day with more visitors and Mr. Bull played several songs. Stephen told Mr. Bull he admired his playing more than anything. Mr. Bull told Stephen he wanted to settle in the United States, and would send for Stephen to select the right concert hall for him.

Alexander Bullitt wasn't the only writer who came to Mammoth Cave. Others asked for Stephen because he knew so much and explained it so well. Once a writer was full of questions at a time when Stephen had a bad toothache. Stephen sent for Edward, a trailer guide who brought up the rear on a tour in Main Cave, to take his visitors out of the cave. Stephen explained that his pain was so intense he could not do a good job guiding. He would make good the following day. I took Stephen to old Mrs. Garvin who put oil of cloves on his bad tooth.

He found the tour members at the hotel the next day and completed their tour with his usual good humor. They gave him a handsome gift of two dollars at the end of their trip.

Artists came to Mammoth Cave and Stephen took them to the most scenic spots and lighted the views for them. One set of pictures was printed in *Rambles*. The Brewer brothers came with an ambitious plan to make oil paintings. Stephen carried along torches of twisted cloth soaked in lamp oil. He'd place the flaming torches behind rocks to light the scene without shining in the artists' eyes. He had a couple of Bengal lights that were extra bright. The management told him not to use many as they were costly.

The Brewers painted one oil painting in the cave, but they were slow painters. Stephen told them he was running out of torches. They made sketches after that of a dozen places in the cave. We learned later from visitors that the Brewer brothers made their paintings into a traveling panorama painting of Niagara Falls and Mammoth Cave. The painting was several hundred feet long, and rolled by so city audiences would see continuous sights of the famous cave and falls. George Brewer would speak eloquently of these natural wonders of America while musicians played.

As Thomas was no longer a baby, I decided I could make a little money if I learned to cut hair. Newspapers left by visitors had pictures of stylish ladies and gentlemen. I cut some of those out and studied them. When a peddler wagon came to Mammoth Cave I bought scissors and two combs. Stephen wore his hair medium long. I urged him to let his hair grow. I told him he would look better with longer hair. His hair was bushy and thick, but I trimmed it to look neat. One picture struck me as most handsome, a man with a black moustache. I asked

Stephen if he would think about growing a moustache because it would make him look distinguished, so he agreed to try it. Mat and Nick made fun of him until he said if they would be nice to me, maybe I would cut their hair.

My next purchase from the peddler wagon was a straight razor, cakes of soap, and a brush. The peddler brought out a bottle he just got from New York, the finest hair tonic. The peddler said it would grow hair. I think it was just rose water, glycerin, alcohol, and red color. I said no thanks, but the third time he came I paid him fifty cents for the red hair tonic.

Stephen laughed when I rubbed the hair tonic on his hair and combed it out. He said, "You should buy a bottle to give to Dr. Croghan. If that stuff will grow hair on him, he'll set you free for sure!"

I told Stephen everything that Lizzy Williams had told me about Liberia. Stephen had picked up hints that Liberia wasn't so wonderful for Negroes. Some were manumitted by their masters and sent there by ship to settle on farms. Only there was no land when they arrived. Some of the settlers were stolen away by native Negroes and never seen again. Overseers robbed some of the settlers. We concluded that Lizzy was right. A few visitors on Stephen's tours had spoken boldly that Negroes should be freed at once. Stephen knew better than to talk with them, so he pretended not to hear or allowed as how he himself was very well treated.

Visitors from outside of Kentucky often asked him about Liberia. He would tell them pretended plans to go there himself one day, if he could buy his freedom or be manumitted by his owner. Many visitors would nod and smile. Such an ambitious servant! All we wanted was to be free, to raise some crops, to bring up Thomas, and to work at the cave for money. And Stephen wanted to explore.

I pinned pictures of ladies and gentlemen with different hair styles on the wall and my hair cutting turned into a regular Saturday night gathering at our house. Guides came in for a trim and a shave. I charged ten cents for a haircut, five cents for a shave. They would swap stories. Alfred said one woman had ordered him to shine his light on the Armchair in Gothic Avenue. Then, "Guide, throw your light into the stone hut." He shrieked in a high voice, sounding out her shrill demands. They came to the Bottomless Pit. "Guide, throw your light into that pit!"

"Yes ma'am," said Alfred. He tossed the lamp he was holding in a high arc. It rose and curled over and plunged into the abyss. It left the tour in pitch blackness. They heard the faint clatter of the metal lamp far away, one hundred ten feet down. After a suitable silence, Alfred said, "That will be five dollars." The barber shop exploded with laughter.

I'll bet Alfred told that story twenty times. The first time I heard it I think I cut a gap in Nick's hair.

Stephen's moustache passed the wispy look after a few months. I combed it out and put beeswax on it. "Now I look like a proper Spaniard," he said. When Stephen's mustache became fuller, several other guides began to grow mustaches.

The other guides used to tease Stephen about his exploring. "You give all that free exploring to the management, instead of just doing your day's work like the rest of us," said Mat. "It makes us look bad."

"I don't explore for the owner, I explore because I want to see where the cave goes. And I don't see how that makes you look bad," said Stephen. Mat said Stephen ought to stay home and tend to his business, not neglect his family like that. It made Stephen hot. "I find the new stuff, and then you find it again and claim you found it first. Exploring means more to me than anything else; it always has. A hundred years from now, who are they going to remember?"

"Not you, not me, not any of us," said Mat. "The only thing that matters is showing up for the tours every morning. When your owner sells your babies down the river like calves, then you will figure out what is important." Mat had loved and married Parthena, who belonged to a farmer over on Flint Ridge, two miles away. The farmer let them marry, provided they lived there. The first three of their children were sold away by her owner — just like my mama, my brother, Addie and Tom Wells. The pain of ripping away your family like that can't be imagined by those who never lived through it.

Late in the fall of 1848 Dr. Croghan returned to the cave after many months away. He looked like a dying man. He shuffled instead of walking briskly as he used to. His eyes had red rims and his hands shook. Isaac, my fetch servant at Locust Grove when I was chief cook there, stayed close by him and carried his kerchief.

Stephen approached him to tell him about some new passages that fanned out beneath Mary's Vineyard. Dr. Croghan seemed not to hear and he didn't ask any questions to indicate his interest in new discoveries. His eyelids were heavy.

"I'm so tired of late, I couldn't get through the day without Isaac to help me," said Dr. Croghan, as he sat down in a rocker on the porch of the hotel. He continued, "I've written into my will that upon my death you and Charlotte, little Thomas, and the rest of my servants are to be manumitted after a period of seven years. During those seven years you'll be paid wages to work here at the cave."

Croghan coughed a dry, wracking cough. Isaac handed him a kerchief. He spit into it and wiped his mouth with a shaking hand. Then he composed himself,

"Where was I? Oh yes, if you save your money you can go to Liberia and settle there. Make a future for yourself. Study law, become a teacher or a doctor."

Stephen asked if there were caves in Liberia. Dr. Croghan didn't answer. He rose, reached out his hand to Stephen. He squeezed Stephen's hand good and fixed his gaze far away. Isaac helped him up and into his quarters.

Dr. Croghan and Isaac left in a carriage driven by my brother, Jim Brown, early the following morning. I saw them leave from the window of the guide house where I was cooking breakfast for the guides and that was the last time I saw Dr. Croghan.

Later, after the New Year, we heard that Dr. Croghan had died on January 11, 1849 at Locust Grove. Isaac had been holding his hand at the end. The doctors treating him said he died of pulmonary consumption, the same disease that had felled so many patients in Mammoth Cave. His brother, George, died just a few days before that. There was great sadness up at Locust Grove and we draped black cloth over the hotel entrance for two weeks in respect of Dr. Croghan.

Joseph Underwood arrived a couple of months later. He gathered the servants in the near empty dining room and read Dr. John Croghan's will. It took a long time to read. Mammoth Cave was to be held in trust for the benefit of his brother, George. If his brother died—which he did—the cave would be operated by a trust company until all surviving nieces and nephews were dead. His relatives were to have the profits from the cave operation. His slaves at Locust Grove and at Mammoth Cave were to be manumitted after seven years. They were to be paid regular hired hand wages in the meantime so they could save up for the time they were free to go to Liberia or elsewhere. The trust company, with Mr.

Underwood's supervision, would hire the cave and hotel manager, who would run the place and keep accounts.

In August an agent of the trust company arrived and set a price on all the slaves. Stephen, twenty-eight years of age, was worth $600. I was twenty-six years of age and worth $450. Thomas Bishop, age six, was worth $100. The agent didn't know about the money in Stephen's box, and we certainly never told him. Our farm wasn't mentioned.

Alfred and Hannah and their four children were also to be emancipated in 1856. Their youngest, Charlotte, was named after me. Mat and Nick and their wives and children were not to be freed because they didn't belong to Dr. Croghan. Mat and Nick belonged to Thomas Bransford in Glasgow, Kentucky. Mat and Parthena lived in a cabin on Flint Ridge. Nick and his wife Rebecca had two daughters by this time: Hannah and their baby Annie. Hannah almost became my daughter because she spent so much time at our place helping with Thomas. I think she liked to get away from her baby sister Annie, who cried a lot. The Croghan estate continued to pay annual rent for the Bransfords' services. I think they were saving to try to buy their own freedom.

Hannah Bransford often begged for Nick or Stephen to take her on their exploring trips. "I'm skinny, I'll fit through the tight places." She offered to carry the lunch baskets. I know Stephen couldn't wait until Thomas was big enough to go.

A couple of years after Dr. Croghan's death, Nick and Rebecca and their children moved onto the farm near ours. It was just beyond the big white oak tree on the corner of our land. On summer days when the hotel was crowded, Mr. Scott Miller, Sr., the manager, said I could do extra work and wait tables at the dining room. That was in addition to cooking for the single guides and making up the cave lunch baskets. If Hannah had not helped me I don't know how I could have done all that.

Stephen was becoming so famous that he was sent on twelve-hour tours nearly every day. He complained that his exploring days were behind him.

In the summer of 1850 a big group arrived from Louisville. They were on a grand tour of the country. All seventeen of them put up at the hotel. Stephen was told that the head of the group was the famous Ralph Waldo Emerson. Mr. Emerson wrote poems and essays. He had been a preacher and a teacher. Stephen said that Emerson and his group were the most enthusiastic visitors he had ever conducted through the cave.

"Where are you from and where are you going?" Stephen asked them as he passed out oil lamps at the beginning of a tour that lasted fourteen hours.

Mr. Emerson replied, "Stephen, where are you from and where are you bound?" Stephen said his roots were Indian and African, that he was born to explore. Curiosity was his middle name (not Lucky after all). Adventure was his calling. He told them he sought to help his visitors transform from tired travelers into fresh youngsters who could be just as surprised at finding a new passage as a new idea.

"I want to lead you into the adventure of a lifetime. You will never be the same after we explore together." Stephen matched his own enthusiasm with that of Emerson and his friends.

The large tour formed a merry band, with Nick trailing behind to make sure nobody wandered off. Nick let Hannah go along to help carry lunch for the big group. Stephen stopped them in the Rotunda and explained the saltpetre making process. He described the spooky atmosphere of seventy slaves mining dirt and driving ox carts. He painted a word picture of flickering torches and glistening skin. They passed the newer saltpetre vats and climbed the stairs to Gothic Avenue (I liked its name Haunted Chambers better.) Where stalactites and stalagmites grew Stephen told how rainwater filled cracks in the rock and dissolved mineral calcium. The drip of water through the ceiling released the mineral to form cave onyx.

Mr. Emerson said, "Stephen, you describe natural processes very well. Did you learn this in books?" Stephen explained that he had read books, but he also explored and discovered things for himself.

"Ah, a self-reliant man of action. That is the best kind!" Mr. Emerson told Stephen he wanted to know everything Stephen knew.

In Echo River Stephen explained how this was the same river that many years before had carved out the upper levels of the cave. As the Green River valley cut down, the river inside the cave cut down. "Are you sure this is the same river?" asked Mr. Emerson.

"The water is different. It changes all the time," Stephen said. On the boat ride the passengers formed a two-part choir and sang "When Stars are in the Quiet Skies." Stephen praised their melodious sound as the last echo died away. "Now that you have practiced some, you will have to sing that song tomorrow. We will go to a place where the illusion is perfect, and I will have a surprise for you."

A gunshot rang out. "Surprise!" said a visitor.

Most of the visitors were exhausted as they climbed the hill to the hotel after the trip but Mr. Emerson still had a spring in his step and he said to Stephen, "What will you do now?"

Stephen said he would walk to his home nearby, kiss his wife and small son, and eat supper. Emerson wanted to accompany him. Stephen protested that his tour would be waiting for him in the dining room. To tell the truth, no white person had ever asked Stephen to invite him into his home. That could lead to trouble.

Mr. Emerson insisted, "I have many questions to ask you, so I won't take no for an answer. Tell me what it is like to be an explorer?"

As they walked, Stephen told Mr. Emerson that exploring is venturing into the unknown. It requires curiosity. You prepare as well as you can, and then you go on and you learn as you go. Sometimes you are stopped by a deep pit or a breakdown. You look for other ways around, behind rocks or through crawlways. Sometimes you need to make a ladder and return to a high passage. The experience renews your mind. It's almost the same way when you explore history or nature in books. Your discoveries are yours. Nobody else sees what you see unfolding, changing, growing.

Mr. Emerson wondered if Stephen was always curious, but Stephen said, "I believe all children are born with a desire to explore. The world discourages exploring and demands obedience. Be like everyone else. Don't ask so many questions. My mama encouraged me to explore, except when I hid in the oven and nearly got burned up. She answered questions as best she could, but she urged me to find the answers myself."

They reached our house as the last rays of a sunset flashed through the trees. I had just lighted some candles when I heard them talking. Mr. Ralph Waldo Emerson was tall and lean. He had big ears and a big nose, but an altogether friendly face. His gray eyes flashed around the room and he looked me over pretty good when Stephen introduced us. Thomas was playing upstairs. I called him to come down and meet Mr. Emerson and I set the table for supper. I had already fed Thomas and eaten my meal in the kitchen.

I told Mr. Emerson that the greens were from Thomas's garden patch in the corner of our garden.

Mr. Emerson paid attention to Thomas immediately. "How old are you son?"

"Six, sir."

"Can you read?" Thomas glanced at his father and me.

"I can read CAT and RAT and HAT and BAT," Thomas said.

Mr. Emerson nodded in approval. "What is the difference between three of those and the other one?"

Thomas puzzled for a minute. "Three of them are alive and the hat is . . . is dead." I was proud of Thomas. We had started to write words on his slate and sound them out. But we had not talked about what the words meant. Stephen had read stories to Thomas when the boy climbed into his lap. Sometimes he would go to sleep, but I enjoyed Stephen's reading even though I knew the stories. Mr. Emerson asked Thomas if he wanted to be a cave guide, like his father. "No sir, I don't like that old cave. Not one bit."

Thomas asked if Mr. Emerson wanted to see his goat.

I changed the subject because I thought I saw a tear in Mr. Emerson's eye, and I asked him, "Do you have children?"

"Alas, our son, Waldo, died at age five, eight years ago. Seeing your Thomas reminds me how much I loved him and miss him." His son was taken by scarlet fever. Mr. Emerson swallowed a couple of times and shook his head.

"I honestly had a wonderful time in the cave," said Emerson.

"When people talk about their honesty, it's time to count the spoons," I said. I was warming to Mr. Emerson, and Mildred's wisdom made him smile.

"Stephen, why do you think God made Mammoth Cave?" said Mr. Emerson.

"I think God made Mammoth Cave for us to discover, explore, and enjoy," said Stephen, "And maybe that's why he brought us together, too."

During a meal of ham, greens, and cornbread, Mr. Emerson and Stephen talked until I got sleepy and went to bed. Stephen said that Emerson wanted to know how slaves could read. He explained that his first master had educated him, and he had taught me. It wasn't against the law to teach slaves to read in Kentucky, but most slaves could not read. Emerson said that slaves needed to learn to read and write and figure. "They will be free one day and will need all the good information and skills they can get."

Stephen asked Mr. Emerson why he thought slaves would be freed. That would go against the money interest of their owner. Most slave owners would never free their slaves. Mr. Emerson said, "God hates slavery and loves freedom. It's not moral to hold slaves and profit by their labor. Couldn't you guide just as well if you were a free man?"

Stephen guessed he could.

"You would keep all the money you earned. I read about you in *Rambles in Mammoth Cave*. You are the king of this cave. Kings are paid handsomely."

Stephen walked with Mr. Emerson back to his room in the hotel. They agreed to meet early in the morning with Mr. Emerson's own surprise.

The surprise the next morning was that three of the tour of seventeen carried armloads of fireworks. Stephen passed out the filled lamps and the two baskets of lunches. They went into the cave past the Giant's Coffin. At the Star Chamber, Stephen had the large tour sit down on rocks. He gathered the lamps and departed leaving them in darkness. They laughed and talked for a time, then settled down.

"Let there be light!" said Stephen in a deep voice.

Nick, stationed in a second side passage, made a good imitation of a rooster's dawning crow, "Cock-a-doodle-doooo." Stephen moved the lights slowly back into the Main Cave, casting light on the starry ceiling. Nick made a "moo" sound like a cow.

"Stop!" said Mr. Emerson. "The illusion is almost perfect. We must make it perfect. He gathered the singers from yesterday in two groups. He had the others lie down on the floor on their backs and close their eyes. He handed Roman candles to four of the men and told them what to do. "Let's begin again," he said.

Stephen gathered the lamps and retreated once more. Emerson then said in his deepest voice, "Let there be lights in the expanse of the heavens to separate the day from the night. And God made the two great lights, the greater light to govern the day, and the lesser light to govern the night. He made the stars also." At this the lights began to creep across the sky and the choir sang the song they had rendered the day before on Echo River, "When Stars are in the Quiet Skies." When the last notes died the men ignited the Roman candles sending balls of colored fire hurtling in all directions. The last green ball shot into the blackness of Main Cave.

The illusion left everyone breathless. Stephen said he learned more about showmanship from Mr. Emerson than he had from anyone else. Mr. Emerson pressed a five-dollar gold piece into Stephen's hand at the end of the trip.

Stephen conducted many famous people through Mammoth Cave in the following years, such as the singer Jenny Lind. None captivated Stephen as Mr. Emerson did. I think Stephen captivated him, also.

# Chapter 24

# Discovering Other Things

Cave visitors sometimes challenged Stephen. He had taken a tour of three men out to the end of Indian Avenue. The tallest of the men pointed to a lump in the wall, saying, "It looks like a hen's egg."

"You can tell it's hard boiled, just try to crack it," Stephen said. They rested in the narrow passage before going on to some domes where they could eat their lunch and get a fresh drink of water. "We could look around these domes, and maybe discover something, or we could go down to a lower level and crawl over to get to Echo River and go out another way. Or we could return the way we came, through Indian Avenue," Stephen said, explaining the advantages and disadvantages of each choice.

"Exactly where are we?" said the tall man, gazing upward at the top of the dome.

"I reckon we are pretty near going under my farm," said Stephen. He took out his compass and told how he had figured out how to look at the direction of travel in the cave, count his steps, and guess where the passage was. "Of course, there's no way to tell for sure."

"Yes there is," replied the tall man, "If you find an entrance, then you poke your head out and look around. From the looks of this dome rising over our heads, you might just hoe the right rock the wrong way in your garden and open up a new entrance." Stephen said if the land looked all the same, he might not recognize where he was when he poked his head out.

"That's an easy one, just kill a chicken and poke the dead chicken out the same hole. Then go out of the cave and look for the circling buzzards," said the tall man. Stephen and the three visitors laughed, but Stephen thought about that trip and how much he learned from cave visitors. He especially thought about how handy it would be to find an entrance to Mammoth Cave on his farm. I told him we could use it as a storage cave, so he'd better get to work and find it.

One day the following year, Rebecca and Nick's daughter Hannah and her sister little Annie were playing outside with our Thomas. He found a baby rabbit and planned to raise it. But they thought if they could find another baby rabbit to keep it company, it would be more fun. They set out to look for another rabbit. They surprised a wild sow pig with babies, and chased her down into Eaton Valley, not far from our house. The pigs squealed as the children crashed through the bushes. Hannah stopped when she felt cold air blowing out of a small hole at the base of a rock face. Hannah threw rocks in the hole and listened. She was eager to move rocks and find a cave, but Annie was tired and they needed to go home. Thomas told Stephen and me about their adventure that evening and he showed us the rabbit. Stephen asked Thomas and Hannah to show him the hole.

After a lot of looking, they found the hole. Stephen cleaned away the earth and rocks and revealed a steep muddy slope down. He climbed down about thirty feet and got beyond the daylight coming in the top of the hole. He came back to the house all muddy to get a lamp. The muddy slope changed to a rock scramble that ended above a ten-foot narrow chimney down to a spring of water. Hannah enthusiastically followed Stephen into the cave, but Thomas waited outside. A low crawl above the chimney ended. Hannah crawled into a low crawl off to the left but it ended also. At the bottom of the chimney Stephen found one way that ended, and another that went on to a small hole that led down. Hannah climbed down the chimney and wanted to climb into the small hole, but Stephen said it was too dangerous. "This is the perfect place to fill our water buckets," said Hannah, "The water is clear and cold, not like the pond."

Stephen found a grapevine and cut it off a tree. He pushed the end of the vine down the hole and put several rocks on the end that stuck out. That way, if he came upon the grapevine dangling down from the top of the dome at the end of Indian Avenue, he would know where he was and just where to find an entrance. Stephen took several tours with visitors to the end of Indian Avenue, but he never found that grapevine. It unsettled him, not knowing where something in the cave was.

Stephen made a ladder to climb down into the hole and set a bucket to collect spring water. Thomas was sent to bring back water, but he complained that it was too dark in that hole, and too hard to climb up the ladder with a bucket of water and the lamp. We mostly drank from the spring pond near our cabin.

I became pregnant again. Since I knew what to expect, it did not slow me down from hotel work or barbering until I was about seven months along. A scary thing happened when the labor pains began to come early. I sent Thomas to Alfred's house to find Hannah, and I lay down. I told Hannah it was too early for me to deliver. Hannah made some hot tea and went off to bring Mrs. Garvin, the midwife, who came about an hour later.

Mrs. Garvin was there when Stephen came home after his last cave tour that day. "Charlotte's baby is trying to come too early," she said. "She must have complete bed rest. Someone else has got to cook and fetch for her. If not, Charlotte's baby will come too early to live. It is up to you."

After Mrs. Garvin left, Stephen climbed in bed beside me and held me in his arms, "I will cook and fetch for you." He said he had enough money set aside that we could make it for several weeks, and he could gather food from our garden. With some meat hanging in our smokehouse, we'd make it. I said what about the manager? He'd expect Stephen to guide.

"Just because you're now getting paid, you're still a slave. You have to obey the manager," said Charlotte. Didn't the cave come first?

Stephen said confidently that I came first and had been first ever since we met at Bell's Tavern. He said to me, "You're smarter than most visitors and just as smart as the best of them. More than that, you can run faster than anybody I know. You know numbers and have learned to read and write. Most of all, you're the friskiest and prettiest woman in the whole wide world. I'm ready to prove it to you!" he said with a wink. I loved him dearly for his sweet words, but mostly because he was as good as his word.

Mr. Proctor, the new manager, said that Stephen could not stay home all the time—he'd have to report for work at least one day a week. "It isn't our busy season, or I couldn't spare you at all. But you must come on Saturdays, our busiest days when visitors ask for you,"

Mr. Proctor said. Alfred's wife Hannah could not come on Saturdays so she suggested Nick's daughter, young Hannah as a helper.

He cooked three meals for Thomas and me every day, plumped up my feather pillow and made sure I was comfortable before he went out with Thomas to do chores or work in the garden. He'd send Thomas back every once in a while to see if I was all right. Thomas often brought me flowers he'd picked, then he'd tiptoe out without slamming the door if he thought I was asleep. For many weeks Stephen cared for me while I rested. He'd brew tea and tell me what he was doing, or report some wise thing that Thomas had said.

Those were the happiest moments of my life, when I could spend time with Stephen and not have to share him with the cave. We talked about our plans for the farm, for having a family, being a good neighbor to our friends who were still slaves or were saving to buy their freedom. We did not talk about freedom much because we could only imagine what it would be like.

Young Hannah was a big help, and she wanted to know everything about Mammoth Cave. She had carried things into the cave a few times, but never was taken exploring. "Did you like exploring in the cave with Stephen? I want to be a guide when I grow up. Even bringing up the back would be all right with me," said Hannah. She relived her excitement when she and Stephen explored the spring cave.

I told her exploring was fun, but I was curious about everything, not just caves. Hearing Stephen tell of his discoveries was fun for me. I told Hannah that maybe some day she could be a guide, but she'd have to be very good at it—like her father—because poor guides didn't work out. She'd have to work hard to get good at whatever she wanted to do. I told her I wanted to learn to be a barber, and kept at it until I was good at it. I could cook and became good at that, even though cooking is not what I wanted to do. I learned to manage the dining room at the Mammoth Cave Hotel because I was good at numbers and could make change. "Some things you do because you want to do them, some because you have to do them. But whatever you do, try to give the best you can," I said.

About one month before she was supposed to be born, our baby came suddenly. By the time Mrs. Garvin arrived, our baby lay dead at the end of the bed. I screamed in pain and grief, we had so wanted that baby, and now I had failed at being a good mother. I feared Stephen would blame me or hate me. Instead, he helped Mrs. Garvin clean me up and change the bed. Mrs. Garvin told Stephen to let me rest a few more days and to guard against a fever, and then she left us three alone.

Stephen tried to smile at me as he said, "I love you more than ever before, Charlotte, and it is not your fault. You did what you could. Mrs. Garvin said that when babies come early like that they often die and it is a mercy of God. I don't agree that God wanted our baby dead, but she is right—you did everything you could." Stephen had tears in his eyes. We both wept and pulled Thomas to us.

My heart filled with tenderness and I said, "No, *we* did everything we could, and we have one another." Stephen stayed with me for another week after burying our daughter in the slave graveyard near our house.

The loss of our daughter reminded us of the loss of Mat and Parthena's babies when Parthena's owner sold them off. Stephen told me something I did not know before. When Mat revealed that Parthena's master was going to sell those children, Stephen talked all the guides—

slave, freedmen, and white—into agreeing to collect a
purse to buy the three children and give them back to
Mat and Parthena. Stephen offered Mat the money they
had pledged to buy them. Mat had then offered that
money to buy the Bransford babies, but the farmer who
owned them refused. He said he was sorry, but the offer
was too late. The children had already been promised to
a man in Nashville. The buyer and his wife were on their
way to pick them up, to raise them as household slaves
on their horse farm in Tennessee." They'll have a better
life there, and I need the money bad," said the farmer.
That farmer was one of the takers in this world.

I was proud of Stephen for offering our money and
getting the guides to pledge that way. Mat and Parthena
were not free and had no prospects of being free. Stephen and Thomas and I were better off than some, and
especially better off than folks who didn't love each
other, slave or free.

Stephen went back to his guiding, and getting home
late more tired than ever. If the next day's trip was in
the middle of the morning, Stephen got up at dawn and
took Thomas off to hunt for a cave entrance on our property for a couple of hours. They did not find anything
promising, but they did find where the saw briers were
thickest and nastiest. They returned home with bloody
scratches on their arms and feet, but no cave or blow-
holes.

At my hair cutting on Saturday night the guides
poked fun at Stephen's scratches: "Stephen lost his
touch finding caves and it looks like he lost his fight
with a wildcat, too," said Alfred.

Nick added, "We're gonna get you a tourniquet so
you can stop the bleeding next time you mess with a
wildcat."

Alfred said, "Just Stephen's luck, a wildcat bites him

on the nose and we have to put that tourniquet around his neck!" Even Stephen laughed and put his hands around his neck and squeezed, sticking his tongue out and rolling his eyes up. Those white eyes sent the room into a laughing jag. "Charlotte, you'd best be careful when you shave Stephen because if that razor slips, we've got to apply that tourniquet right here and now!"

Stephen's success at raising a purse to buy Mat's children, even though it did not buy the babies, did something else. It brought the guides together to where they considered him a leader. They asked him to approach Mr. Proctor, the manager, and ask for equal pay for equal work. Stephen told Proctor: "You pay the white guides more than the freed men. And you don't pay the slave guides anything at all. We just want what's fair, because it takes the same amount of work no matter what color we are."

At the barber shop the following Saturday the guides asked Stephen what Mr. Proctor had said about equal pay. "He said the authority for paying guides comes from Mr. Underwood, and his hands are tied. 'If I had my way, you'd all get two dollars a day and meals also. But I am not the boss man.'" Mr. Proctor said what he could do is set up a guides' beneficial fund, and that every month the money visitors contributed to that fund would be distributed to all the guides, share and share alike. None of the guides bragged about how much he had been paid privately by visitors at the end of a trip, so there wasn't much hope the fund would amount to much.

Stephen told me how much visitors gave him. We put the money in a metal box that Stephen buried out back in case our house burned. Stephen always wanted to buy more land for our farm, and he wanted to buy some books for Thomas to read as he got better at it. Thomas wanted a book on how to raise chickens that could fight back when a hawk came down to grab them. And we all enjoyed it when Stephen brought back a left-behind newspaper some nights and read to us by the light of the fireplace.

One article in a Louisville paper described the Compromise of 1850, the Clay Compromise. It strengthened the 1793 Fugitive Slave Act, saying that federal officials must catch and return slaves that escaped from slave states to free states. It offered a sum of money for every slave captured and returned. We told Thomas about Cato and how he had tried to run and was caught. Wherever Cato was, he could not hope to flee to the north where slave catchers were fanning out to catch slaves and collect money from the government as well as any rewards that owners might pay. Thomas said that since we would be free one of these days, why talk of running away? Our boy didn't appreciate what it was like being a slave in Mississippi or other plantation states.

# Chapter 25

# Stephen Remembered

Iremember the 1850s at Mammoth Cave as wonderful times and sad times. For me, the wonderful part was living with Stephen and Thomas on our farm, and being freed. For Thomas, the wonderful part was turning from a baby to a child who grew to be a big help with farm chores. Thomas would run with me once in a while and he was good at it. He also became strong friends with Hannah, Annie, and the other Bransford children. The Garvin children joined them. It helped when I made extra money working at the hotel and barbering.

The sad part for both of us was that Stephen worked for twelve hours most days guiding tours in the cave. He seldom went cave exploring because there was land clearing, planting, harvesting, butchering, and fence mending when he was not guiding. Stephen also took sick and died and that was the saddest of all. But I am getting ahead of my story.

My barbering on Saturday nights brought out the guides, especially those who had discovered something wonderful in the cave and wanted to brag about it. One of those brag sessions was about domes. Of course every guide knew about Stephen's discoveries of Gorin's Dome and Mammoth Dome—the biggest domes. Which dome was the prettiest was easy to argue about. Stephen said Charlotte's Dome was the prettiest, but he hadn't found it yet. He may have said that to get in good with the barber.

Stephen had showed me the dome he wanted to name after me on one of our exploring trips to River Hall. We walked up the hill from River Hall and walked to the right and then the left, into a high passage. It was not very wide but was comfortable walking. Near the end we crawled through a window in the left side of the passage and stood on a flat place looking up and looking down. Water cascaded from the ceiling and struck the orange walls of the dome with sparkling drops that glistened and flashed light. The water fell into a tumble of rocks in the bottom. The dome was about forty feet in diameter and over a hundred feet from top to bottom. Because it was the right size we could see all the walls, and that made it more beautiful than the larger domes with far reaches hidden in shadows. I was pleased that he intended to give my name to this beautiful place.

Nick Bransford teased Stephen, "You've been poking in those crawlways under Cleaveland Avenue. I know because I have seen your name or initials in nearly every one of them but you haven't found any domes lately."

Mat added, "I think he's lost his touch, so busy showing off the old stuff he hasn't got time to find and show the new stuff."

The talk about domes vexed Stephen a lot. Around 1855, he said to Thomas, who was about twelve, "Let's go find something in Mammoth Cave." Thomas said he would just as soon not go. He said he had farm chores to do, and would rather work outside than in the cave.

"I need to weed the garden and take some flowers over to the hotel. I asked if I could plant some flowers near the door, and the manger said go ahead." Thomas loved gardening.

Thomas had been to the entrance a few times, and always complained about the wind from the cave and how cold it was. Stephen let it go that time. Thomas never talked about the cave, but Stephen sure made up for that!

Stephen returned one night from guiding two tours. He pulled out some coins from his pocket. He slammed them hard on the table and said, "Ten cents from the morning tour and fifteen cents from the afternoon tour. Not enough!" Stephen was hot about how stingy people were getting, "It is like a slave who earns wages when rented out, everything for the master and chicken scratch for the slave." I suggested he needed an exploring trip to take his mind off being an exhibit in a showcase.

The next morning, he said to Thomas, "Come on son, we are going into the cave."

"What for?" the boy asked.

"Because I said so. And I want to take lamp oil to the Snowball Room. Mr. Proctor said I should do it if I can get someone to help, so you are it." Thomas complained he did not want any part of a long trip in the cave, but Stephen insisted: "I haven't time to argue."

It was very late that night when I climbed down the ladder from upstairs to meet them on their return from the cave. Stephen had a look of cold fury on his face. Thomas scowled and it looked like tears had streaked down his cheeks. I set out some cold cornbread and mo-lasses and two apples. They ate them in silence.

Finally Stephen said, "This boy won't ever make a cave explorer or a guide, not even a trailer bringing up the rear and wiping women's noses. He's worthless."

Thomas blurted out, "Who wants to be a damn mule slave for nothing? I never want to go in that cave again. Dad tried to kill me in there. I was sick and tired, and he said: 'We must go on. I'll leave you here if I have to. If I find another way out, I might come back for you next week!' I never want to go into Mammoth Cave again!" Thomas stormed out the doorway.

I asked Stephen what happened. Stephen fumed and fussed, then took a swig of coffee. He said that he and Thomas had each carried a large can of lamp oil into the cave. Thomas kept insisting the rope was cutting into his shoulder and to slow down. They had to keep going so they could look at a place that Stephen had in mind to explore after they dropped their load. It took them five hours to reach the Snowball Room by way of Echo River. There was no time to eat, so they set off toward the end of Boone Avenue and went past a deep pit on the left, to a place where the passage ended at a drop-off. A tiny ledge along the right wall would be unsafe to cross. They looked way down and saw another passage far below, but there was no way down and no place to tie a rope. Thomas continued to whine and complain that he was hungry and tired and wanted to go home.

Thomas retreated in Boone Avenue about a hundred feet to a sandy place down at one side of the passage. While he lay down and waited for his father, he felt a breeze. It came from ahead in the direction where he had just left Stephen. Thomas crawled in the little sandy passage to try to warm up. After a hundred feet of crawling he came out on a ledge half-way down to the lower passage they had seen from above. He called to his father, whose light glinted above. He told Stephen about the bypass that would let them reach the bottom. They met and climbed together down to the bottom.

Stephen and Thomas then set off along a tall canyon

with few footprints. They came to Stephen's name on the wall next to the name RONDEAU and a date, 1843. There was another name, J. A. Creighton, 1848. Stephen had come here before with two different visitors, but they reached this place through another way, a terrible climb down into a pit. On the 1843 trip the ledge they crossed to reach the hole had let go and crashed to the bottom of the pit. Stephen would have lost a visitor if he had not grabbed Rondeau's hand in time. Creighton had been an exploring fool, too fearless for his own good. He insisted they cross to the hole where the fallen ledge used to be. After that, Stephen had vowed never to take such a scary risk again, and that he would try to find the new route that Thomas had just discovered.

As Stephen and Thomas followed the main passage they stopped suddenly. From a narrow side canyon leading off from the left wall a strong blast of cold air struck them. "Big cave!" shouted Stephen. They edged sideways through the narrow canyon. They walked into an enormous chain of domes, one right after another. Their lamps could not light up the top and they heard water falling some place beyond. They went down a slope to the end of the last dome where a lively waterfall sprinkled into a pool, splashing water in every direction. The walls of the dome glistened with water running down them. Grooves in the walls guided the water into drips that made musical sounds when they fell into the pools on the floor. Stephen and our son drank deeply from the pool, getting their heads and backs soaked from the falling water. After they filled their water bottles they turned back.

Stephen told Thomas he was a real cave explorer now. Nobody can make a discovery like that and be the same afterward. Their discovery was wonderful, better even than digging through Sparks Avenue mud into Mammoth Dome. He was glad Thomas had seen what it was like to make a big discovery. But Thomas said, "Who cares? I won't ever go in that cave again. It's too dark, and too long, too tiring, and too cold."

I think Thomas broke Stephen's heart that day. Stephen hoped his son would grow curious and turn into a real explorer, a guide to follow in his father's footsteps.

Stephen told me that night, "I don't want anything to do with that hateful boy again. If he won't go in the cave, he's no son of mine. Mat's boy Henry is only seven and he wants to be a guide."

I said, "Mammoth Cave doesn't go where you want it to go, and you love that old cave. Why would you stop loving our son because he won't go where you want him to go? He's not Henry."

Stephen went off to bed and it was the next day before he replied, "I am sorry I blew up at Thomas and at you. I hate disappointment. Raising a farm hand is not my idea of a future, when Mammoth Cave has so many places to discover and enjoy. I'll tell Thomas that I am sorry, and that I do love him."

I said, "Dr. Croghan's will promised to set you free, so you can set Thomas free, and help him be a man right now, help him make his own choices."

Stephen said, "Yes, Dr. Croghan promised to set us free after his dying. Why didn't he free us sooner?"

I said, "Better late than never. We have to live now, not yesterday."

Consumption was all around us. It took Sally, many members of the Archibald Miller, Jr. family, and Dr. Croghan. That disease felled the patients in Mammoth Cave, and three of them were buried in the guides' cemetery beyond the hotel. We heard that people all over the county were dying of the disease. Also cholera was spreading and killing people in Glasgow.

On January 12, 1856 Mr. Underwood called us all together and said that we had reached the end of seven years and now we were free. He wrote out free papers for each of us and told us to guard them well. We must show the paper to anyone who demanded to see them. "This is a time to celebrate," Mr. Underwood went on, "Larkin Proctor and I have butchered a pig. Mat started the fire last night and that pig has been turning on the spit. It's barbecue time!"

We cheered and waved our free papers. Alice Garvin began to clap her hands and dance wildly. The rest of us clapped and rocked back and forth. Thomas ran out the door to gather the folks for the big feed. Alfred's wife, Hannah, shouted "Hallelujah, hallelujah!" and joined the dancing with more spirit than Alice. Freedom for some of us was celebrated by all of us, and women brought food to go with the barbecue. Those kids screamed and yelled, and they all went back for seconds. Mat and Nick were there, smiling, but quiet. They had no reason to celebrate. They were still slaves.

During that seven-year time that we waited for freedom, the slaves had been paid wages so they could save something to go to Liberia or someplace else. Stephen was now being paid two dollars a week to guide, and he took in extra money that visitors would give him after tours. I filled in as manager of the hotel dining room some days. Late in 1856 Mr. Proctor, manager of the hotel and cave, hired me to be the manager of the dining room for one more dollar a week. I had to buy new clothes from the peddler wagon for that job, and then later I bought cloth and got Mary Garvin to sew me some nice dresses. I made a little extra money in gifts from visitors and more money from barbering on Saturday nights. Since I could write with pen and ink, I made a little money writing letters for others.

Thanks to our savings, we were able to pay a little money to show good faith, and then signed a note with Robinson Shackelford to buy more land to increase the size of our homestead to seventy-five acres.

In the spring of 1857 Stephen began to complain about getting old and feeling tired. He often returned from the cave so tired he would stretch out and go to sleep without eating his supper. I thought being free would liven him up for exploring, and maybe set him into going back to the dome he and Thomas had found. He told no one about that dome—it was a secret. Once or twice on Saturday night Mat or Nick asked him what was beyond the end of Boone Avenue. He would just shrug and say that was the end of the cave. Alfred told him he just might see for himself next time a visitor paid to go to the limits of the cave. I doubt if the guides believed Stephen or Alfred.

By June, Stephen was so sick he could not go to the cave to guide tours. Mr. Proctor asked about him and said he was not able to pay a guide who would not show up for work. I tried to get Dr. McMillan to come from Three Forks, but he never showed up. I gave up my job at the hotel and stayed home to tend Stephen.

"You need to get back to the hotel, they need you," Stephen said. I told him I belonged here with him. Had he forgotten how he nursed me when I had lost the baby? We had never felt so close as that time when he gave up everything to comfort me. Now it was my turn to comfort him. Stephen had prided himself in knowing the cave, in confidently guiding men and women over the gloomy trails, and engaging in conversation on any and every subject visitors might bring up. Now, I must be the confident one. It was my turn to read stories aloud from newspapers that Nick dropped off at our cabin.

There was a terrible story in a Cincinnati newspaper

about a slave woman, Margaret Garner. She escaped from Kentucky to Ohio with her husband, four children, and his folks. Slaveholders and U.S. marshals trapped and captured them. Margaret slit the throat of her baby daughter and tried to kill two of her boys with a shovel to prevent their return to slavery. The court verdict was that she must return to her master. She made one last desperate attempt to escape and threw herself and one child into the Ohio River. She was recaptured, separated from the remains of her family and sold down the river to a planter in the Deep South.

I choked up and cried at that poor woman who just about gave up everything to be free, then lost just about everything else in the end. I think some of me died when I read that story. Stephen wept with me, recalling some of the things that had happened on the farm where he grew up near Glasgow. Stephen's tears fell on my arms when I held him. I think I did replace Mammoth Cave for him at the time when Stephen knew he had explored his last. We truly belonged to each other, and I gained strength from the strength and encouragement Stephen was showing me. He had taught me to discover hidden things, such as the tears of grief and disappointment and the tears of wild joy and happiness of a cave explorer. I taught him endurance and persistence, how to love at a distance or up close. We were one in every way.

Stephen's eyes began to grow dull and sunken in his face. He ate less and less. For a while he was able to sit up and eat bread dipped in gravy, but later he would throw up his food. I remembered how Sally Lively had taken sick, and near the end she had sweated and shivered.

I bent close to hear Stephen whisper, "The cave will go on when I'm gone, but I'd love to know what happens. Promise . . . Promise you'll tell me someday."

He said he dreamed about all the places he wanted to revisit, to check behind breakdowns for undiscovered passages. "Oh Charlotte, there's so much more I must find."

On that last terrible day, Stephen clutched my hand and whispered a rasping order: "Go at once to Nick Bransford and tell him I want to deed the farm to him." I asked why. "Because I am dying and I want you to have this farm. But colored women cannot own property. I trust Nick, so I want him to own the farm so you can live here and he'll watch over your interests." He spat up blood. I sent Thomas to run as fast as he could to find Nick, but he was in the cave and would not come back home until evening.

Once he was out of the cave and heard the news, Nick picked up the farm deed and the Shackelford note and went to Franklin Gorin's house to arrange for the property transfer. In our cabin, my tears for Stephen splashed on his hand while Thomas held his other hand, and we both wept and moaned that we could not soothe Stephen, our dying husband and father. My heart cracked like it did when Addie and Tom Wells were led away at the slave market in Nashville. I cried just as I did the day that I left Stephen behind when I was taken from Mammoth Cave to Locust Grove. Together we had wept at the misfortune of poor Margaret Garner and her baby dead by her own hand.

Stephen died that July night, and a good part of me died with him. Thomas ran to fetch Nick and Rebecca and Alfred and Hannah. The men laid Stephen out in the barn to cool.

The next day Mr. Proctor stopped by to say that Stephen should be buried in the guides' cemetery. He had some of the men digging a grave for him and at three o'clock in the afternoon a flatbed wagon arrived from Mammoth Cave pulled by a chestnut horse. Mat had nailed together a coffin for Stephen and they hoisted it onto the wagon. Thomas placed a beautiful rose colored hollyhock stem on the coffin. All of us walked behind the wagon to the cemetery. Franklin Gorin and his wife joined us at the hotel, along with Mr. Proctor. Stephen's funeral procession was as sad as any I ever knew. We all cried.

At the graveyard, Mat asked God to take Stephen and have him search out all the unexplored caves in heaven. Mr. Gorin tried to speak but he choked up and couldn't go on. The men lowered Stephen into the ground.

Nick began to sing, "Swing low, sweet chariot, coming for to carry me home. Swing low . . ." Alfred and few of the other guides joined the slow sad song, but Nick began to choke up and the others stopped singing. For the longest time I heard sobbing and sniffling. Thomas put his arm around me. Nick put his arm around me. The men shoveled earth on the coffin and one by one people gently squeezed my hand and drifted away.

Between my tears I said to Thomas, "Your father loved to be in the cave more than above ground sometimes, and now he is in the earth with his cave. We'll never forget Stephen's love. I know he loved us more than the cave and I have you to prove it. His love will always be with us."

We turned away from Stephen's grave and headed home. Thomas said, "Race you back to the house."

We ran and ran.

Tombstone of Stephen Bishop, donated by James Ross Mellon, is a refurbished Union soldier's marker carved in Pittsburgh, PA in 1881. The date of death is wrong; it should be 1857.  Photo courtesy of Chuck DeCroix.

# Epilogue

Charlotte's fictional narrative ends in 1859, two years after the death of Stephen. Oliver H. P. Anderson, who entered Mammoth Cave on October 20, 1842 and stayed until January 11, 1843, died in 1845. Thomas Bishop, Stephen and Charlotte's son, died of an unknown cause at an unknown date as a teenager; the last mention of him was an 1860 Census record listing him as a farmhand of William Miller, Horse Cave, KY. Charlotte became the wife of the widower Nick Bransford a few years later. Nick continued as a guide at Mammoth Cave until his death in 1894. Charlotte Bransford died in 1897. They had no children together.

Stephen's grave marker is a Union soldier's tombstone that was purchased by James R. Mellon. A millionaire when he visited the cave, Mellon was so struck by written accounts and Charlotte's descriptions of Stephen's accomplishments as a guide that he ordered the unclaimed tombstone refurbished and placed over Stephen's grave in the old guides' cemetery at Mammoth Cave. It can be seen to this day. The headstone shows the wrong date for Stephen's death. It should be 1857, not 1859.

It could be coincidence, but Stephen's map of the

cave shows a side passage near the end of Indian Avenue that was later shown to extend beneath Stephen and Charlotte's farm. The 1907 cave survey shows that Edith's Avenue contains an identical configuration to a 1990s cave survey, both of which lie beneath the Bishop farm site.

W. Stump Forwood in 1870 published a guide to Mammoth Cave, *An Historical and Descriptive Narrative of the Mammoth Cave of Kentucky*. In it he quoted a letter from Franklin Gorin, first owner of Stephen: ". . . I placed a guide in the cave—the celebrated and great Stephen—and he aided in making the discoveries. He was the first person who ever crossed the Bottomless Pit. After Stephen crossed the Bottomless Pit, we discovered all that part of the cave now known beyond that point. Previous to those discoveries, all interest centered in what is known as the 'Old Cave' . . . but now many of the points are but little known, although, as Stephen was wont to say, they were 'grand, gloomy, and peculiar.'

"Stephen was a self-educated man; he had a fine genius, a great fund of wit and humor, some little knowledge of Latin and Greek, and much knowledge of geology; but his great talent was a perfect knowledge of man. There was not any Indian blood in Stephen's veins. I knew his reputed father, who was a white man. I owned Stephen's mother and brother, but not until both children were born. Stephen was certainly a very extraordinary boy and man. He knew a gentleman or lady as if by instinct. He learned whatever he wished, without trouble or labor; and it is said that a late professor of geology spoke highly of his knowledge in that department of science."

Three monumental lifetime accomplishments of Stephen stand out:

First, Stephen was a driven and productive cave

explorer. He set the standard in the United States for insatiable curiosity that pitted his courage and tenacity against formidable cave obstacles. These included exploring cold underground rivers that could flood, pushing muddy crawlways where only the smallest caver would fit, and traversing around deep pits where loose handholds and slippery footing could plunge the explorer to his doom. He ordered the confusing cave into a three-dimensional picture in his mind's eye.

Second, Stephen set the standard for modern cave guiding. He educated those entrusted to his care and he engaged, enlightened, and entertained them. His fame as a skilled interpreter spread during his lifetime and he was always in demand by repeat visitors and those who had heard of his prowess. Franklin Gorin's moving tribute to Stephen — the man — summarizes a most accurate assessment of his humanity and curiosity.

Third, Stephen was the economic engine that made Dr. John Croghan prosperous when his family's fortune was declining. His Croghan estate trust initially supported nine nieces and nephews, until the death in 1926 of Serena Croghan Rodgers, the last of the Croghan beneficiaries. Trust property was purchased by the Mammoth Cave National Park Association.

Ultimately, Stephen's legacy was the public demand that Mammoth Cave become a National Park, and Mammoth Cave National Park officially became a reality in 1941. While Stephen didn't invent or create Mammoth Cave, he stimulated others for more than a century to prove Mammoth Cave the longest cave in the world. The United Nations Educational and Scientific Organization (UNESCO) has designated Mammoth Cave National Park a World Heritage Site and an International Biosphere Preserve. This is a universal acknowledgment of its value. It is the highest honor that can be bestowed upon any place on earth.

It could be argued that Stephen was a product of the Romantic Era in black literature, a time surrounding the U.S. Civil War when almost superhuman qualities were ascribed to persons of color. And it could be argued that Stephen and Charlotte and the rest of the slaves at Mammoth Cave had it better than their counterparts who were owned and exploited, often under cruel conditions. It is unarguable, however, that slavery was and is a prison. Any argument about the size of cells is foolish. What Stephen achieved was a world class accomplishment for mankind.

He was—as Mildred said—a giver.

# Acknowledgments

Many people gave freely of their time and resources to aid in the writing of this book. I thank them all. To those whose names I have omitted, I apologize. I alone am responsible for errors of omission and commission. Perhaps this is an odd comment for a historical fictional story, but I don't claim it to be the whole history or truth.

First, thanks to Superintendent Patrick Reed of Mammoth Cave National Park, where much of this story is set and where many records of Stephen Bishop are housed. Bob Ward and Joy Lyons gave access to National Park Service interpretive, guide, and scientific resource personnel, Jerry Bransford, Chuck DeCroix, Keven Neff, Colleen Olson, and Rick Olson—who provided essential checking and criticism. Scott House, president of the Cave Research Foundation, helped reconstruct the most probable route by which Stephen crossed the Bottomless Pit.

I am indebted to Executive Director Carol Ely of Locust Grove, KY, a Louisville Park District Preserve. Docent Nancy Lee devoted many hours to showing me around, answering questions, and providing research materials from her personal collection. Philip DiBlasi provided slave records and information about archaeology work at Locust Grove.

The Cave Research Foundation allowed access to the CRF's *Mammoth Cave Gazetteer and Database*, compiled by Michael Sutton and Sue Hagan, and maintained by Scott House. It is a valuable reference that combines place names, trip reports, and other data regarding the Mammoth Cave System. CRF also provided me with the *Bibliography of Mammoth Cave and the Mammoth Cave Region* compiled by Michael Sutton, Sue Hagan, and Ray Mansfield. This database of many thousands of references is maintained by Scott House. The *CRF Cartography Trip Report Data Bank*, also maintained by Scott House, was invaluable for clearing up ambiguities within the cave. Stan Sides, a past president of CRF and a teacher of the history of Mammoth Cave exploration, and historian Norman Warnell provided critical comments and corrected numerous errors. Janet Smith and Hilary Lambert contributed careful editing. Richard A. Watson has provided detailed editorial criticism, encouragement, and friendship since 1954. Lynn Brucker, Emily Davis, Bonnie Delong, Cooper Fleishman, Michael Nardacci, Bill Steele, Gerald VonderBrink, and Lucy Weir made useful comments.

Thomas Kopp, a caver and professor at Miami University, Oxford, Ohio, took me under his wing to help me understand slave literacy issues. Janet Stuckey, Head Special Collections Librarian at Miami University, made the entire special collection of McGuffey Readers available to me. At the William Holmes McGuffey Museum in Oxford, Ohio Curtis Ellison, Interim Director and Beverly Bach, Curator, answered questions about the availability of McGuffey Readers and sources of songs of the era. Dr. W. Sherman Jackson, professor of American Constitutional History and Law, supplied insight on slavery in Kentucky and how the wide local

variation in laws and customs made slavery a most peculiar institution.

Norman Warnell showed me the former Bishop farm
site, located beyond the materials storage area at Mammoth Cave National Park. He answered many questions
about families residing in the area.

Carridder Jones, a playwright and author of short
stories based in Louisville, made important suggestions
and critical comments as the manuscript developed.

This novel is an amplification of the section "Stephen
Bishop" in Roger W. Brucker and Richard A. Watson,
*The Longest Cave*, Southern Illinois University Press,
Carbondale, Illinois, 1976, pp 265–273. I consulted many
sources while checking the background of Stephen Bish-
op and the Croghan family. The best source for histori-
cal information about Stephen Bishop is Harold Meloy,
"Stephen Bishop: The Man and the Legend", in *Cavers,
Caves, and Caving*, Bruce Sloane, Ed., Rutgers University
Press, New Brunswick, New Jersey, 1977, pp 265–291.
Meloy, the "Historian of Mammoth Cave", wrote many
historical articles and collected the information con-
cerning Stephen Bishop in one chapter. The best source
for information about the Croghan family is Connor,
Eugene H., M.D. and Samuel W. Thomas, Ph.D. "John
Croghan (1790–1849); An Enterprising Kentucky Physi-
cian", Vol. 40, No. 3, July 1966, *The Filson Club History
Quarterly*, Louisville, Kentucky, pp 205–234. The best
source for the history of Bell's Tavern is Thomas, William L., "A brief history for the Three Forks Tavern; the
builder, subsequent owners and operators," February
15, 1999, a manuscript in the vertical file of Park City,
KY Library. The best source for information about slave
guides at Mammoth Cave is Joy Medley Lyons, *Making
Their Mark: The Signature of Slavery at Mammoth Cave*,
Eastern National, Fort Washington, PA, 2006, 71 pp.

Roger W. Brucker with Stephen Bishop's wall signature in Salts Cave. Franklin Gorin and Stephen visited Salts Cave in 1839 and 1841. Salts Cave became a part of Mammoth Cave in 1972. Photo by David Carson.

## About the Author

**Roger W. Brucker** has coauthored four nonfiction books about cave exploration in the Mammoth Cave area. He is an Honorary Life Fellow of the National Speleological Society and winner of its highest honors, including the 2004 Spelean History Award and 2009 Arts & Letters Award. He is a founder and past president of the Cave Research Foundation. For 25 years he taught the Speleology course for Western Kentucky University at Mammoth Cave National Park. He has been called one of the greatest cave adventure writers. Roger resides in Beavercreek, Ohio, with his wife Lynn. Visit his Web site at **www.rogerbrucker.com**.

## What Reviewers and Readers Say About Other Books by Roger W. Brucker

### The Longest Cave
by Roger W. Brucker and Richard A. Watson

". . . a primer of self-reliance and self-worth,"
— NEW YORK TIMES

**A Wonderful Story**
". . . recently I bought *The Longest Cave*, which I am now reading for the second time. As soon as it was delivered I read it all the way through on consecutive nights and then immediately started reading again. Thank you once again for writing this book. It is a wonderful story which I am bursting to tell anyone who will listen."
— REVIEWER: Stuart Woodward, Yokohoma, Japan

**Captivating, Awe-Inspiring, and Incredibly Exciting**
"If you like adventures, if you like caves; If you like drama and suspense, or if you breathe in and out and have a pulse, you really ought to read this book. The story of the years it took to connect the Flint Ridge/ Mammoth Cave systems, it sweeps the reader into the wonderfully obsessive world of the Flint Ridge cavers. A great book. Strongly recommended.
— REVIEWER: Emily Ohlin, Chicago

**The All-Time Number One Cave Adventure Book**
"Fiction should hope to be so true . . . the reader feels as if he is crawling, climbing and squirming along with them. Read this book!
— REVIEWER: John Tudek, Caver

## Trapped! The Story of Floyd Collins
by Robert K. Murray and Roger W. Brucker

". . . offers fascinating glimpses of Collins as an eternal adolescent who seemed at home in a subterranean world, and a clan whose rural simplicity was marbled with dark conflicts."
—NEW YORK TIMES

"The Story of Floyd Collins' entrapment in a Kentucky cave makes for chilling and exciting reading."
—LIBRARY JOURNAL

"Of the countless articles, books, TV shows, and even a musical about Floyd Collins, none is finer than "*Trapped! The Story of Floyd Collins.*
—CINCINNATI POST

". . . Ranked the third largest news story between world wars . . . topped only by Charles Lindbergh's crossing of the Atlantic . . ."
—EL PASO TIMES

## The Caves Beyond
by Joe Lawrence, Jr. and Roger W. Brucker

"This excellent book is by far the best written on the adventures of exploring a single cave . . . This is really a terrific book, and if I had to single out the most enjoyable caving book in my library, this would be it."
—Chuck Pease, EXPLORERS LTD. SOURCE BOOK

"It is impossible to read these pages without recognizing the insatiable drive that spurs man onward or realizing how frustrating it is to turn back when you can see with explorers' eyes that there are caves beyond. But never completely solved logistical problems, the growing fatigue that becomes overwhelming—that invisible but insurmountable endurance barrier—and the paralyzing uncertainty as to where you are in the uncharted maze, combine to make the caves beyond unconquerable."
—Charles E. Mohr, Past-President, THE NATIONAL SPELEOLOGICAL SOCIETY

## Beyond Mammoth Cave
by James D. Borden and Roger W. Brucker

"This book tells the whole truth . . . With books like this there will never be a shortage of cavers."
—NATIONAL SPELEOLOGICAL SOCIETY NEWS

". . . all the ingredients of high adventure, remote surroundings, physical hardships, clashing personalities, and the elation burn of important discoveries."
—LEXINGTON HERALD-LEADER

". . . more plot twists, secrecy and intrigue than a Tom Clancy novel."
—COLUMBUS DISPATCH

"I've read a lot of outdoor books, but this has got to be, honestly, one of the most fascinating."
—Steve Horstmeyer, WKRC-TV

"There is much in this account for the armchair caver as well as the active caver to plunge into and enjoy."
—LOUISVILLE COURIER-JOURNAL